CURSED DAWN

KISSED BY BRIMSTONE BOOK FOUR

LEIGH KELSEY

INSANELY PRETTY SPECIAL EDITION HARDBACK!

If you're like me and LOVE a stunning collector's edition, check out this GORGEOUS Fae of the Saintlands hardcover, with brand new covers, colour illustrations, and the chance to unlock foil and SPRAYED EDGES!!

Find the hardcover exclusively on Kickstarter!

CURSED
DAWN

LEIGH
KELSEY

BLURB

We have ten days to break the curse, or my mates and I kill each other.

Time is running out, and every day we come closer to the end. We finally have Wane back, but with the clock ticking down and grief eating me whole, it's hardly a victory.

Cronus has won, and he knows it. I can't kill him when my world just collapsed. If the Labyrinth broke me, the Damned Realm crushed what was left into dust. Exactly like Cronus crushed my mate when he unmade him. Who cares what the prophecy inked on my back says? Or what great and terrible future I'm supposed to have?

The only thing I want is to keep my mates and I alive. But with monsters freed from Tartarus, vicious gods in our way, and a titan hellbent on devouring me whole, I'll need more than magic to break our curse.

I'll need a miracle.

NOTE

This series contains mentions of past abuse and sexual assault that could be incredibly triggering for some readers, so please proceed with caution. It also contains references to miscarriage. Don't hesitate to skip this book if it's safer for your mental health.

This series also contains some spoilers for the Lili Kazana trilogy, which takes place a year before this series, but only minor spoilers for the events of the story (nothing character-wise is spoiled.)

Leigh x

For all my bookish masochists, who love books that make them suffer

PART I
TORMENTED

CHAPTER 1

*A*sh from my dead mate clung to my knuckles as I curled my fingers into fists. They were shaking. They hadn't stopped shaking since Wynvail died in my arms. This ash and the blood staining my clothes, crusted on my arms, was the only thing left of him.

"Almost there," Emlyn soothed, rubbing his hand up and down my back. I didn't have the heart to tell him the gesture was pointless because I was entirely numb.

I kept my eyes on the cracks in the pavement as we walked across Edinburgh. I didn't know how we'd gotten here, didn't particularly care. I only looked up to count my mates, to make sure we hadn't lost anyone else.

Harvey. Wane. Kai. Emlyn. And Wynvail was dead.

What was the last thing I told him before he died? I couldn't remember. But I remembered all the times I'd called him a monster, called him evil, and said I hated him. I did—I still did, even now—but I couldn't ignore the part of my heart that loved him, too.

"Are you sure this house is safe?" Wane asked warily, his voice low but not quiet enough to stop me hearing.

"Don't," Harvey sighed, skimming the back of his hand down my arm in the place of a brush of his wing. They were glamoured away, so humans didn't run screaming from the sight of us. Let them scream; who the fuck cared?

I hunched my shoulders, my arms wrapped around my middle. I was covered in blood—all of us were. So much that we'd got a few wary looks *and* a well-meaning woman who asked if we needed help. Kai hissed in her face, summing up how I felt about someone talking to me, expecting me to form words.

My mate was dead. He died *in my arms,* and even that wasn't enough; Cronus had to unmake him. He had to turn him to dust and then snuff *that* out until there was no part of Wynvail left. My nostrils flared with faster breaths. A keening sound got stuck in my throat; I hugged myself tighter, digging my fingernails into my skin.

I wanted him back.

I hated him, and would happily break his nose, but I wanted him back. He was my psychopath. Mine to kill. I hadn't even—gods, I hadn't even properly *kissed* him.

"We should be more worried about whatever the fuck that was under the Damned House," Kai muttered, glaring at everyone and anyone we passed. "Cronus will send that thing after us."

"Do you know what it was?" Emlyn asked Wane, his voice heavy and tired, matching the deep lines on his face. "Did Cronus ever talk about it?"

I lifted my head to watch Wane shake his head, long chestnut hair matted to his head and hanging, grimy and lank, around his face. His whole body was covered in filth from the tunnel cell he'd been locked in, his clothes ragged and old. Blood had soaked into the back of his shirt. Blood that still flowed now. I wanted to ask if he was in pain, but I couldn't find the energy to open my mouth.

Had I been unmade, too?

"Here, this looks right," Emlyn murmured, running his hand up and down my back. I hated not having my wings to wrap around myself; I felt bare, exposed. "It's that house with the black railings, isn't it?"

Harvey muttered his agreement, and we all shuffled up the terrace's three checkerboard steps to the front door—and promptly realised we didn't have a key.

"Shit," Harvey hissed, rubbing his face and looking as exhausted as I felt. Like I was dead inside.

"I'll kick the door in," Kai offered, hungry for violence.

He lifted his foot, but dropped it back to the step when the lacquered black door of the house next door creaked open and an ageing, elegant woman popped her head out. She fit into a place like this, unlike us. Her hair was in silver curls, her slim body draped in fine, beaded silk, and pearl jewellery clung to her throat and fingers.

"I've got a key," she told us, reaching up into a basket of bright pink flowers that dangled from her porch stoop. "Wynvail said you'd be needing it. He didn't say anything about you being beaten to hell, though." She slid a look in our direction, missing the flinch that rocked me at hearing his name spoken so casually. "It's not gangs, is it? I don't want anyone starting shit on my doorstep."

I barely blinked at her coarse language.

Emlyn shook his head, at a loss for words for a moment. "Not gangs. We were—attacked."

The woman clucked her tongue. "Crime in this area's shocking lately. Here you are." Emlyn accepted the key with obvious surprise.

"You must be Halwen," she added, her eyes on me with curiosity and a touch of worry. "Beautiful and tough, exactly like he described you. You're lucky, having a man like that. I need a man who'll buy me a house, too. I had to start a multi-million business and buy this one myself."

She smiled, expecting us to laugh, and seemed to belatedly notice the sombre mood. "Where *is* Wynvail? Not with you?"

I screwed my eyes shut. I couldn't stand it—hearing his name, listening to this woman talking about him like he was amazing and kind and generous. Like he was coming back.

I need a man who'll buy me a house, too.

I swallowed the knot in my throat and croaked, "The house isn't mine."

"Oh, it is," she disagreed, a furrow in her wrinkled brow. "He put it in your name, didn't you know?"

My breathing cut out, heat gathering in my face and burning my eyes.

"Oh, shit, I've said something wrong," she breathed. "If that man's hurt you, you just tell me and I'll go and lamp him."

I blinked. Appreciated the sentiment, and added the new wording to my vocabulary.

"He's dead," I told her, and took the key from Emlyn, throwing open the door.

I didn't look back to see the woman's reaction to Wynvail's death; I threw the key on the table in the hall and took the steps upstairs two at a time.

The living room was still a mess; through the open door, I saw the artwork and photo frames lying on the floor, the takeaway containers spilled across the rug where Cronus's pit of darkness had knocked them off. I glanced quickly away, memories assaulting me. I'd lost the dagger he gave me during the fall into the Labyrinth.

My body ached all over, and my ass was still throbbing from getting fucked hours ago, but I pushed myself to my limit, clinging to whatever strength I had left. I didn't stop until I found his room.

His scent wrapped around me like a chokehold, and the

tears burning my eyes finally overflowed. Gods. I started to shake.

Beautiful and tough, exactly like he described you. You're lucky, having a man like that.

The first tears fell as I kicked off my boots, and I curled up on Wynvail's bed, letting grief swallow me whole.

CHAPTER 2

I slept as long as my body would let me, refusing to move from the bed even when the sun set and rose again. I didn't bother to eat or shower. I snarled when Emlyn tried to wash me with a warm cloth. I was covered in Wynvail's blood; it was all I had left of him.

His blood, this house, and the dagger—the dagger he bloodied himself breaking a shop window to give to me. The dagger I'd traded away like it was nothing.

I buried my face in the pillow when a new wave of keening cries hit, my stomach cramping as pain squeezed my whole body. I'd been sick so many times that my mates had put a bucket next to my bed. I threw myself over the edge now and vomited bile, the gross stuff burning my throat until I tasted blood.

When the nausea passed, I spat the awful taste out of my mouth and rolled onto my back with a pitiful moan. I hadn't felt this sick since Kai and I challenged a massive, green demon to a drinking contest back in Vhadell.

I wanted to go back to that time, when the only thing I had to worry about was where money was coming from this month and if Em would be mad that we scuffed up the kitchen floor on the way in.

But that wasn't true. We'd been terrified, practically every second, that Cassander Locke and his mercs would find us. That his *hunter* would find us. Wynvail. All that time he'd chased us across Hell, and I thought he was trying to kill us. Instead, he was following orders. But Locke's or Cronus's? I didn't know if there was a difference, didn't know where Locke's vileness ended and Cronus's began.

I jerked upright when the door creaked open, irrationally thinking it was Cronus prowling towards me. Even if I didn't know what he looked like, I'd built an image in my mind—a smug, oily smile, cruel eyes, an inhuman face and ... I was picturing Cassander Locke. Fuck.

I rubbed my face when I saw it was Wane padding across the threshold, something hesitant and brittle in his expression and a tray in his hands.

"I can't eat," I told him, my voice croaky and raw. It hurt to talk.

"I can't either," he replied, a sad smile curving his scarred cheeks. There had been softness in that face before, but now there was only hardness and a deep, carved pain.

I scrubbed my face harder and shifted aside to make room for him.

"I'm sorry," I rasped, my throat burned raw, "I've been so focused on my pain that I forgot about yours."

"I'm fine," he replied, setting the tray down beside me and sinking onto the bed with a groan.

"Try that again without lying," I said, faking a smile.

"I'm free," Wane said after a too-long pause. "That's more than I ever hoped for."

I shuffled closer, casting a disinterested eye at the sandwich and muffin on the tray. "You should have known I'd come for you."

He smiled, as fake as my own smile, and turned over his arm so I could see the inside of his forearm. Now the grime of that room was washed off him, I could see the white scars layered on top of each other, hundreds upon hundreds of them, from his fingers up his arms and to his neck. There were even a few faint lines on his jaw. And on the inside of his right forearm was a curse mark. Not the same as mine, but obviously by the same tattooist. The lines were shattered, like something had exploded it apart.

"Wane," I breathed, hovering my fingers over the dark ink, my heart crushing in my chest. "What did he—"

"He cursed everyone to forget me. He was the only one who knew about me—and Andryas, his servant and enforcer. The curse broke when you remembered me."

Andryas. I committed that name to memory, already planning his death.

I was so focused on the curse branded on his arm that I jumped when Wane touched me, folding my hand between his.

"Sorry," he murmured and began to drop my hand. I scrambled to hold onto him, my fingers shaking.

"No. I—I'm just so used to not touching you," I admitted, trying so hard to push through the numbness icing my entire chest so I could *feel* something. I should have felt something right now with Wane beside me, finally safe. I held onto his hand tightly, my throat burning and stomach roiling again.

"Touch me as much as you like," he replied, his voice tight and raspy as he gazed at me. "I don't—I don't remember what Locke did every time I'm touched now. That fear was tortured out of me years ago. *Shit,* I shouldn't have said that," he rushed out when I flinched.

"I want to know," I breathed, flicking a tear off my cheek and inching closer to him, my eyes on the brutal lines of his face. He was too thin, too poorly cared for. We'd change that.

It was my job—to take care of him, to give him everything he needed. My heart thudded hard in my chest. I'd done a piss poor job of that so far.

Wane shook his head hard, rich chestnut hair flowing freely now, not plastered to his head. I was starting to feel like a gremlin beside him, dirty and ragged. "It's—you shouldn't know, Haley. I don't *want* you to know. You can never unhear it."

"I can never unsee you in that room," I murmured, seeing it now, the dark walls, the piss bucket, and wane folded up in the corner, covered by a scrap of shadow. "I want to know, Wane. You're mine; what happened to you happened to me."

He squeezed my hand, linking our fingers and killing me with the simple touch. It had been so fucking long since I'd touched him. *A hundred years.*

A tear dripped off my chin and splashed our hands, sliding over a scar he'd carved into the back of his hand. My name, always my name.

He wanted to take her name from me.

"He—killed me," Wane whispered. "Over and over. And when he didn't, he ordered Andryas to do worse things." I jerked, sucking in a breath. "Not rape. He never even threatened me with that. But—you can see what he did to me. I'm ruined."

"That's not what I see," I replied in the same soft tone, turning his face so he met my eyes. The misery and self-hate in his silver eyes killed me. "I see someone he *tried* to ruin. He failed. You're here, still breathing, speaking to me, bringing me sandwiches."

Wane laughed. His eyes creased, his cheeks curving, his dimple appearing. I made him *laugh.* Hot tears rushed down my cheeks, and I couldn't take it anymore; I threw my arms around him and hugged him tightly.

"Tell me to let go if you need me to," I breathed, shaking as I clung to him.

"I'm okay," he promised, folding his arms around me, so warm against me. "You have no idea how much I need this, Haley. Every day, I imagined this. I dreamed of you holding me, telling me everything would be okay now, that I was safe. It was the only thing that kept my dark thoughts at bay. But I —I *hate* that I could only touch you for a few minutes when we were together. I hate that I wasted so much time."

"You're traumatised, and triggered by touch, Wane. That's not wasted time. Do you think I ever loved you any less because you have tight boundaries? I never did. You always respected my needs, so why is it a bad thing that you had needs, too?"

He held me tighter. "I just—being alone for so long in that room, all I wanted was to have you close. Being alone and without you was a thousand times worse than what happened when you touched me. I wanted to go back in time and do everything differently."

"You told me once that *what ifs* are a special kind of torture."

He sighed, unable to argue with his past self. "I know. I just missed you so much."

I melted into him, resting my face on his shoulder and letting his sweet scent drown every sense until I could breathe again. "You know I'm going to kill him for what he did to you, right?"

Wane's chest jumped with a soft laugh. "That's the fourth promise I've had in twenty-four hours."

"Good. It's a family murder, the whole gang's involved."

His next laugh ruffled the baby hairs at my scalp. "Just like old times."

I smiled, but it still felt strange and frozen on my face, and I was one sharp motion away from throwing up again.

"Haley, I—" Wane began, softer. Careful. "I'm sorry for how I treated—him," he breathed, knowing I couldn't stand hearing Wynvail's name right now. "I didn't realise—I've had a lot of time to think today, and I was wrong. When I said he wasn't your mate. I was wrong."

My stomach cramped. I pressed my face into Wane's shoulder, inhaling short, sharp breaths as I rode out the nausea. "It's okay."

"It isn't," he disagreed, barely louder than a whisper. He wrapped his arms tightly around me, and I only realised I was waiting for his wings to enfold me too when I remembered, with a sick jolt, that they'd been severed from him.

I dove for the edge of the bed, getting to the bucket barely a moment before more bile burned up my throat. This wave passed quicker than the others, with Wane rubbing my back and his soul wrapping around mine.

"I said all those awful things to your mate," he murmured, his voice husky and broken from years of screaming. "And he just accepted them and—and he freed me."

"Cronus ordered him to," I rasped, reaching for a half empty bottle of water on the bedside table. I couldn't even say who'd brought it; I'd been so out of it since I passed out in Wynvail's bed yesterday.

"No," Wane disagreed softly, pulling me back to the bed and settling my head on his chest when I stopped throwing up. "Didn't you hear what he said? His self-preservation instincts kicked in. He could have fought it. But he chose to lead you to me in that house, and let you free me, even knowing he would—"

"Die," I finished, guttural and low.

Wane held me closer to him, ducking to press a long kiss to the top of my head, his warmth seeping into my icy skin. "He was a good person, and I couldn't see past his creation to realise that until it was too late. And I can't tell him I'm

17

sorry, but I can tell *you*, and you deserve that apology, Haley."

"He's a dick," I muttered, refusing to use the past tense. "He probably wouldn't accept your apology anyway. But I'm not mad at you, Wane. I'm—I don't feel anything."

"You're in shock," he corrected, which made a lot of sense. "And we're all going to be here for you when it wears off."

Not all of them.

"I didn't even like him," I muttered. "I wanted to kill him myself. Who should I care that he's gone?"

"Because he's your mate, and he might have been a dick, but you're a good mate. Your heart is so big."

"My heart's a dick, too." How dare it make me fall for a villain? "I wish I could cut it out."

Wane ran gentle fingers over my hair.[1] "Please don't hurt your heart, itzaia. I'm very attached to it."

My eyes were hot, tears burning them, and a lump the size of a golf ball formed in my throat. I'd been desperate to hear that name for so long, desperate to hear *him*, his voice, to feel him against me, his arms around me.

No, *this* was more than I dared to dream of.

"What do you need?" I asked, pushing off his chest and scrubbing my face free of tears. "What can I do to make this easier for you? And don't try to bullshit me that you're fine. You've been locked up and tortured for a century; this is a huge adjustment for you. So tell me what I can do."

"You can eat that sandwich," he replied hesitantly, his eyes on the grey sheets of Wynvail's bed under us. Like he was shy to ask. Or afraid. Embarrassed? Ugh, my chest being a lump of ice was starting to piss me off; I needed to feel his emotions so I could understand him and take better care of my mate.

"What?" I asked, and cleared my throat when it came out thick.

Wane flicked a tentative glance at me, shadows of suffering cutting into his cheeks, making him far more gaunt than he'd ever been before. I still saw the shape of my Wane in him, but it was like Cronus had chiselled away any softness. "You're in pain, and that overrides my pain. Mate thing," he added when I began to argue. "I can't focus on myself when you're tormented. And you haven't eaten anything in two days, Haley."

Shit, it had been two days?

"So *please*, eat the sandwich," he finished.

When he asked so sweetly, how could I deny him? I propped my back against the cushions, reaching for the plate. I slid a sly look at him at the last minute and broke the sandwich in half.[2] "If I'm eating, so are you, zivai."

His eyelids fluttered, lashes casting deep shadows on his gaunt cheeks. "Fine," he sighed, meeting my sly smile with one of his own.

When he took the sandwich too easily, biting into it, I narrowed a stare on him. "You knew I'd bargain, didn't you?"

"I knew it was a possibility," he agreed, a light entering his eyes that made me want to sob like a baby.

I ate my sandwich in slow, gradual bites so I didn't throw it up. Wane and I shared the rest of the water between us, both struggling but too stubborn to admit defeat. He thought Cronus had broken him? When he could speak and smile and look at me like that?

"The muffin is a step too far," I said after a long moment, the two of us sharing a comfortable silence. We might have been apart for years, but our bond had been whole and unbroken this whole time. He'd never once forgotten me.

He laid another kiss on my forehead and moved the tray off the bed, lifting his arm to let me cuddle close.

"Thank you for eating," he murmured, brushing a soft touch down my cheek with a scarred knuckle.

"Right back at you," I replied in the same tone. I swallowed and said, "Wane, I—"

"If you even *think* about apologising for anything that was out of your control, I'll be forced to silence you," he cut in, making me blink. Reminding me that Wane had always been introverted and tentative, but never timid when it came to me.

My whole chest was numb and icy, but my body flickered with a slow-creeping heat. "Oh, yeah?"

His thumb brushed the dip under my bottom lip. He held eye contact for so long that my stomach squirmed. "Yes."

I swallowed. Licked my bottom lip and said, "I'm sorry it took me a hundred years to come for you."

"Alright, you asked for it," he warned, and grabbed my hips, hauling me up his body so he could kiss me hard enough that my head spun.

I broke the kiss quickly. "Wane, I taste like vomit and sandwiches."

"The most shocking thing is you think I care," he replied, and gripped my hair hard enough to keep me in place for another deep, powerful kiss.

I groaned and melted, my heart soaring and part of my soul healing as he kissed me fiercer, taking full control of me. I needed this, needed someone to control me so I didn't have to think or feel. I needed the distraction and the connection more than I'd realised.

When Wane caught my bottom lip between his teeth, I couldn't think of anything but him. He licked the dimples his teeth made and surged back into my mouth to claim my tongue, leaving no part of me in doubt that I belonged to him.

When he finally released me, panting, I could only blink.

His rapid, laboured breaths hit my skin in waves of heat as he kissed my cheek, my jaw, my neck, almost obsessive in the way he covered me with his lips.

"Wane," I groaned when he pressed me into the cushions and covered me with his body. A surprising hardness met my hip, making my whole body flash hot and cold. My pussy ached. "Can we—not here?"

Not in Wynvail's bed, not when I never got to be intimate with him. It was a cruel reminder of what I'd never have. I understood what Wane meant about wasting time. I'd been so fucking stupid.

"Anything you need, itzaia," Wane murmured against my collarbone, leaving a long, adoring kiss there until I felt like crying. He gathered me against his body, my legs around his waist, and lifted me off the bed.

"How are you so strong?" I asked, a furrow pinching my brows. "Shouldn't you be weak?"

"Cronus has no use for weakness of any form. If my body had wasted away, he'd have ended me. But every time he killed me, every time I returned, I came back stronger."

"Is that a titan death thing, or an archdemon thing?" I asked, clinging to him as he carried me down the hall to the bathroom. My stomach tightened at the thought of showering off the blood covering me. If it hadn't been Wane holding me, I'd have squirmed out of his hold, but every moment I had with him was a goddamn gift. I'd lost him. I couldn't bear to break contact with him for a second now.

"I'm not sure," he replied, his mouth in a thin line as he shuddered open the bathroom door.

I traced a finger over the sharp edge of his cheekbone and down to that frown, brushing carefully, still so sure I'd trigger him and have to let go.

But whatever Cronus had done to him had replaced that trauma, so much worse and more harmful than twenty years with Cassander Locke. Like a killer whale swallowing a shark.[3]

"Archdemons are hard to kill, but I've never heard of death

making them stronger," he went on, setting me down on the wide marble counter beside the sink. This room was the bathroom of my dreams, all white marble and classy black accents —and pink cloths and towels.

Because Wynvail hadn't just bought this house for me. He knew me so obsessively that he'd decorated it for me too, every single piece something I loved.

I remembered him being furious with Kai for muddying up his rug and my eyes stung. He was protective of the things in this house because they were gifts for me.

"Haley?" Wane murmured, haunted silver eyes fixed on me, wide with worry. He cupped my face in warm hands. "Hey. Where did you go?"

I blinked fast, a lump back in my throat. "This house is mine."

He tucked a lump of dirty hair behind my ear. "And you can't look at anything in it without remembering your mate."

"Yeah," I squeaked out, determined not to cry again. "I never knew—any of it. I thought I was a challenge to him, a prize he wanted to claim. But this? It means I was always —more."

It hurt so much to say it out loud. The thoughts had been circling my head constantly for the two days I'd been in his bedroom.

"And I know I have the house from him, but ... I don't want to take this shirt off. The blood is *his* and—and it's proof he existed. Cronus unmade him, but if his blood is still here, then I—"

"I know," Wane said gently when I struggled to finish. "Kai figured it out. That man's knowledge of you is scary," he added, making me smile even if I couldn't feel the answering emotion in my chest. "Here, we thought you could put a piece of your shirt in here."

A lump grew in my throat, my face hot with near-tears as

Wane grabbed a pair of scissors from a drawer, and from his pocket he drew a long silver chain with a glass vial dangling on it. I didn't know what he planned, but the fact they knew I couldn't let go of the shirt and had thought of ways to help me, to soothe me, meant so fucking much.

"It's meant for tiny gemstones, but who cares?" Wane murmured, his eyes on me, nervous like he was waiting for me to break. Maybe I was already breaking, right before his eyes. Or I'd broken on the driveway outside the house in the Damned Realm, when Wynvail died in my arms. "What if we cut off a piece of your shirt, and you can carry it with you always? You'd always have a piece of him that no one could take away."

I sniffled, pressure gathering in my face, right over my eyes and cheeks. I could do that. I could take the shirt off if I carried a piece of Wyn with me. Wane was right; no one could ever take him from me then.

"Okay," I croaked, swallowing as I met Wane's worried eyes. "Thank you."

"Thank Kai, he's the genius," Wane deflected, sending a gentle brush down my soul. "Which piece should we keep?"

I looked down at the stained mess of my clothes. Gods, I was a mess. Holding Wynvail to me while he bled out from a neck wound meant I was *covered* in blood.

"This," I rasped, sliding the shirt over my head and wincing at how much it stank. I'd worn it for days in the Labyrinth. Oh gods, I—I stole this shirt from a wardrobe in this house and taunted Wynvail about stealing his shit. But he'd bought it for *me*, all this time. No wonder he looked so amused.

My vision blurred as I cut a piece of fabric, Wane helping me place it in the vial and pushing the stopper in. He sealed it with a tendril of shadow.

"So it'll never come open accidentally," he told me, and dropped the chain around my neck. It beat against my breastbone, a solid reminder that Wynvail was real. He might have been created by Cronus, but he was every bit as real as the rest of my mates. "And we're going to have a memorial ceremony. Nothing formal or fancy, but—Emlyn said you might need it. And for what he did for us, for *me*, we owe it to him to remember him."

"Don't—" I began, trying to push the words past my swollen throat. "Don't stop saying his name. I know it hurts me, but if we stop saying his name, he could be forgotten."

Wane slid his arms around me, exhaling a rough breath when I wrapped my wings around his back. "We owe it to Wynvail to remember him."

It was like a stab wound in my chest, but I meant it. We needed to say his name. I wouldn't have his name be a taboo. I wrapped my fingers around the vial, part of me settling at the physical proof of my mate's existence.

"What?" I asked when Wane's attention fixed on my stomach. "Oh." My curse mark. "Yeah, that."

He let out a heavy sigh, stroking the backs of his fingers over the black ink. "We need to find who gave us these marks."

"And kill them?" I asked hopefully.

"And get them to undo them," he corrected with a mild laugh, kissing my cheek. "But yeah, we can kill them, too. Why not?"

"This one is nullified by the line here, but the mark cursing me to kill you guys ... I don't know how to stop it." I swallowed, but when Wane pulled me close, the tension in my shoulders melted away. He was here, home, scarred but safe.

"We'll figure it out," he promised, shadows flickering around him, the silken texture brushing my bare chest. I arched into the touch.

"You should save your strength," I chided him. His shadows had been so faint when we got him out of that room; judging by the thicker mass of them around us they were healing but slowly. He couldn't use them to fully hide himself yet.

"Or," he countered.

I drew back, frowning until I met his silver eyes and glimpsed the desire turning them a shade darker.

"Or?" I asked breathier than I intended.

His shadows stroked up my sides, caressing my neck, kissing the edge of my jaw. "Or I can show you how I spent most of the last hundred years."

My heart beat harder. "How?"

"There wasn't a single day where I didn't picture all the ways we'd been together in the past, and the way the others would make you gasp and cry. The way your whole body flushed a beautiful shade of pink when you got close to the edge. With their hands, mouths, and bodies, I learned your body. I couldn't touch you for ten years, but I paid attention to every minute thing that gave you pleasure. And for the last century, I spent hours thinking about how I'd use that knowledge if I ever got to touch you."

I shivered, my pussy hot and pulsing. "Fucking hell, Wane."

He smiled, and it was all wickedness. "So I can put these shadows away and just help you get clean. Hold you while you fall asleep again. Or I can keep the shadows out, clean you, fuck you with every ounce of shadow, love, and hunger in my body, and *then* hold you while you fall asleep."

"Where did this dirty mouth come from?" I demanded, clutching him closer, wrapping my legs around his hips.

"I told you. I planned how I'd give you pleasure, and I know the effect dirty talk has on you."

I groaned. "You're trying to ruin me."

He grinned like we hadn't been murdered, kept apart a hundred years, and tortured. Dimples appeared in his cheeks. "Of course I am. Good girls like you deserve ruination."

I groaned. It was official. Wane van Khama was dangerous.

CHAPTER 3

WANE

*T*here were a hundred things I wanted to do to Haley, a thousand ways I wanted to pleasure my mate. I didn't know where to start. I wanted *everything.*

She arched against me when I slid her off the counter, the fabric of her trousers clinging to her deliciously. I didn't care that they were filthy; they were on her body, so they were beautiful.

"Gods," she breathed when I sank to my knees before her, tugging down the zip of her jeans with my teeth. I held eye contact, never once looking away. I'd been kept from her for a hundred years; I never wanted to look away.

Every time I filled my vision with her, I reassured myself she was here, she came back, too, she wasn't dead. I'd hoped, all this time. I hadn't let myself doubt for a single second. But I was scared I was the only one left alive. Scared I'd be alone forever.

I pressed long, indulgent kisses to her hips when I tugged

the dirty jeans off her, and grazed more kisses over the curves of her thighs. My chest expanded with arrogant pride when Haley let out a choked sound, her fingers diving into my hair.

"Something you want, itzaia?" I asked, holding eye contact as I peeled the dirty denim off her, discarding them entirely.

"Now that you mention it, you *could* move your head a little to the right," she replied, her voice neutral but failing to disguise the dark need in her smoky eyes.

"Here?" I asked, teasing her by moving my mouth the wrong way and delighted by the low, needy sound she let out. A little bratty, a little sulky, and all *mine*. I'd dreamed of coaxing that noise from her long before we were ever separated; for ten years I'd tortured myself by watching, never able to touch her.

Now, my skin didn't crawl, my stomach didn't roil, and a century of being locked away with only my thoughts of company had forced me to face my memories. To dismantle them until they couldn't hurt me anymore. They couldn't stop me smiling against my mate's thigh, or skimming my scarred fingers up the backs of her legs, paying special attention to the sensitive spot behind her knees that made her shudder.

I knew each and every one of her weaknesses, and that knowledge made my smile hook a little deeper.

"Oh, *fuck*, don't look at me like that," Haley groaned, tightening her grip on my hair. "I thought you would be a slow, gentle lover. I should have known better, with the way you kiss."

I grazed my teeth a little closer to her pussy. "And how do I kiss?"

"Like the world is ending," she breathed, reverent and soft. "Now, kiss my pussy already."

"Okay," I agreed mildly, keeping those dark, stormy eyes locked on mine. *"Beg."*

That one word had a gloriously violent effect on Halwen.

Her stomach hollowed when she sucked in a breath, her tongue flicked over her bottom lip, her eyes darkened another stormy shade. A desperate little noise left her mouth, and her hips jerked forward in an involuntary motion; when I stroked my palms up the backs of her thighs to fill my hands with her ass, her legs shuddered.

"Please," she rasped. Her breathy voice was so damn sexy that my cock throbbed furiously, imprisoned in my pants. *"Please,* Wane, I need your mouth on me."

I kissed her hipbone in reward, and drank down the frustrated whine she made, loud enough to travel further than the bathroom.

"Need my mouth *where?"*

"You're just being mean," she complained.

"That's not an answer to my question," I pointed out, my voice making her breathing come faster, shallow.

When I let go of her ass and leaned back, like I was about to stand, both her hands shot out and gripped my shoulders. I didn't care that her fingertips dug into the wounds of my severed wings. The pain made everything sharper, gave a clarity that made every sensation more devastating. Sound, touch, smell, sight, taste—gods, I could taste her already.

"Wane, please. *Please.* I need you to touch my pussy. I've needed you for so long, waiting any longer will actually *kill me."*

Fuck, her pleas were so pretty. And she was right; she'd waited long enough. I hooked my fingers under her underwear—silkier and smaller than anything she'd worn a hundred years ago—and tugged them down her thighs. She stepped out of them eagerly.

"You beg so beautifully," I told her. Her breath caught on a whine.

I laid a lingering kiss on the patch of hair between her thighs, the scent of her fucking devastating me. I couldn't hold back a groan, and I hoped Haley didn't realise she had true and ultimate control over me. Sure, I could give commands and harden my voice, but if she asked, I'd do anything she wanted. I'd bury my face in her pussy until I suffocated, bring her pleasure with my fingers until my arms cramped, and fuck her until my legs gave out. There was no part of me that wasn't wholly, entirely hers.

"Tell me everything else you want, itzaia," I ordered, knocking her legs wider. "I want to hear every single thing you need from me. If you stop talking, I stop feasting on your pussy. Do you understand?"

I was close enough to watch her pussy throb, for her scent to coat my senses until my mouth watered.

"Fuck," she gasped, fingers digging deeper into my back. I revelled in the pain, blending it with a taste of euphoria when I swiped my tongue through her pussy. The hot, silken texture of her arousal spiked the flames of my lust until it was a full damn blaze. I swallowed it greedily and went back for more, drowning myself in her taste.

"Wane, I—I want—*that*," she moaned when I flattened my tongue on her clit, stealing the move directly from Emlyn. "Oh, gods, that feels—"

"Tell me," I ordered, flicking my tongue against that swollen bud until my face dripped with her need. Every drop on my scarred skin cleansed me, gave me new life. I bit back a desperate litany of adoring words, and said, "Or I stop."

"Please don't stop," she rushed out, thrusting her hips in a shuddering motion that made need pulsate in my cock. "It feels so good, Wane. I love it when you—lick my clit and—how am I supposed to talk when you're doing that?" she whimpered.

She wasn't, but I was thoroughly enjoying her attempts.

I smiled and sucked her clit into my mouth, keeping the suction light. I was self conscious that I'd done something she hated for a second, but she threw her head back with a cry. She stumbled, so suddenly that I had to catch her.

"Lean against the counter." I helped her sprawl over it, and the moment she was braced on her elbows, no longer in danger of falling, I fastened my lips around her clit and sucked in harder, rolling pulses.

When I darted a look up at her, her mouth was open on shallow, panting breaths, and her face was flushed and so beautiful it hurt. Possessiveness and fear gripped me in equal measure. No one would take her from me. *No one.* She was my whole world, the best thing to ever happen to me.

She'd been silent for too long. I pulled my mouth away—and jumped in surprise when her hand dove into my hair, grabbing a fistful of strands to shove my face back in her pussy.

I didn't recognise the low, rumbling sound that escaped me, but it made her back arch.

"Please, please don't stop," she babbled. "Please, Wane, I'm so close. I—I need it so badly. I need to come, please can I come?"

"My beautiful mate," I breathed against her pussy, my lips dripping with the taste of her. "Of course you can come."

My voice came out even—I'd learned to hide every bit of emotion under Cronus's cruel hand—but inside I was losing my goddamn mind. *She was going to come? Because of me?*

My hands shook where I gripped her ass, and I unleashed myself on her, devouring every drop of arousal. I ate her like a madman, like an addict, like I'd die without another taste of her. I used my whole mouth, and I didn't know if this technique was right, had never learned this from anyone; this was instinct and need driving me, dark and pure.

I wanted every damn part of her to be mine, wanted to cover her in my touch like I was covered in her name, until there was no doubt who she belonged to.

"Wane!"

Her hips bucked when I glided a finger through her slickness and slid inside her. *Fuck.* Her pussy was so hot, and so goddamn soft that I lost my mind, my cock throbbing wildly. I'd imagined this so many times, but the fantasies were grey compared to these violent sensations.

She quivered around my finger, so I added another and moved my mouth faster, more desperate with every moment. She was going to come—on my face, around my fingers. She was a gift and a treasure and she was mine. She was really going to come.

"Please don't stop, don't stop, don't stop," she chanted, digging her fingers into my shoulders, tension winding her body into one taut, desperate line.

I groaned against her clit, the taste of her, feel of her, *sound* of her wrecking me. The tension in her body snapped, her wings flaring wide and knocking bottles off the counter. I didn't give a shit if we broke them. She grabbed my head in both hands, tugging on my hair as her body shuddered, her shout filling the room and echoing back to drive me twice as crazy.

Her pussy gripped my fingers in tight, forceful pulses, scalding and dripping and making every part of me ache to be inside her, feeling that around my cock.

She came all over me, fucking *drenched* me with her needy thrusts, and all I could think was *I really made my mate come.* With *my* hands and *my* tongue, not a surrogate's or a fantasy. *Me.* Mine.

My knees hurt from the cold tile floor, but I didn't stop eating Haley until her legs stopped shaking and her loud cries turned to little whimpers—I'd learned that years ago from one of her needy tantrums when one of the guys stopped too soon. She'd squirmed, knocking a candle off the bedside table, and nearly burned the safe house to a blackened crisp. My mate was deadly when it came to her pleasure.

"Wane," she gasped now, her hips jerking against my mouth one last time, "Wane."

I pressed a final kiss to her clit as she slumped against the counter, her eyes fluttering shut. Her chest rose and fell with long, slow breaths, her expression calm. Fuck me, she was beautiful.

I withdrew my fingers, instantly obsessed with the gleam of her on my skin. Her arousal and cum was a siren song; I wrapped my lips around my fingers and groaned at the explosion of her taste—sweeter than before, deliciously smoky, and nowhere near enough.

I'd just devoured her pussy, and I needed more. If I got lockjaw, I got lockjaw; some things were more important.

"Wane," she groaned, her eyes flying open when I lifted her onto the edge of the counter, spreading her legs. Her teeth met her bottom lip when I sank my fingers back inside her, moving slowly so I could watch the play of expressions on her face.

"I love you," I blurted, my heart beating so hard in my chest. "I love you so much I can't breathe. I don't care what I have to do to keep you with me; I'll burn down empires and start wars if I have to."

She blinked fast, her grey eyes shiny. "And I'll end those wars to keep *you* with *me*," she replied, reaching for my face to draw me in for a kiss, and freezing when she noticed the blood on her hands. "Shit, Wane—"

"I've spent a hundred years apart from you," I breathed, "and you think I care about a little blood? Drain my body dry; if I get to hold you close and make you come, I don't care."

"You're crazy," she hissed, but she groaned when I withdrew my fingers and sucked them clean before gliding them back inside her.

"Crazy and yours," I countered. "Now kiss me, itzaia. Taste yourself on my tongue."

Her whole body shuddered, her pussy clamping down around my fingers as she slammed her mouth into mine.

The force with which she kissed me made my head spin, the sweet smoke of her on my tongue driving me wild. I fucked her with my fingers, greedy for her next orgasm.

"Another," I groaned, ordered, begged against her lips.

She grabbed my hair in a tight fist, kissing me deeper, and I matched the ferocity with my fingers. The wet sounds of my hand meeting her pussy made my cock painfully swollen inside my pants.

I opened my mouth to tell her to take out my cock, but Haley proved she was the mate of my dreams, the greatest woman on the planet, because she stole my words with a kiss full of growls and teeth, and wrenched my pants open.

I swore against her tongue when she gripped me in a squeezing fist. My eyes rolled back.

I'd never been touched by anyone except myself. All those other times, that awful cot in the basement, the pain, the fear —that didn't count. That wasn't sex. I'd erased it from my story; my life started the moment Harvey and I escaped.

"Eyes on me," Haley commanded, breathless and husky.

I followed her order and fell into her blazing stare. There was so much love there, so much need and rage and affection that it didn't match the cold burn of icy numb coming from her soul. When the shock wore off, she was going to be a force of nature. The whole world would burn, and it would deserve every second of judgement.

"You're here with me," she panted, squeezing my aching shaft. "Only me."

"Only you," I agreed, and slid my fingers from her pulsating heat, filling my mouth with her taste until my eyes fluttered, heavy-lidded. "I'll never get enough of your taste, itzaia. I want to fall asleep with it on my tongue every night and wake up with your pussy riding my face every morning."

Her mouth dropped open, smoky eyes darkening further, and her fingers stroked up and down my cock, thumb swirling over the tip. She was touching me, stroking me, *finally.*

"That dirty mouth is going to kill me," she said, her voice high and tight. I could hear the desperation in her tone, could hear how badly she needed me. *Me.*

Whatever expression I wore, it made her throat bob and her thighs tremble when they clutched me closer.

"No more fingers," she begged in that breathy voice that made my balls ache. She pumped my cock in her hand, dragging a deep grunt from my throat. "I need you. Please, Wane."

I grabbed my desperation in a chokehold and forced out, "Need me where, itzaia? Use your words."

Her eyes rolled, a convulsion going through her body. "I need your cock. I need you to fuck me so hard that we break this counter. I need every inch of you inside me, so I forget every moment we spent apart. I need you to fuck every dark thought out of my head, and fill me so deep that I lose my mind. I'm yours, Wane. I've *always* been yours."

She reached between us, spreading her pussy with two fingers. My dick jumped uncontrollably in her hand, my breathing a quickened mess. Shit. I understood why dirty talk ruined her now. I bit back a whimper, watching a drop of needy arousal drip from her. Matching precum slid down my length.

When she used her grip on my cock to lower me to her entrance, I dragged together every last scrap of control I possessed, and asked, "Did I say you could put me inside you?"

She shook, that tremor the exact reason why I fought for composure. She *loved* me being in charge. I heightened her pleasure with every calm word and cold command, and this second orgasm was going to be explosive. And I would feel every second of it around my cock.

I kicked my trousers off, ripping my shirt over my head and delighting in Haley's rough groan.

"Every part of me is marked with your name, itzaia. This body is yours. The soul inside it is yours." I bowed over her, my lips brushing hers with every word. "You own me, inside and out."

She swallowed, her pupils so wide, swallowing the smoke grey of her irises.

"Here," I said harshly, struggling to keep it together as I covered her hand with mine, guiding her thumb over the underside of my cock. "Feel it?"

Her head fell onto my chest. Her hips lifted off the marble counter, a deep throb making howling need crack through the numbness in her soul.

"You—" she panted. "Are you *insane?*"

"I'm yours," I countered.

"You carved my name *into your cock?*" She sounded outraged, her breath hot on my chest.

I smiled, running my thumb across the back of her hand. "It's yours; why wouldn't I?" She groaned, those cracks widening. "But it's an old scar, fully healed. I want it drenched in your desire. I want you throbbing around your name. I want you to come all over my scar."

Her back arched again, hips leaving the counter for longer. She was so desperate, her need dripped all down the worktop and coated her inner thighs. I wanted to cover my face in her flavour, but sinking inside that wetness would be every bit as heavenly.[1]

"Please," she whined, wrapping an arm around me. "It hurts; I need you."

One brush to her clit, and she'd shatter. Hopefully, I'd last longer than one stroke inside her; a hundred years of planning and fantasies, and that would be embarrassing as fuck.

"Hold onto me, Haley," I murmured, releasing her hand so I could stroke my thumbs over the flushed tips of her nipples. I wanted to taste them, but I couldn't do everything this first time. We had more time together. I'd make love to her every day.

Her arms locked around my neck, and she blinked wide eyes up at me, eager for another command, desperate for her pleasure. *I love her so fucking much.*

"My soul," I breathed, kissing her quickly. "Remember what I said about my shadows?"

She blinked, so needy she was dazed. "Huh?"

A grin crossed my face. "Watch my cock, itzaia. Watch what I'm going to fill your needy pussy with."

She groaned so loudly it nearly undid me. But I panted through gritted teeth and encouraged my shadows to flow, guiding them around my legs, wrapping in circles until I was half flesh, half darkness. They reached my cock and shadows grew from the tip, a long, writhing tongue of velvet dark extending my cock by four inches.

"Inside me," she panted, trembling hard. *"Now.* I want to feel it, I need to feel you, I—"

She dug her fingernails into the back of my neck, and threw her head back on a cry as my shadow cock stroked through her wetness. It was as solid as a real cock but far more flexible. When it filled her, Haley's eyes glazed over and her pussy clenched hard.

"Oh, it's—*oh.*"

Now, she understood. While my flesh and blood cock stretched her, my shadow cock undulated inside her, finding all the weak spots that made her body buck and her cries fill my ears. I fucked myself into her with shallow thrusts, the sheen of arousal that coated my cock making me absolutely feral.

She was dripping with desire *for me.* Wane van Khama. Her mate. Her shadow.

I fed her more of my cock, sinking teeth into my bottom lip when her pussy stretched around my base, taking all of me. Drenching the scar I'd carved into my skin like I told her to. The noise that came from me was wordless and inhuman. This felt … a thousand times more intense than I imagined.

Haley dug her heels into my ass, grinding me deeper, her eyes blown wide. I knew I must look equally stunned, equally needy. My shadow cock writhed inside her, searching, ruthless, for the spot that would make her shatter. I'd watched her body react to her other mates finding that spot to know it was her undoing.

I guided my magic in a slow swirl, applying pressure, and was caught by surprise when Haley's eyes rolled back. A rush of pleasure deluged my soul from hers. Holy fucking shit, that felt too good—our combined pleasure was deadly.

I grunted, slowly withdrawing and driving back into her heat. *Fuck,* that felt good. Too good. My balls ached; I panted, holding my orgasm at bay through sheer will, my teeth bared.

"Wane," she whimpered, testing my control with my name in that high, pleading tone.

I screwed my eyes shut and fastened my mouth to her throat, my teeth and tongue obsessing over the taste of her salty skin as I rolled my hips in slow, shuddering thrusts.

"Faster," she pleaded.

I picked up the pace, pleasure boiling dangerously. But whatever Haley wanted, she would have. And the throaty sounds she filled the bathroom with were worth it, even if they made my balls ache, and my cock throb inside her. Her pussy was *incredible,* gripping me like a vice but so soft, and so fucking slick. I'd never felt anything this good before.

My hips snapped into her thighs, the sound wet and forceful, and my breathing came faster, heat coiling tight in my gut. My shadows writhed faster inside her, always returning to that place that made her moan, stroking it every time I drove my whole length into the hot clasp of her pussy.

When she rippled around me, her cries louder, I buried my cock to the hilt inside her and roared my pleasure. Both flesh and shadow cocks spasmed, darkness lengthening, thickening until she cried out at the new stretch.

Yes, itzaia, every part of this pussy is full of me now. Every part of it is mine.

"Ah," she gasped out, her hips bucking off the counter, pussy squeezing me so hard my eyes crossed. I kept coming; I couldn't stop.

I buried my teeth in her shoulder, muffling my groans as I ground my cock inside her, guiding my shadows to that sensitive spot and making them shudder like vibrations. No one had taught me this, but I'd had a long, long time to contemplate how I could use my magic on my mate. Her reaction was so much better than I imagined, her cry so much louder.

Her legs locked around me, breathing fast and sharp, and when she came, the convulsions were so powerful that they ripped another orgasm from me before I'd even come down from the first. I was so sensitive, all I could do was whimper when she kept coming, but I didn't stop my shadows caressing her for a damn second. If I died from overstimulation, so be it.

Her next sound was choked and short, her inner muscles milking my cock from the tip of my shadows all the way to the base. Coming all over my scar of her name like I'd told her to, because she was my good girl.

When she stilled, I pulled my mouth from her throat and gritted my teeth, my cock too damn sensitive.

Her eyes were shut, her body slumped against the wall and dark wings splayed—and panic hit me fast. But she was breathing, and there was only pleasure and relief in her soul. Smugness bloomed then, a grin crossing my face as I embraced the final flutters moving her pussy around me.

I'd made her come so hard she blacked out. Good. She deserved nothing less.

I tentatively withdrew from her pussy, a sharp breath whistling through my teeth at the way she clung to my cock. It was right on the edge of pain, and I couldn't decide if I couldn't bear it or wanted more.

Fuuuck. When my shadows slid out of her, cum overflowed her pussy, oozing over the countertop. A dark sound vibrated my chest; I stared at my cum coating her pussy. *Mine. Fucking mine.* And there was the proof, dripping out of her, *marking* her. It was primitive, but I didn't care. I stroked a finger through our combined fluids and pushed them back inside her where they belonged.

Haley's eyelids fluttered, lashes parting as she gazed at me like a lazy, satisfied queen.

"You passed out," I told her, guiding more of my cum inside her.

"You don't have to sound so smug about it," she whispered. "Are you—pushing your cum back into me?"

"Yes," I agreed.

She laughed, rubbing her face. "Psycho."

I raised an eyebrow at that remark, gliding my fingers out of her and pressing them to her lips. "Suck."

She groaned, and obeyed, swirling her tongue around my fingers like they were my cock. I was too spent to throb, but I couldn't hold back a soft curse.

"Wane?" she murmured when I dropped my hand.

"Yes, Haley?"

"I love you."

I smiled, my chest so full of affection that it ached. "I love you so much, it should be impossible."

"Is this the part where you take me into the shower and wash me clean?"

I kissed her, soft and loving. "No, Haley. I'm nowhere near ready to wash myself from your body."

She trailed a low, proprietary stare down my body. "Hate to break it to you, zivai, but you're looking a little limp there."

I grinned. "My cock is," I agreed, enjoying the flash of panic and lust across her features when I added, "But my shadows aren't."

Her whole body arched when I filled her with a thick tendril of darkness. I made her scream my name so loudly there was no doubt everyone in the house heard her.

CHAPTER 4

HALWEN

I slept so deeply I probably snored, my body relaxed and satisfaction burning every ounce of stress from my body. I woke up around dawn, my face on Wane's bare chest and my eyelashes glued together. I didn't bother getting up; I rolled over, pulled his arm around my waist, and fell back asleep.

I didn't recognise where the dream took me at first. There was only a blank wall across from me when I groaned and sat up, but apprehension rolled down my spine like ice water.

The ground began to quake, shaking my body so hard that the feathers on my wings shuddered, my hair lashing my back and shoulders.

And then the sound came, arrowing deep into my bones, carving through my skull until it was all I could hear. My thoughts were drowned out by the noise, my breathing silenced. Stone ground on stone, violently loud, so *familiar* that I flinched and forgot I was dreaming.

I scrambled to my feet, my knees already weak, hands shaking. I was boxed in. Stone walls stretched to the sky on every side of me. I was back in the Labyrinth.

I threw myself into the closest wall, my arm and stomach blazing with crimson light as the magic buried in my curse marks reacted to my terror. I couldn't think straight, couldn't use logic to escape. I hammered on the stone with my fists until skin bled and the bones in my fingers snapped.

When the wall finally fell, Wynvail was on the other side, laid in a pool of blood where he'd bled to death because I was too slow.

I WOKE WITH A GASP, MY WHOLE BODY JERKING AND MY HEARING sensitive and sharp. I strained for the deep, groaning sounds of the Labyrinth, held my breath and waited for the roars of monsters and the screams of my mates as they died.

Wynvail was dead. He wasn't coming back.

I covered my mouth with my hand, my bottom lip wobbling and tears flooding my cheeks and soaking the pillow.

Wane and I had slept in his room; he hadn't asked for an explanation when I said we couldn't sleep in Wynvail's room. I didn't want anyone's scent to drown out my mate's. Because he was never coming back.

He was ... dead. He—sacrificed himself for Wane. Let himself be unmade. Because I needed Wane, because I was so deeply unhappy without him that Wynvail felt it through our bond.

But also because Cronus had done such a thorough job in convincing Wynvail he was worth nothing. He thought I needed Wane more. He thought I'd be fine if he was dead.

I bit my bottom lip when it shook uncontrollably, and not

even Wane's arm around my waist could hold the emotions at bay. I'd fucked up. By telling him over and over that I hated him, that he was a monster, and I wanted him dead—I'd fucked up. Because I only half meant it, and Wynvail had died never knowing that.

I slid out from under Wane's arm; it was a testament to how badly he was still hurt that he didn't even stir. It was probably the first deep sleep he'd had in years. In decades.

I brushed a lock of mahogany hair from his face, my bottom lip shaking as I stared at Wane, peaceful in his sleep. But there was no hiding the scars all over his body, and the damage I felt deep in his soul. Cronus had killed him over and over, exploiting an archdemon's near-invincibility, making sure it wasn't a true, final death so he could bring him back for even more torture.

I was going to hunt Cronus down and repay every bit of vile, inhumane pain he'd dealt every one of my mates. But I didn't know how to do that without him killing all of us first. I'd died once; I didn't plan on dying again.

I kept an eye on Wane, checking he didn't wake as I dressed, pulled on my boots, and grabbed my leather jacket. He needed to rest and heal. And I needed to outrun my nightmare.

But there was no escaping the gnawing ache in my chest. It was eating through my numbness, until Wynvail was all I could think of. All I could see was him punching his hand through a shop window and handing me a dagger because his alphas had hurt me and he didn't know how else to apologise.

It was all I could think of. The dagger he'd given me. The dagger I traded away like it was worthless.

I couldn't breathe, couldn't function. I had to get it back.

CHAPTER 5

*B*y the time I reached Iarlon, the sun was setting, but time was different here. It could have been sunrise in Edinburgh, could have still been pitch black night. Either way, I knew my mates were going to be furious when they realised I'd gone. I couldn't think straight; it only occurred to me that I'd put myself in danger, and been completely stupid by leaving *alone*, when I flew over the gates to the capital and landed outside the palace.

But it was too late to back out now, and the ache in my chest gnawed deeper, spreading until my whole body hurt. I needed the dagger. I needed—needed Wynvail back.

"Move," I barked at a cluster of winged women loitering in the pale hallway I stalked down. My skin crawled, needles stabbing into my pores. They were just standing there, sharing pictures. *Chatting.*

My eyes burned with tears, but rage beat against my breastbone until I wanted to kill them. I'd failed Wynvail. I let him think he meant nothing to me. He died thinking I could live without him; he didn't even tell me what would happen when we all walked out of that place with Wane. He didn't give us a chance to find another way. He accepted his fate. But *I* couldn't accept it.

One of them women twisted towards me, scowling at my tone. I saw the picture they were looking at—a squash-faced new baby with dark skin and cute tiny horns. My gut clenched. Yet another way I'd failed my mates. I could never give them a child. Ten years of failure and loss slammed into me hard enough to make me stagger.

Trembling, I ploughed through the women, their wings brushing mine, soft but abrasive and cutting my nerves to shreds.

"The fuck's wrong with her?" one of them muttered.

I hunched my shoulders, tucked in my wings, and marched on, scanning every corridor for the pink-skinned woman I'd traded for the jacket on my back. She wasn't in the dining hall, the library, the gym, or any of the training rooms.

I shook harder with every moment. Failures mounted with every second. Where was she? I needed my dagger. I *needed* it.

"Hey, are you okay?" a man called when I rushed past him, probably because my breaths were loud and wheezing. I didn't bother to see who it was. "Slow down, a little."

"Can't," I bit out, shoving open the door to the kitchens and scanning the busy room. Not here.

"Whoa, wait a second," the infuriating man said, his voice so gentle and pacifying that it made me want to punch his teeth in.

I spun to face him with my fangs bared, a growl so loud and threatening in the back of my throat that someone dropped a pot in the kitchen behind me.

The do-gooder currently testing my patience was the hybrid angel-demon I'd met in the gym—the pretty, long-haired redhead who was one of Queen Lili's men. I couldn't remember his name, or if he'd ever told me it.

"Get out of my way," I growled, ploughing past him and

storming down the corridor. I had five places left to check before I lost my mind entirely.

I was relieved when I glanced behind myself and found the corridor empty, the irritating redhead gone. Good. I didn't need help; I needed to find the pink woman and get my dagger back. It was *mine.*

I finally found her in a common room where a group of soldiers and guards were playing cards. The same game the alphas had played in Kalador before I killed them all.[1]

I stalked across the warm, busy room, not seeing the den-like decor or the demons lounging on plush green sofas, scrolling through their phones or reading books. I only saw *her.* She looked exactly how she had last time, but in a grey denim jacket this time.

I tore the black leather off my back and threw it down on the table, scattering the cards and money stacked on the polished wood.

"I need my dagger back," I snarled, too far gone to be friendly. My whole body vibrated, blood whooshing in my ears and thumping in my chest as my magic responded. *"Now."*

The pink woman sat back in her seat, her mouth pressed in a flat line. "Fuck off. It's mine now; we traded for it, fair and square."

I'd liked her the last time we met. Now I just wanted her dead.

"I need it back," I repeated, my voice gravelly. A final warning.

She scoffed, rolling her eyes to her friends like I was being ridiculous. *My mate was dead!*

I grabbed hold of the magic boiling inside me and poured it into her heart, squeezing so hard that she shot out of her seat and grabbed her chest.

"I *need* it," I ground out, my hands shaking violently. Her heartbeat quickened, pulsing through my magic, filling my ears. "My mate gave it to me."

"Then why did you trade it?" a man at the table growled, grabbing his friend. Or girlfriend. I didn't care.

"Because I hated him then, but now he's—he's—gone." My whole body shuddered. Hot tears burned my eyes, spilling down my cheeks in a rapid flow even as rage pounded faster. I failed him.

I lost my grip on my blood power; her heart slid from my control and resumed beating rapidly. "Please."

"Did you say your mate died?" a woman breathed behind me, footsteps padding closer until I whipped a glare at her and she froze. This woman was small and birdlike, tawny and wide-eyed. "How are you still breathing?"

Killing them will kill me.

Not necessarily. You already died once; there's no telling the effect their deaths could have on you.

"Maybe I'm not," I replied, my anger rapidly forsaking me. I shuddered, cold replacing my fire.

"Daina," the birdlike woman said sharply, glaring past me at the table's occupants. "Give the woman her knife back."

Daina made a throaty sound, and I turned back to face her when she dug the dagger from inside her denim jacket. She held it out to me with long pink fingers, looking pissy about it.

I launched back at the table and snatched the blade from her, my fingers trembling around it. It was exactly as I remembered, the scabbard covered in pewter forget-me-nots, each one lovingly cast. I squeezed my fingers around it, clutching it to my chest and half hoping it would cut me.

"I missed this jacket anyway," Daina huffed, saving face after obeying a petite, wide-eyed woman half her size. She threw me a vicious glare. "Now get the fuck out of our—your highness," she blurted, her eyes darting behind me and widening.

My shoulders slumped, a new weight crashing onto my chest. I had my dagger back, I'd undone that failure, but now I would be thrown in the dungeons for threatening half the palace. Maybe I'd have an adjoining cell with Bevan.

My mates would be furious and scared and stressed. Now, I'd failed them too.

"Everyone out," Lili's calm voice cut through the silence, and motion blurred around me, chairs scraping the floor as they were pushed back, sofas creaking as their occupants jumped out of them.

I turned slowly, my heart hammering fast, the numbness fully worn off. And *oh god*, the pain it had been masking was enough to make my knees buckle. I grabbed the back of an overstuffed armchair to keep myself on my feet, and ignored the strange looks thrown my way by everyone rushing to leave the room.

"If you're going to throw me in the dungeons," I said in a dead voice, "just do it. I don't care."

"What the fuck happened?" a coarse voice snapped.

Renna stalked into the room behind Lili, with—with Tali right beside her. There was also a woman with a long, silver braid and tanned skin who I didn't know, but she followed, too.

I swallowed. Licked my dry lips. Renna fixed her sharp gaze on me, making it clear she expected an answer.

"Wynvail's dead," I said in that same empty tone, staring at the knife in my hand.

"And?" Renna demanded, crossing the room with long strides. "Don't we hate that bastard?"

"He's my mate. And he's dead."

"Oh, honey," Lili breathed, sympathy softening her whole expression, widening her brown eyes.

Honey. *Honey.*

That word echoed louder than a death knell, and an axe of brutal pain hacked my chest open.

My knees finally gave out; I crashed into the carpet, tears landing on the dark swirling fabric.

Awful, hiccupping sobs possessed my body, and I didn't know how to make them stop.

CHAPTER 6

I ended up bundled onto one of the huge, squishy sofas, Tali's massive red head resting on my knees as she made low, soothing sounds to comfort me. I couldn't stop the tears flowing, couldn't seize control of my breathing long enough to make the sobs stop.

Someone stroked my hair, and it made me cry harder. Even Renna was quiet, not snapping for once. No one pressed me for details until I stopped choking on my own breath, until my cries died out.

I jumped when a warm hand uncurled my fingers from the first where my fingernails bit into my palm, and a teacup was pressed into my palm by the woman with the silver braid.

"Who are you?" I asked, surprised by the scratchy quality of my voice and how quiet it came out.

"Asta," she replied, patting my hand before she backed away, sitting on the arm of the chair where Renna loomed, turning over a small knife in her purple fingers. "Renna's wife."

"Oh." I was so wrecked that I didn't respond to that news appropriately. It was a different sort of numb in my chest now; before, ice had blocked off my emotions. Now I was hollowed out, all feelings cried out until I struggled to feel anything but gnawing loss.

"Drink your tea," Asta ordered, her voice soft but steely.

I didn't bother to argue; I brought the cup to my mouth for a sip—and choked on the taste of moss and mould. "Ugh, that's awful."

Renna pointed her knife at me, but she obviously felt bad for me because she didn't verbalise her warning.

"Nothing healing ever tastes good," Asta replied good-naturedly, nodding at my cup again. "It'll soothe your emotions for an hour or so."

Well, in that case... I lifted the cup and chugged it like a pint of ale, not stopping until there were only a few leaves in the bottom.

I felt the effect almost instantly, and the clarity was brutal. My bottom lip wobbled. I couldn't hide under numbness or grief anymore.

I might as well get the interrogation underway.

"Go on," I choked out, setting the cup on the floor at my feet and—accepting the salted cracker Asta passed to me. Where did she even get it from?[1] "Ask the questions I can see you're dying to."

"What happened?" Renna exploded, like she'd been barely keeping the question in. "The last time you were here, you wanted Wynvail dead and now you're broken over his death? Did he have a personality transplant?"

"Renna," Asta chided, giving her wife a disapproving look that, to my immense surprise, made Renna sigh and shoot me an apologetic look.

"No, it's a fair question," I murmured, clearing my throat and staring at the cracker uneaten in my hand. Lili leaned closer, nothing but sympathy on her tanned face. "I did want him dead. I hated him. I called him a monster and—" My throat tightened, my voice a squeak. "I called him so many awful things. I stabbed him, for gods' sakes."

Tali's head vibrated on my knees, her question a gentle rumble. *What changed?*

My bottom lip wobbled; I pressed my mouth thin until I had it under control. "We went to find Adhiti, but instead—Adhiti's been dead for years. We found a titan. Rhea. She was captive, and tormented, and—and she used me as a tool for her suicide."

A hot tear spilled down my cheek. Lili leaned across and brushed it away, the touch, the friendship, doing far more to heal me than getting Wynvail's knife back.

"She's my great grandmother. I'm—I'm descended from a titan."

"Shit," Renna breathed, subdued for once.

"And the whole reason Wynvail set up Alphaven and started collecting alphas was because—because he had to. He was made, not born, and—I'm telling it out of order." My breath shuddered when I inhaled. "The cave started coming down around us. We were going to die. And then Wynvail showed up and got us out. He took us to a safe house, but—"

My hands shook, every word painful. I tasted blood.

"Rhea killed herself to escape her captor. Another titan had imprisoned her there. Cronus. And he—he stole my mate from me a hundred years ago. My Wane. He made me forget, cursed him so no one would remember him. Even Lucifer forgot him. Cronus is—he's a monster. Never Wynvail. He's a villain and a bastard, but not a monster."

"How did he die?" Asta asked, a furrow on her pale brow.

I scrubbed my face, and shoved the cracker in my mouth because I was sick of holding it. It tasted like ashes, like nothing.

"Cronus was pissed off that Rhea died, and that Wyn came to save us. So he—punished us. He tore a portal through the floor of our living room, and sucked us into the Labyrinth."

"*The* Labyrinth?" Renna exploded, jerking forward in her seat so suddenly that she dropped her knife. It plunged into the floor tip-first and shimmied there.

"I don't—want to talk about what happened in that place. I can't—I haven't even processed. We all nearly died so many times, and Wyn, he was—he was like one of us. Cronus commanded him to kill my mates, to break me I think, so I was easier prey."

"He didn't kill them, did he?" Lili asked gently, her eyes wide and sad.

I shook my head. "The stupid idiot helped us. And we—we fought our way out of there, half-dead and broken. And then we went to find Wane."

"The mate Cronus had captive?" Renna clarified, speaking the words like she couldn't quite believe them. Like she doubted the titans were real like I had.

I nodded, my throat tight. "I thought Cronus would be furious if we found him, freed him. But it was what he wanted all along."

My throat closed up so tightly that I couldn't speak. I flicked tears off my cheeks, jumping when Tali began to purr a low, comforting sound.

"Wane was bait, wasn't he?" Asta asked, figuring it out faster than I had. I didn't realise it until Wynvail started to—until he—died.

I nodded, sniffling. My whole body shook. "When I crossed the threshold with Wane at my side, my magic flared. Like a—a trigger. Wyn said it broke the seal on Cronus's prison. On Tartarus."

"*Shit*," Lili gasped, and flew to her feet. "I'll be back. Tali, you're on cuddle duty."

Tali leapt up onto the sofa when Lili rushed out the door,

laying half her massive, furry body over my legs and purring a deeper rhythm of comfort.

I needed to finish the story, I had to end it. The words clawed up my throat, digging in like barbs that fought me with every syllable, but I spat them out.

"Wynvail knew it would kill him, but he did it anyway. Because I needed Wane. He'd outlived his usefulness to Cronus. The only reason that monster made him in the first place was to push me to that moment, so my magic would shatter the seal. I don't even know how I did it, or if I can —undo it."

"We'll figure it out," Asta assured me, kindness swimming in her hazel eyes.

"He died in my arms," I rasped. "And then he just—he turned to dust. Like Cronus wiped out every trace of him."

It was silent for so long after I said that. Even Tali's purr died.

"No wonder you needed the dagger back," Renna said eventually.

My lips trembled. "I just want him back so I can hate him again, because this—this hurts too much."

"He's your mate," Renna replied, her sharp edges worn blunt. "It's unspeakable to lose part of your soul. Of course you need him back."

"But I *hated* him," I choked out. I hated myself for it, would always hate myself for it. "And I treated him like shit."

"Because he was a dick," Renna said comfortingly. "Anyone would have hated him."

"You can hate someone and love them at the same time," Asta added, and I got the sense the couple were counselling me.

It's not your fault he's dead, Tali rumbled, butting my stomach with her head. I swallowed and said nothing. *It's not your fault,* she repeated harder.

"Feels like it," I croaked.

Tali shook her furry red head, her eyes so big, so full of worry and pain on my behalf. She began to say something, but her head snapped to the side a moment before emerald green magic blasted through the door and part of the wall, slicing it into shards that collapsed to the floor with an almighty crash.

Renna and Asta jumped up with matching defensive positions, both drawing a knife so fast I didn't see where they came from. Magic shook the room, and I thought it was theirs until Emlyn stormed through the door and I felt the unstable power coming from *him*.

It scythed through three chairs and a table until they fell apart too, and Emlyn strode through the wreckage, his blue eyes fixed on me with bright, red-hot rage.

CHAPTER 7

*M*y bottom lip wobbled, a sick, oily feeling twisting my stomach when Kai, Harvey, and Wane strode through the room after Emlyn, sidestepping the severed bits of furniture.

"Back the fuck up," Renna spat, lifting a violet hand in warning. Not the hand holding the knife but another where deep red magic pooled like blood. She and Asta cut off Emlyn before he could reach me, and Tali leapt off the sofa to crowd me behind her, a low menacing growl baring her teeth.

"Don't rip his head off," I pleaded, and cleared my throat when it came out tight and squeaky. "He's my mate, Tal-Tal."

"This caveman's *your mate?*" Renna demanded, holding her hand further in front of her, red magic dripping through her fingers. "I thought you said they weren't feral anymore."

"Fuck off," Kai spat. He was so angry that my knees knocked together, my hands shaking so hard.

"Move," Harvey growled, his beast close to the surface.

"So you can hurt my friend? In your dreams," Renna laughed, deep and coarse.

"Yeah, tell 'em, babe," Asta encouraged.

"If you keep me from my mate," Emlyn replied in a voice so deep that the walls shook. Or maybe that was Kai losing control, his snakes going haywire. "I will kill you so thoroughly there won't be a single scrap of your flesh left to bury."

"Threaten my wife again," Asta breathed, so calm that I shuddered in primal warning. *I dare you.*

"Stop," I rasped, my voice too weak for the shout I tried to form. But my mates paused as if I'd yelled, and that seemed to make the power couple stand down.

I blinked, and Wane was in front of me, his body wreathed in shadows. I jumped hard, my heart slamming into my ribs, but I slumped into him when he pulled me into a tight hug. He made soft, *shhh* noises, holding me close, and I fell apart.

"Make one move to hurt her, and I'm castrating you, no questions asked," Renna warned someone. Phantom pain chased through my bonds from the guys, and I managed a weak smile.

"Why did you leave, Hales?" Emlyn growled.

My stomach twisted, sickness crashing through me in waves of nausea. He was angry at me. Like he'd been angry at me the day we were killed.

A low, mournful cry swelled in my chest, and I couldn't stop it escaping.

"I'm sorry," I breathed, my breath catching halfway through and making the words a sob.

"Don't," Harvey sighed, and my shoulders hunched, pain spiking through me. They were all angry at me. He didn't even want to hear my apologies, and I—I'd been so selfish, running off in the middle of the night. "She's here, she's safe. We've done this once before; I don't want to live it again."

Harvey brushed past Tali, my friend hovering protectively close, her teeth still bared. When he wrapped his arms around me from behind, forgiveness and care in the touch, my knees buckled.

"I-I wasn't thinking," I choked out. "I'm so sorry, I didn't think, I just—I needed the knife. I gave it away like it was nothing and it's *not* nothing, he was *never* nothing and I—"

Warm fingers turned my face, and Kai leaned close, pressing a long kiss to my forehead. "Shh, it's okay. It's okay now, my rose."

"Em's mad at me," I choked out, a fresh wave of tears burning my eyes before they flooded down my face.

"Em's *scared*," Wane corrected gently, stroking my side with a shadow-wreathed hand. "We all are. You were just *gone*, and there was no trace of you."

"You thought Cronus took me," I realised, my shoulders sinking and shame curling through me. "I should have realised."

"Hales," Emlyn murmured, closer than before. Tali must have finally let him through. "I'm sorry for shouting."

Harvey made a rolling motion with his hand, and Em sighed, scrubbing his face because—those were tears trickling from the corners of his eyes. My stomach plummeted. I'd made Emlyn cry.

"I'm not angry at you, I don't want you to think I am. It's just so hard to have you out of my sight after the Labyrinth, let alone to find you gone. I'm sorry I made you cry."

"I'm sorry I made *you* cry," I choked out, my bottom lip wobbling when Wane pressed a kiss to the side of my neck.

"We'll leave you to talk," Asta said from behind the wall of protective muscle and magic. *"Won't we*, Renna?"

"Not willingly," Renna muttered. "But fine."

"Thank you," I croaked. I'd been gifted a lot of amazing friends since I was reborn, like the universe was looking out for me.

"Tali," Asta warned. "Come on."

If they make you cry again, I'm eating their feet, Tali grumbled, nudging Harvey aside so she could lean up and lick my face in one wet, gross swipe of her sandpaper tongue. *Men can survive without feet; I'm being generous.*

"Ugh, Tali," I groaned, wiping her slobber off my face with a shaking hand.

She backed up, giving each of my mates a narrow-eyed glare. Except for Wane, possibly because he hadn't shouted at me. Or because the animal part of Tali could sense he was suffering right now.

I dared to meet my mates' eyes, expecting anger and disappointment but finding neither. Fear and frustration, but no anger. Em's blue eyes were still watery and pained.

"I didn't mean to scare you," I told him, my voice hoarse. "I just—" My bottom lip wobbled violently, and Em rushed forward. Harvey shuffled aside so Em could hug me, and I trembled in his arms.

"No more running off on your own," Kai said gently. "Even if your head's fucked up and you're breaking down, take one of us with you. Yeah?"

"Yeah," I agreed, my throat closing up. I shouldn't have come here on my own. Their heat bled into me, thawing my icy numbness. "I didn't want to wake you up. After everything we've been through, you need sleep."

"Fuck sleep," Kai hissed, his forked tongue snapping out. "I'll sleep when I'm—safe and Cronus is dead."

"Nice save," Harvey whispered.

"Shut up," Kai muttered, making me smile.

"So you're—not mad at me?" I asked, holding Em closer.

"Shaken, but not angry," Emlyn replied, squeezing my side, never taking his eyes off me. Like he needed to reassure himself I was okay.

"Why did you sneak out, Sugarplum?" Harvey asked, his voice carefully soft.

I swallowed, flexing my hands, and panic hit so severely

that I recoiled. "My dagger, I've lost it—no, please gods, it can't be gone. I need it, *I need it*, I can't—"

"Is this it?" Wane asked, leaving my side for a moment, and reappearing with his hand held out, my pewter knife secure in his bronze fingers.

My face crumpled, and I nodded, crying ugly tears. I clutched the dagger to my chest, my body shaking again.

"Oh," Kai breathed, understanding and sadness bleeding through his soul to mine. "The dagger Wynvail gave you."

I nodded, my bottom lip shuddering and my nose running, tears racing down my cheeks.

"That's why you came here," he murmured, carding gentle fingers through my long hair. "You needed to get it back."

"I gave it away; I was so stupid," I rasped, staring at the knife, telling myself I hadn't lost it, it was still here. "I don't—I don't have anything else—"

"Shh," Emlyn murmured, pulling me into a bear hug that dwarfed me in heat and comfort.

Harvey pressed himself flush to my back, dropping slow, calming kisses on my shoulders. Kai stroked my hair until I could draw a long, shuddering breath. Wane folded his hand around mine, shadows caressing my knuckles. Like they could all sense the fractures in my sanity, the breaks in my soul.

Losing my mate should have killed me. Instead, would I deteriorate like my mates had without me all those years? Would I forget Wyn? Would I forgot how to speak and love and do anything except fight?

"What if I turn feral?" I dared to ask, gripping the dagger until my knuckles turned white.

"You brought us back," Emlyn reminded me, worry deep in his blue eyes. "We can bring you back, too."

I swallowed, and nodded. That seemed optimistic, but he wasn't wrong.

Em wiped a tear away and leaned closer, kissing my cheek

in a long brush. He pulled a face and asked, "What do you taste of...?"

A laugh rose unbidden from the depths of my stomach, the sound relaxing the wall of tension and tightly-coiled muscle around me, relief hitting my bonds.

"Giant panda tongue," I told Em.

His face wrinkled further, a cute furrow in his scrunched nose. "Yuck."

I laughed again, my cheeks aching with a smile after crying so hard. "The good news is you met my best friend and she didn't eat you. That's positive."

Wane's hand tightened around mine. "You don't mean *actually* eat...?"

"Oh, I do. I watched her eat a guy. She crunched his skull like a bar snack."

"Shit," Kai breathed, a little shudder running through him. "The friends you choose, my rose..."

I sniffled, brushing tears and panda slobber off my face. "Yeah, well I chose you fuckers. Did you think I'd pick normal besties?"

"She has a point," Harvey said warmly, sending a brush of affection down my soul that made tears threaten my eyes again.

"I won't leave you again," I promised now I'd calmed down and could think clearly—for now. Grief was still messing with my head. I knew it wouldn't ever stop. "I fucked up."

"You're forgiven," Emlyn murmured. "And if you needed your friends, you only had to say, Hales."

"Kinda rude that we're not your entire world, but okay," Kai muttered, joking. Or I thought he was joking. Actually I wasn't sure.

"I didn't plan any of this," I told them. "They sort of just ... swaddled me in hugs and crackers before I could stop them. It's nice to have girlfriends, though."

"No sex," Kai hissed, his eyes glowing.

I rolled my eyes. "Possessive psycho. Two of them are married to each other, one has a whole parade of scary men, and Tali's a giant panda. Calm your tits, Malakai."

Kai grabbed his chest in both hands, faking being affronted. "Me and my tits will *not* calm, thank you very much."

I snorted.

Wane lifted our joined hands and brushed a kiss to my knuckles. His soul was a tangle of panic, pain, and relief, but it was bundled up in sympathy and love, sharper and clearer than the other's emotions. "Can we go home now you've got your dagger?"

"Yeah," I breathed, double checking it was still in my hand. "We can go home."

We'd be safe in the Edinburgh house.

But safe didn't make a difference when the clock was ticking down, and our curses were still unbroken.

A week left—that's all we had. A week until we killed each other.

CHAPTER 8

"We need to find the person who tattooed me," I said the next night, brushing creases out of my pillow until it was a perfectly flat surface before I laid my head. "Or a curse expert like Ashboren told us to."

"Who's Ashboren?" Wane asked, laying on his side facing me, with a chunky wrap of bandages around his chest. It did nothing to stop the wounds on his back bleeding, and neither had any of the lotions or salves we'd tried. Neither had Harvey's healing power.

"An alchemist," I replied.

"Grumpy old fucker," Kai muttered, knocking Harvey's hand aside so he could touch me.

"He was only grumpy because you all broke his shit," I pointed out, relaxing into the expensive mattress. "And he helped us. The stone he gave us worked."

"The stone you *bought* worked," Emlyn corrected. Yeah, he had a point. Ashboren hadn't given us it out of the goodness of his heart. I still needed to thank that old bastard, though. He'd given me my mates back.

"So we find a tattooist or a curse scholar," Harvey murmured, his soul aching and voice subdued.

I felt the weight too, the press and crush of Wynvail's absence. The remembrance ceremony we held tonight had helped, but barely. At least we acknowledged what he'd sacrificed, even if Kai *did* go off on a rant about all the ways he'd fucked with them and allowed others to torture them.

I had to make it convincing. I couldn't let Cronus realise I only took you three so he couldn't keep you.

But that excuse only went so far. Wynvail should have protected them. Instead, when we first met he'd been so dead set on claiming me as his that he'd been willing to let my other mates die. Or kill them himself.

He was a bad person and a good person in the same body. I hated him. Loved him. Missed him.

"And then what?" Harvey finished.

"We threaten them into helping us," Kai suggested seriously, making Wane laugh softly, his breath ruffling my hair.

"We could try asking," he suggested with a yawn.

"He's right," Emlyn agreed, stretching his arm carefully across Wane's body so he could stroke a light touch down my wing. "We'll ask first, and threaten them if they refuse."

Kai grinned, like he'd won. I pinched his hand where it rested on my side, earning a hiss. He flicked out his forked tongue, eyes narrowing like I'd challenged him.

"Whatever you're planning," Em said tiredly. "Don't."

"I'm not planning anything," Kai replied innocently. Not a single one of us believed him.

I was surprised by the sudden scorch of desire through Wane's soul; he guessed Kai's intentions long before I did. My body responded to his lust, heat travelling through down my body until it reached my clit, making it throb.

"What *are* you planning?" I asked Kai, turning to face him

and absently brushing Harvey's wing where it rested on my thigh. He shuddered.[1]

"I'm undecided," Kai replied casually, as if his red eyes weren't smouldering with heat. He flicked his tongue out again, tasting me on the air. Or teasing me with what he had planned. "I'd be interested to get the guys' opinion. Do you think we should fill all her holes with cock, or get my tail involved? Either way, we should give her so many orgasms that she can't speak."

"Or until she passes out," Wane added mildly.

I slid a smirk in his direction, remembering how fucking good his shadow cock felt.

"Wait, what?" Harvey blurted, his eyes wide. His hand flexed on my hip.

"Yeah, he fucked me so good I passed out," I told him, with a grin curving my cheeks.

"Nice," Kai praised and lifted his hand. I shot them *both* a glare when Wane high-fived him.

Even Emlyn looked impressed, and something like affection softened his eyes when he looked at all of us. "Would you rather sleep, Hales?"

I snorted. "No. When have you ever known me to turn down orgasms?"

"Never," Harvey answered my hypothetical question, wrapping his wing around me and tugging me closer. His breath rippled down my neck, making me shiver, suddenly sensitive. "Our mate is a greedy girl when it comes to pleasure."

I didn't mean to smirk. But... "Is that a pun?"

I felt his confusion through the bond.

"When it *comes* to pleasure."

He groaned, nipping my shoulder. "That's awful, Sugarplum."

"Don't be mean. Em, tell him not to be mean." I twisted to

pout at my big, cuddly mate, but my heart skipped a beat when I saw the heavy desire darkening his blue eyes a shade. He was a little rumpled and devastatingly handsome, his teeth bared behind his beard in a wide smile. Soft sleep clothes fitted to the shape of his body, tempting me to trace his shape, and wicked, wicked plans churned behind those eyes.

Em didn't tell Harvey not to be mean. He glanced at Kai and said, "I think we should give her all our cocks *and* your tail."

"Um," I breathed, lifting my hand. "How?"

Emlyn just chuckled, the sound dangerous and sexier than it had any right to be. "We'll be generous and let you choose what goes where, won't we, boys?"

I shuddered at them ganging up on me.[2]

"It's only polite," Wane agreed.

I dropped my head onto the pillow with a groan. He was going to kill me sounding so dominant and in control.

I watched Harvey and Kai exchange a surprised glance. Yeah, Wane was far more involved than he used to be. He'd normally have slid out from the pile of limbs and roaming hands, retreating to a chair where he had a good view. I remembered all the times he'd watched them fill me, fuck me, and reduce me to a sweaty, whimpering mess, stroking his cock the whole time. Sometimes he waited for them to move away and spilled himself across my body. I groaned at the memories, heat pounding through my clit.

Harvey grinned suddenly, sitting up beside me to gaze down at me. He swiped his thumb along my jaw and brushed my bottom lip. "Oh, Haley. We're going to destroy you."

I whimpered, so fixated on Harvey that I didn't notice Emlyn had moved until he rolled me onto my front and pulled my ass into the air. I didn't know what he was planning. My anticipation mixed with nerves, tingling through me deliciously. Goosebumps covered my body.

I was only wearing a long t-shirt and underwear for bed, so it was easy work for Em to bare my ass, the shirt falling into the dip of my back. The soft graze of the fabric made me shudder, and I tried to look over my shoulder to see what Em was doing, but Kai's palm flattened to the spot between my shoulder blades, keeping me pinned to the bed. Magic shuddered around his palm and into my skin, the scratch of invisible fangs making my back arch further.

"Gods, Kai."

He laughed, ducking over me to drag his real fangs along my shoulder with only the fabric between us. It would be a useless barrier if he decided to bite me. I was acutely aware that he hadn't bitten me since we'd been reborn; I hadn't felt that rush of endorphins and venom heighten my pleasure for a hundred years.

"Lift up, Hales," Emlyn murmured, his voice gravelly. "Make room for me."

I had no idea what that meant, but Kai had it covered. He manhandled me into the middle of the bed so Emlyn's body could fit under me, and I realised his nefarious, sexy plan when Em's hips slid under my face, his thick cock bobbing against my lips. He was already so swollen, dripping precum. He must have practically ripped his clothes off, he'd undressed so fast.

When I flicked out my tongue to taste a drop, his cock jolted and he groaned, his big chest shaking my stomach.

I wasn't sure if his mouth dragging along the length of my pussy was a punishment or reward, but either way pleasure stroked all my nerve endings. I reciprocated by dragging my lips up the thick vein in his shaft, sucking the underside of his tip. For every lick and suck I made, his tongue swirled and lapped at my pussy, his pace unhurried and indulgent.

I jumped when a soft, wet tongue glided over my ass, my heart slamming into my chest. It thrust past my tight muscle before I'd even processed there being a second tongue.[3] I recognised Harvey's boldness. Or Kai's gluttony. But shit, Wane had been more forward and commanding lately. Okay so I had no idea who was tongue-fucking my ass. Why was that so hot?

I groaned when Em's tongue thrust into my pussy at the same time my mystery mate buried their whole tongue in my ass. The sensation was completely insane—cool and wet and soft and firm all at once. I groaned around Em's cock, sucking hard, my eyes slamming shut. I grabbed his thighs, gripping so hard I left imprints in his skin.

"Fuck, that's hot," Harvey grunted, too far away to be the man whose tongue curled inside my ass to flick new spots. I tore my mouth off Em's cock to pant, gripping the base so hard I probably strangled off the blood supply. He roared against my pussy, sending tremors through my clit, and my back arched. When a hand pushed me back down, tongue driving deeper, I knew it was Kai.

"Shit," I gasped when Em's tongue stroked through my wetness to flick my clit, over and over like he knew I was close. How was I so close to orgasm so fast? Goddamn, these mates were sex magicians.

When Kai's tongue moved deeper, the forked ends taunting the sensitive walls of my ass, I grunted, guttural and deep.

The bed dipped on my left. *Oh, fuck.* I shuddered, both holes clenching as a slow, velvety hand stroked down my back. No, not a hand. A shadow.

When a weight sank into the mattress on my right, both twins pressing against me, I ascended to a whole new level of pleasure. I sucked Em's cock just to muffle the scream I made when I came.

My hips jolted hard with every wave of pleasure, my eyes blown open. I gagged around Emlyn's cock, accidentally taking him deeper than planned, and my throat squeezed his tip. Em groaned, the sound so deep and visceral that it made my climax soar higher. My mouth filled with the taste of his cum. Panting, my head spinning, I swallowed everything he gave me, knowing that drove Em absolutely crazy.

I grabbed the sheets under me as Em and Kai pushed me even higher, stroking both tongues inside me. Em's groans filled me, not stopping until my powerful spasms turned to quiet tremors and a rough breath punched out of me.

"Fuck, guys," I groaned, turning my head to rest it on Emlyn's thigh, his cock slipping out of my lips. His leg was squishy enough to make an excellent cushion; I should have done this before.

"That's the plan, my rose," Kai replied, withdrawing his tongue from my ass.

"I'll get her ready for you," Wane offered, his voice an electrifying mix of softness and cold, hard command.

Emlyn shimmied out from under me, ignoring my muffled noise of complaint as my cushion retreated. I'd been comfy, dammit.

I opened my mouth to voice my grouchy protest, but the noise choked off in my throat when a long, slim finger pushed into my ass. I grabbed the sheets, bunching them in my hands.

When the finger thickened, my wings shuddering involuntarily in response to the new sensation, I realised it wasn't a finger. It was a shadow. And with Wane controlling it, I didn't know how thick or deep it was going to go.

"Wane," I rasped, the burn and stretch only making me eager for more. My pussy ached, throbbing, empty. I was pretty sure arousal dripped out of me, pleading, desperate.

"Gods, you're beautiful," he said in a low voice just for me.

A long, sensual stroke down my soul drew a whine from my throat, and his shadow began to slowly move, swirling across every sensitive spot just inside my tight ring of muscle.

When he found an especially devastating spot, his shadow shuddered fast, vibrating against the weakness until I fell onto my forearms, my face mashed to the mattress and my eyes rolled back. It wasn't the first time I'd had something in my ass, but the way this felt, it was brand new all over again. I'd never experienced anything like this. My mouth popped open, tongue lolling out.

"She's gonna come again," Kai realised. "What are you doing with that thing?"

"Jealous?" Wane taunted.

His cockiness made my hips buck, and I choked on a cry as his shadow was pushed deeper in my ass. Frantic, I slid a hand under me to circle my clit.

Someone groaned. More than one person. When two fingers plunged into my pussy, satisfying the needy ache with fast thrusts, I sank my teeth into the covers and climaxed so hard that not even a moan came from my frozen body.

"I can feel your orgasm through the bond," Harvey groaned, telling me it was his fingers in my pussy, stroking fast and deep. Oh *shit*. Being touched by both van Khama twins at once fucking *broke* me. My whole body convulsed, my pleasure so intense that I couldn't breathe.

I barely felt when they slid out of me, or when the twitches died down, or when I resumed breathing in rough pants. When I opened my eyes I could only stare, blink, and unclench my teeth from the sheets.

"Here," Kai murmured, using the soft voice he only used for me. "Come here, my rose."

I didn't know much right now, but I knew I was incapable of moving.

I recognised the arms that gently lifted me and settled me against Kai as Emlyn's, and knew the slow, loving stroke brushed down my hair was from him, too.

Kai's snakes came around me like a firm hug, and his

fingers carded through my hair when I dropped my head onto his shoulder. I got deja vu. This could have been a hundred years ago. Things always got intense when we were all together, not just one-on-one, and Kai was our designated cuddler. He always held me while I floated back to Hell—or Earth in this instance—and helped me piece my mind back together after they exploded it with extreme bliss.

"You are so fucking beautiful," he murmured, pressing a kiss to my temple. "I've never seen anything as sexy as when you come, my rose."

I sighed when a soft kiss met the arch of my back and slowly, lightly trailed up the dip of my spine. With Kai stroking my hair and kisses covering my skin, I could fill my lungs with air and flex my fingers against Kai's chest. His skin was feverish and hot. His dick was also hard behind my ass, though he was ignoring it so he could take care of me.

"Drink this, Sugarplum," Harvey said, and I lifted my head off Kai's chest to see a glass of orange juice held out to me.

I smiled. It really was like old times; they knew exactly what I needed, like a hundred years of pain and misery hadn't passed.

"Thanks," I murmured and accepted the cold glass, draining half of it in one go.

"Good girl," Harvey praised, kissing my cheek. Warmth spread through my chest, and I sighed, a weight melting from my body. Their care was even more euphoric than the orgasms.

I finished the rest of the juice and couldn't resist wiggling against the erection resting on my ass. Kai must not have expected me to, because his fingers tightened reflexively in my hair and he grunted.

"Insatiable," he teased me, nipping my ear and snaking his magic fully around my waist so he could lift me, settling me so his cock brushed my pussy instead. "There, writhe against me, greedy girl."

Lust burned a sudden fire in my pussy, my clit throbbing. It reminded me so much of one of our early days, when he kissed me for the first time. It had been one hell of a kiss. I needed another right now.

He groaned when my lips slammed into his, and I mirrored the sound when someone pressed close to my back, gentle fingers teasing all the sensitive spots on my wings. Shit. That touch to my wings was dangerous; my pussy throbbed wildly, my clit swollen so badly that I reached down to take care of the ache.

"No," Kai chided, catching my wrist. "Hands on my shoulders, my rose. And didn't I tell you to writhe against my cock?"

Goosebumps rippled down my spine. I followed his instruction immediately, and the friction against my clit made my eyes roll back. I knew it would be intense again far too quickly, but he was right—I was greedy. I didn't care.

I chased my pleasure, forcing my hips to move slowly when I really wanted to move fast and frantically. But I couldn't handle fast right now.

As if sensing my thoughts, hands settled on my hips and feathery wings brushed my own.

"Slow," Harvey murmured, setting my empty glass on the bedside table and guiding my hips in languid rolls. "You're not allowed to come again until we're both inside you."

My mouth opened in affront. "How is that fair?"

"Take it or leave it," Kai cut in with a smirk, his eyes fixed on my chest as I moved in sinuous motions. "We can stop right now..."

"No," I muttered, glaring at the smug, handsome bastard as his hands wandered up my front, skimming my ribs on their way to squeeze my boobs. "I can wait."

"It's going to kill you, isn't it?" he asked, a fang poking free as he grinned.

"I can wait," I repeated, a sulky tone entering my voice. "It takes more than a few touches to make me come."[4]

"Well, in that case..." Harvey murmured, his wings stroking over my own and a soft, blunt cock grazing my ass. I sucked in a breath, stilling my gliding movements over Kai's cock. "You can handle this easily, can't you, Sugarplum? Since it takes more than a few touches to make you come."

I bit my bottom lip, bowing over Kai until my spine arched when Harvey sank into me. He moved in slow, shallow thrusts, gaining an inch every time, and each inch drew a new breathless sound from me. He panted, too, each breath laced with a snarl, and claws tipped the hands at my waist when he pulled me back onto him.

Oh shit, too much, too *full*—

Kai leaned up to taste the cries on my lips, kissing me deeply and slowly, him and Harvey overwhelming me with sensations. Burning fullness, euphoric pleasure, deadly antici-pation of what came next, and desperation for more hands on my body, more kisses.

My head floated. All I could focus on were my body's reac-tions, the pounding in my clit, and the way Harvey glided over a sensitive spot inside me over and over.

Every rush and spike of bliss through my body was echoed through the bonds, and their need flowed back into me, Wane's especially sharp, not a single mental wall shielding me from the force and ferocity of his lust. When someone's fingers linked with my own, warm lips brushing the very tips of my fingers, I cried out. Fuck, why were they so sensitive?

"Haley," Kai murmured, his lips brushing my ear, his voice calm and grounding. "Stay right here with us."

I let out a soft moan in reply when Harvey stilled in my ass, my muscles clenching around the fattest part at the base of his cock. He was so deep, so thick. Oh god, I couldn't take any more.

"Take a deep breath for me, sweetheart," Kai went on, his voice so gentle and the caresses on my chest and ribs every bit as sweet. "That's it, just like that. Let go for us, Haley." His hands wandered over my shoulders. "Let go of all your tension here." They travelled up my neck, massaging my nape. "And here." They trailed down my back between Harvey's body and mine. "And here. Lay against me, my rose, stay nice and relaxed for us."

By the time he was done, I was in a trance state, my breaths slower, my body so lax that when Harvey withdrew and thrust back inside, the pleasure was *so* much more intense. It flowed through every part of me until my toes curled.

"Just like that, our beautiful mate," Emlyn said beside us, his voice throaty and rough. "Fuck, you're exquisite."

Em, and his fancy words. I smiled, even that movement slow and languid.

"You're soaked," Kai groaned, inked fingers dipping between us and stroking my pussy. He brushed a kiss to my temple and rasped, "You're going to feel like Heaven."

I tensed automatically when he guided the tip of his cock inside, but I forced each and every limb to relax until I melted between Kai and Harvey. I was rewarded by a powerful shudder as Kai's cock stroked all the best spots in my pussy, like he'd memorised every one.

He moved as slowly as Harvey, careful of me, but the pace let me appreciate every second of them inside me. Both of them together, thrusting and shuddering inside me, stretching me until the feeling made my head spin—my pussy clenched hard, my ass squeezing too.

"Holy fuck," Kai breathed, hands roaming, touching me wherever he could. I splayed against his chest, giving myself over to the sensations they coaxed from my body until there were no ebbs and flows of pleasure, only constant euphoria.

Harvey groaned when Kai's strokes increased, driving us both higher until my legs shook and I gasped for air.

"Breathe, Haley," Kai ordered, his voice hard enough that I instantly obeyed with a moan.

Hot skin brushed me everywhere, wrapping me in warmth and endless, endless pleasure as Kai fucked me. Harvey stretched my ass, staying perfectly still and grunting whenever I throbbed around him. His hands gathered my hair, moving it aside so he could place hot, wet kisses on the side of my throat, his snarling sounds so much closer, louder. They drove me insane, pushed me higher. My toes curled when Kai moved even faster.

"Gods, those sounds," Wane breathed. "Are you going to come again, itzaia?"

I moaned my reply, trembles moving through my body, my pussy and ass squeezing around their cocks in a frantic pace. My climax was building slowly, threateningly. My breathing quickened.

"So fucking wet," Kai hissed, dragging his tongue up my throat, and sucking on a spot just below where Harvey's lips obsessively kissed me. I swore their tongues connected against my skin, and my hips bucked involuntarily.

"Stay relaxed, my rose," Kai panted, his breathing racing, chest stroking mine as he adjusted me above him, widening my thighs. "That's my good girl."

If I was wet before, I was fucking *soaked* now.

Harvey whispered a curse, and I didn't know why until something soft touched my pussy, rubbing in slow, broad strokes. Gathering my arousal, I realised, when that same thing brushed my pussy.

"Oh, shit," I gasped, digging my fingernails into Kai's

shoulders. I remembered his teasing from before about giving me all their cocks—and his tail.

"My rose," Kai breathed, and pushed the silken tip of his tail into my pussy. *"Mine."*

It was a good thing I had permission to come, because the moment his tail *and* his cock stroked my inner muscles, pressing against Harvey's cock through the thin barrier, I fucking detonated.

Kai and Harvey wrapped their arms around me, keeping me still so I didn't hurt myself as my body bucked wildly, my eyes rolled all the way back and my mouth open on low, moaning cries. Intense didn't begin to cover how good my climax was. Impossible, insane—those came closer.

"That's our girl," Emlyn murmured, watching, simmering with love and pride. "You're so beautiful when you come hard for your mates."

I whined, my wings trembling now. I threw my head back onto Harvey's shoulder when he circled his hips, taking me higher. Not to be one-upped, Kai fucked me with his tail, using it to stroke his own cock.

"Fuck. Now, Wane," Kai hissed, his voice so gravelly.

Harvey shifted above me, lifting his body from my sweaty back, his cock shifting to a new position in my ass and ripping another wave of shudders through me. *I'm going to die. This will kill me.*

I cried out with a mess of disappointment and bliss when Kai's tail slid out of me, grazing all my weak spots obsessively. Why was he leaving me? I wanted his tail? Now I knew how full I could feel, I'd be empty without—

"No, no, *too much!*" I shouted when his tail was replaced with something much broader and far hotter. How were they even *doing* this? What mangled creature of a position were we in, for another cock to push inside me, my pussy aching, stretching, sucking at both cocks with powerful ripples.

I knew the breathless grunt that came from behind me, and I knew the hands that landed on my hips, too. Wane. *Fuck.* I was—they were—Kai, Harvey, *and Wane.*

A whining cry burst from deep in my chest, and I held onto Kai tighter, shaking uncontrollably. Oh gods, oh gods. I hadn't come down from the last orgasm, but with Wane slowly, so slowly, thrusting into my pussy, another climax barrelled into me.

Every one of my mates groaned, bliss and devastation crashing from soul to soul until the bed sank and Emlyn growled, a proprietary hand stroking what he could reach of my shoulders. Those fingers traced individual feathers in my wings until my body locked, my hips bucked, and I came so hard I stopped breathing.

Oh gods, this was—it—

"Yesss," Wane breathed.

Kai sank his teeth into the skin between my neck and shoulder and moaned.

Harvey could only let out a choked sound as my ass strangled his cock in ruthless contractions. Each one sent a blinding wave of pleasure through me, until I floated so high I didn't know if I'd ever come down.

I didn't care if I never did.

Emlyn roared, sucked into the endless loop of our pleasure and release through the bond, and I was pushed impossibly higher.

Wane's shadows tipped his cock with velvet wickedness, and I rose higher still, my mouth hanging open on a choked scream.

"Stop that," Kai bit out.

"Why?" Wane panted. "Scared it feels too good?"

Kai just grunted, clutching me tight, his hands the only thing tethering me to Earth. I floated so high, my body a heated mess of spasms and cum and shuddering, rapturous pleasure.

I'd never felt this—all of them. Never.

I speared my soul for Emlyn in the bond, needing him closer, needing more than a single touch on my back. I needed to feel him pressed against me like everyone else. I needed—

He answered my plea with a rush of love and reassurance, and his warm, soft body moulded to my side. I exhaled in relief.

I needed—needed Wynvail. But right now, I floated so high that that thought couldn't hurt me. So I didn't even try to come back down; I closed my eyes, relaxed against my mates, and let the sky carry me far away.

CHAPTER 9

I startled out of a nightmare some time before dawn, the sky still dark blue beyond the little window in the safe house bedroom. My heart hurled itself against my ribs over and over, and I panted like I'd just run a marathon.[1]

My hands shook where they were tucked between my chest and Emlyn's. I didn't know what woke me—I was ripped into consciousness right as Wynvail was about to die, pleading with me to save him—but then the bedroom door creaked, followed by a quiet, chiding hiss.

It didn't take longer than a second to figure out it was Wane. Everyone else was soft and muted in the bonds, where Wane's soul was spiky with panic, and loud with hatred and— shame. I hadn't felt those emotions from him once since we broke him out of the house in the Damned Realm, but they were familiar.

Harvey shifted behind me when I pushed down the covers and carefully crawled out. I glanced back to find he'd cracked open a silver eye. No doubt sensing Wane's distress too, in the psychic twin way they had.

"I'll take care of him," I whispered, leaning over to kiss his forehead. "Go back to sleep, Buttercup."

"I'll sleep when you both come back to bed," he murmured, stealing a quick kiss from my lips.

I wasn't going to get better than that; we were both worried about Wane. He'd been too normal, too unaffected by spending a hundred years tortured by Cronus and his minions. That level of suffering left a dark stain, and I knew acting as if nothing had happened was probably Wane's coping mechanism, but I couldn't help but worry he was burying a lifetime's worth of trauma beneath a mask.

And masks only lasted so long before they cracked.

I pulled on clean knickers and one of Em's shirts, and padded out of the bedroom, managing not to wake anyone else even when I hissed viciously at the soreness in my ass and pussy. My mates had cleaned me up, though, so I didn't drip cum as I closed the door softly behind me. That was a positive.

I took a deep breath, pausing in the moonlit hallway. I needed to settle my own emotions if I was going to help Wane out of the dark feelings emanating from him, but my nightmare still had its claws sunk into me.

I rubbed the sleep from my eyes, and clenched my jaw when emotion threatened to weaken me. My lungs were full of the ever-present scent of this house. Wynvail's scent.

He'd spent time here, and a *lot* of time if the saturation of his scent was anything to go by. His ghost was everywhere, reminding me of what I'd lost. I couldn't breathe without remembering his absence. But I had to pull myself together.

I found Wane in the living room on the second floor, his arms wrapped around himself and shadows thick around him. The only parts of him visible were swaths of bronze skin on his arms and throat, and his hardened silver eyes when he spun at the sound of a floorboard creaking under my careful footsteps.

I didn't say anything as I crossed the room, standing beside him by the window. The very edge of the sky was beginning to lighten, stained purple and pink, but the moon had yet to retreat. Edinburgh was beautiful in the morning, the silhouettes of hundred-years-old buildings making the city almost mythical.

I didn't dare touch Wane, not with the jagged emotions filling our bond. But I snuck a glance at him, and my eyes snagged on the back of his grey shirt where the fabric was soaked with blood even through his bandages.

"I haven't felt like this in years," he said finally, his voice gravelly. He sucked in a long breath, his eyes fixed on the city. "I think it's—fuck, it sounds awful to say it out loud, but—I think it's being around everyone again. Being around Harvey. I dreamt of—*him*."

"He's dead," I told him, keeping my voice careful and soft. "I promise, Wane, he's dead. Wynvail killed him."

Wane glanced at me sharply, messy chestnut hair dancing around his face and making him look so much like Harvey. "What?"

I sighed, pain burrowing into my chest as Wynvail returned to the forefront of my brain. "Wyn found out what Locke did to you and Harvey, and he killed him."

Wane scrubbed a hand over his face, pale overlapping lines forming my name on his skin. "And I treated him so awfully."

"If it helps, I stabbed him a bunch of times," I said with a faint smile. "Pretty sure I did worse damage than you."

Wane laughed so quietly I wasn't sure it counted. "I don't want to go back to the way I was," he admitted, his brown throat bobbing. "Barely touching anyone, scared of every loud noise, jumping at my own shadows. Hiding. Deprived."

My heart shattered to hear him admit that he'd spent all

those years, the whole ten years we lived together, alone and craving touch, unable to accept it without remembering his abuse.

"What can I do?" I asked, clearing my throat when it came out raspy.

Wane's gaze drifted to the living room with its manic décor. "Do you think this house has a training room?"

"Wynvail decorated it for me; of course it has a training room." The words sliced through my chest, but I forced a smile.

"Can we spar?" Wane asked, sounding so vulnerable that I wanted to wrap him in my arms and squeeze him.

I nodded, swallowing the lump in my throat. I could do nothing about the sheen over my eyes, though. "I'm always up for kicking your ass, Wane van Khama."

Van Khama. Never Locke.

The edge of his wide mouth curved up, some of his shadows thinning as he held out a hand. "Let's go find it, then."

I slipped my hand into his, rubbing my thumb over his scarred knuckles.

"And—Haley? Don't let go, even when it's hard for me. I need to fight this, and I need to win."

My stomach cramped. "Okay," I agreed even if that sounded impossible. I was his mate; I was hardwired to protect him, to fulfil every one of his needs. Ignoring him if he needed me to let go would be near impossible.

His body locked, even his fingers taut with tension as we ventured into the hallway, poking our heads into every new room. We finally found a wide, low-ceilinged space on the third floor that was obviously meant for fighting; mats were propped against one wall, another was full of windows, and the remaining two were covered in wooden sticks, swords, daggers, and whatever the hell else Wynvail had gotten his hands on.[2]

"I need—" Wane began, clenching his jaw as a wave of nausea rippled through him. I fought the impulse to release his hand. "I need your hands on me. So no weapons."

"Okay," I agreed worriedly, bringing his hand to my mouth for a quick kiss. "No weapons."

"Touch me as much as possible," he rasped, his voice already hoarse from a century of torture but now? Gravelly, deep, and rife with pain. His eyes were distant too, not entirely seeing me.

"Wane..."

"Please, itzaia," he breathed.

My heart tightened. I nodded, taking a steadying breath. This was going to be as hard for me as it was for him, but if this was what Wane needed, I wouldn't hold back.

I stepped into his personal space, pushing down my instinctual flinch at the blind panic in his soul, his emotions completely open to the bond. I brushed a quick kiss to his cheek and whispered, "I meant what I said, Wane; I'm gonna kick your ass."

He laughed when I drew back and released his hand so I could curl both mine into fists. The sound was raspy and weak, but defiant as fuck. Strength poured through his soul, and I reached for my battle calm, pulling it over me so I could assess his stance.

I dove at his left, but I must have been too obvious—or Wane just knew me inside and out—because he caught my fist in both his hands and wrenched me closer. His lips landed on the sensitive spot behind my ear, making my breath catch.

"I win a move, I get to kiss somewhere on your body. You win, you get to kiss somewhere on mine."

"Can I kiss your cock?" I asked, because I knew it would make him laugh, which it did.

He rolled his eyes, drawing back. "Not now, greedy girl."

A shudder went down my spine, and my poor, sore holes clenched. *No more,* they pleaded. *We can't take it, please.*[3]

Wane's eyes darkened like he'd followed my train of thought back to last night. Or like he sensed the sudden pump of arousal in my soul. I hadn't planned to distract him with sex, but hey, if it worked...

I took more time with my next strike, feinting left again before diving right—he knocked my wrist aside, grabbed my waist, and spun me so my back smacked into his front.

He shuddered hard, trauma tearing through his arousal, but he ducked his head and kissed the spot on my shoulder where Em's big shirt had ridden down.

"Kick my ass? Oh, Halwen," he taunted, spinning me free.

My head spun, but I smirked, riding out the dizziness. "That's *it,* van Khama. You're going down."

"Hmm," he mused, clenching his fists at a wave of brutal nausea. "Good idea; maybe I'll leave my next kiss on your pussy."

My mouth fell open in outrage. So *he* was allowed to kiss my pussy, but *I* couldn't kiss his dick? How was that fair?

I yelped, so distracted that I missed Wane darting toward me, his body moving with unfamiliar strength but a grace as familiar as my own reflection. He was always fast, but he'd honed that speed somehow. He snapped the side of his hand into my shoulder, silver eyes flashing with victory.

I grinned right back. *"Oh, no,* I lost. How *awful.* Looks like you're kissing my pussy." He rolled his eyes, smirking right back until I teasingly said, "Kneel," and every bit of light bled from his face.

"Shit," I breathed, recoiling so hard my soul hurt when I realised I'd triggered him into a memory.

When he trembled, his knees weakened, I followed him to the ground.

"You're at the safe house in Edinburgh. You're not back

there. I'm here, I'm Haley. I'm right here, Wane, and I'm not going to let anything happen to you."

I wrapped my arms around him, curving my hand around the back of his head, and pressed kisses to his temple to calm him—

But I was making it worse. I was still *touching* him, blindly following instincts that would only harm him.

"Oh gods, I'm sorry," I breathed, letting go of him instantly. Horrified at myself. *I* did this, threw him into a memory so dark, I couldn't even fathom what it felt like to relive it.

"No!" he croaked, throwing his arms around me and squeezing so tight it was hard to breathe. His panic spiked, even worse than before. "I can—I can fight it. I *have* to."

"You're right here with me," I murmured, settling my arms back around him and running my fingers through his hair. It always helped me when my mates stroked my hair. And I didn't know what else to do. I was lost. I needed to help my mate, but I didn't know how to stop hurting him. "He's dead, Wane, he's dead."

His fingers flexed against my back, and he sucked air through gritted teeth. "He's dead."

The memories would never die, though. Not when he looked at Harvey, at all of us, and saw what had happened in that basement.

I laid another kiss against his temple, my hands trembling as I stroked his hair and—

"That's an illegal move, Halwen Vakhara," he rasped, taking a deeper breath. "You didn't get a hit on me; you didn't win any kisses."

I could have cried hearing the life and colour return to his voice.

I shoved all my horror down, and gave him an innocent look when he drew back, composing himself with enormous effort. "*Oh no,* I broke the rules. Just *how* will I make up for it?"

He huffed a rusty laugh, giving me a wry look. "You didn't get enough cock last night?"

"Enough to last a lifetime," I groaned, following his lead when he climbed to his feet, pushing hair back from his face. "But I could stand to have some of those kisses you promised my pussy."

"I said *maybe*," he reminded me.

My mouth fell open. No but—that wasn't—

"Mean, Wane. *Mean.*"

His next smile came a little easier, but the shadows were thick in his eyes *and* clinging to his body, wrapping him in a protective layer. At least his magic was healing after Cronus had cut out a swath of shadows, though. There were more every day.

"Alright," he said, stretching his arms above his head and proving just how mean he was when his grey shirt rode up, exposing a mouth-watering strip of bronze skin, his hip bones tempting me to run my tongue along them.[4] "If you want it, you have to win it, itzaia. Land a hit on me."

"Easy," I scoffed.

Except he was faster, aided by shadows, *and* he knew me scarily well. I lost, which *should* have meant he kissed me somewhere, but all it really meant was he turned into the world's biggest tease.

By the time we wrapped up the sparring session, we were both sweaty, I was worked up, and Wane's trauma was kicked far enough away that he felt safe returning to bed.

It took me an hour to shut off and fall back asleep, but I didn't mind. It gave me more time to run my fingers through Wane's hair while he laid his head on my chest, and reassure myself he was here, alive, and as stubbornly brave as ever.

He let out a deep sigh in his sleep. Cronus might have broken him, but he was healing. And as long as I was his mate, I wouldn't let a single person hurt him ever again.

CHAPTER 10

I winced when a thump came from the room above us, my left eye squinting shut.

"They'll be fine," Emlyn said, smiling at me across the coffee table in the living room. Laughing at me.

"I know," I muttered sulkily, holding the mug of coffee he'd made for me in both hands so the heat could work its magic on my nerves. Kai and Harvey were upstairs taking advantage of the training room Wane and I found. By the thuds coming through the ceiling, they were beating the shit out of each other. In other words, business as usual. At least they couldn't destroy my weapons cabinet this time.[1]

But watching them die had made me ultra clingy and a teeny, tiny bit protective. Not to mention it was amplified by everything that happened in Alphaven, them not remembering me, *and then* nearly losing them in the Wailing Caves *and* the Labyrinth, and now grieving Wynvail. I was touchy and sensitive, and I didn't like having them out of my sight.

But deep down, I knew Em was right. They'd be fine.

I took a sip of hot coffee, sighing at the perfect blend of bitterness, cream, and sweetness, and propped my feet up on the coffee table. If he saw me, Wynvail would turn over in his grave. If he'd had one, and Cronus hadn't turned him to dust. Misery churned in my chest; I took another drink because everyone knew coffee solved everything.

"Come here," Em murmured, his blue eyes gentle on me as he stretched out his arm, showcasing a perfect spot for me against his side.

I took little convincing, and crossed the cosy room to snuggle into that spot. Em's warmth bled into me, offering instant comfort, and the touch was especially reassuring. I sighed, resting my head on his shoulder.

I'd missed this so much—lazy mornings, full of soft words, long hugs, coffee, and homemade breakfast. My eyes burned, but I pressed my face into his neck so his libraries and leather scent filled all my senses, fighting off the emotion.

Em was content to not speak, my quiet mate an introvert through and through. Just spending time in the same space, our breathing synced, our bodies pressed close, was his ultimate love language.[2]

"I'm worried about you, Em," I said after long minutes of comfortable silence, my cup now empty except for cold dregs and Emlyn tracing soft patterns on my bare thigh. I was still in the shirt I'd stolen from him, and I didn't miss the flash of male satisfaction when he first realised what I was wearing.

"Me?" he asked in a low voice—the gravelly softness of early mornings and late nights.

I set my cup on the low table and tilted my head so I could look at my mate. "When you're struggling, you keep all your thoughts locked up. Harvey will get into fights when he's stressed, Kai explodes into rants and yelling, Wane's getting better at talking about what's bothering him, but you Em? You try to deal with everything yourself so it can't touch us."

He ducked his head, his big chest heaving with a sigh. I

couldn't help but notice his shirt clung to every delicious curve of his body.[3]

"I don't want to worry you," Emlyn said, meeting my gaze with a mix of apology and unyielding stubbornness. "You're all going through enough without me—"

"Having a mental breakdown because you kept everything bottled up? I agree."

He exhaled a laugh of pure exasperation, rubbing his hand over his salt-and-pepper beard. "It's not natural for me, Hales."

"I know," I murmured, pressing a kiss to his shoulder, his skin heated through the thin cotton. "But you won't hurt me by telling me what you're struggling with. You'll hurt me by locking me out."

His throat bobbed, his hand returning to tracing my thigh. A giant crash came from upstairs; I dreaded to think about what those bastards had done to my lovingly created weapons room.

"You've confided in me before," I pointed out. Many times. He just preferred not to, protective to a fault.

"That was different," he said, giving me a long, searching look. "That was before the tunnels and the fighting pit and the Labyrinth. Before you were in debilitating pain over losing your mate."

"It's not debilitating," I said quietly, curling my hands around the vial pendant I hadn't taken off since Wane helped me make it. "It was rough when we first got here, but I'm getting better."

I could get out of bed now, and eat, and talk, not just stare into space with dead eyes, picturing Wynvail being unmade. That was progress.

"Hales," Em breathed, squeezing my thigh, his fingers hot against bare skin. "You're not okay."

"No," I agreed begrudgingly. "I don't think any of us are."

"As long as you're beside me, I'll be fine," Emlyn promised, blue eyes pleading with me to drop it.

Naturally, I didn't.

I swung my leg over his and settled myself on his lap.

"Stubborn, thoughtful, infuriating man," I huffed, taking his face in my hands, my palms tingling at the brush of his beard. It was softer than when we lived at the palace.[4]

Emlyn's lips flicked up on one side, and I saw defeat in his eyes, twinned with amusement. "Must you always win, Hales?"

"Yes," I said, and dropped a kiss on his lips, lingering longer than I intended. "I must. Now talk to me, Emlyn."

He leant back against the sofa with a deep sigh, his hands rising to my hips. It was so damn hard not to writhe against him.[5]

Em's tongue flicked out to wet his bottom lip and he gave me a reluctant glance before he asked, "Everyone we knew is dead, aren't they?"

My shoulders sank, ice water dumped on my desire. I rubbed my thumb over his cheek in slow passes. "Yeah. They're gone."

He nodded, his throat bobbing. My heart ached. "All our family, our friends—there's no one left."

"There might be someone," I said gently. "But the chances are low. Tali's still around, but you never met her."

"Tali's the panda that wanted to eat us?" he clarified.

I groaned. "She could have made a better impression. I swear, she's normally friendly and she never bites."[6]

"She threatened to bite our hands off."

"Oh good, you understood that part."

He laughed, but his expression sobered way too quickly. I ran my hands down his neck to his shoulders, stroking where he was taut with stress.

"Em, your mum and dad—"

"Gone," he cut in, a hand wandering from my waist to my

forearm. "And unless we figure out how to stop this curse on us, I'm going to lose everyone who's left."

"Someone, somewhere can read this curse," I tried to reassure him. "We just need to find them. As soon as everyone's eaten, we'll go back to Hell and—"

"Cronus will put a target on our backs," Em finished tiredly.

He was right, and I hated it.

"We can't sit here and wait to kill each other," I said, as gently as I was able. "I won't let you lose me, Em."

And the thought of losing *him*, and of dying again, scared the shit out of me. Ashboren said young demons weren't studying curses anymore, so we needed someone old. Ancient even.

"I can't stand being away from you," Em blurted, his fingers wrapping around my forearm, right over the skulls and flowers disguising the curse mark. "I can't settle when you're out of my sight. I—I'm petrified something bad will happen to you, that Cronus will come and steal you from me the second I'm not there."

Oh, Em...

I hugged him close, pressing a kiss to his soft, salt-and-pepper hair and holding him for long, long moments.

Em didn't break down in tears, didn't even shake, but I felt the turmoil crash through his soul, powerful enough to break through the ironclad walls he kept between me and his emotions.

"We'll break these curses, come back to this safe house, and live happily ever after while someone else kills Cronus. He's fucking with all the wrong people—he stole Poseidon's hippocampi, and gods know who else he's pissed off. Let someone else kill him."

Emlyn trailed a fingertip from the top of my spine to the

bottom. Following the prophecy inked on me. My heart seized.

"I'm choosing to be delusional," I informed him.

Prophecy? What prophecy?

"Delusional sounds good," he agreed, as if there weren't a thousand plans and backup plans and yet more emergency plans spinning around his clever mind. "But if we can't stop this—"

"We can," I argued, kissing him.

Emlyn's throat bobbed. He met my gaze, sombre and sweet. "I'd rather live four short weeks with you than any lifetime without you."

I blinked fast, my throat closing up. "Me, too," I croaked.

I rested my head on his shoulder, our arms around each other as another ominous thud came from above us.

"If those fuckers are doing the whirling tornado, I'm going to neuter both of them."

Emlyn's laugh ruffled my hair. "I bet they've intended something even worse."

I groaned. "Don't."

Em laughed, his hands finding my back and sliding down to palm my ass. My pussy clenched, instantly paying attention.

I drew my chest from his, planning to roll my hips against his cock, but we both shot off the sofa in a panicked rush when a massive puddle of black tar melted through the wall and pooled on the carpet in front of us.

Faster than we could react, the tar rose and resolved into the form of a tall, muscular man with giant black wings. In the place of bulky gym-bro arms to match the rest of his body, he had—I shit you not—fifty dragon heads all spitting fire.

I froze, unable to believe what I was seeing.

Emlyn went nuclear.

CHAPTER 11

*E*m wasn't kidding when he said he couldn't handle the thought of me in danger. A giant, dragon-armed man spitting fire in the middle of our living room was a pretty big fucking danger.

The monster didn't move towards us, just watched with something like surprise on his inky, surprisingly human face as Emlyn roared and magic splintered the room around him. It cut through the coffee table and shattered my empty mug. My heart leapt into my throat and a soft sound of surprise escaped me. Fuck.

I jumped out of the way, not fond of the idea of being sliced down the middle. Em felt ... out of control. Completely ruled by terror.

Wane must have sensed my panic, because he came bursting into the room with shadows swarming around him and a knife already in his hand. I let out a rough breath.

The fiery dragon monster snapped his attention to Wane when the knife flung end over end and drove into his shoulder, narrowly missing a fiery, long-necked dragon. Fuck, how many of those things even were there? Fifty? *A hundred?* I'd seen snakes as hair, but dragons as arms? This was some kid's creepy crayon drawing come to life.

"Wane," the monster spoke, the noise dreadful and ominous. Every one of his black dragons spoke at the same time, too many voices overlapping for my head to process. I gritted my teeth, edging around the dismembered coffee table.

"You shouldn't be able to get in here," Wane replied coldly, stalking across the room to my side. The thuds of fighting upstairs stopped, followed by frantic footsteps down the stairs. "This house is shielded.

"Against threats," the monster agreed, almost ... smiling? Weird. "I bear you or your family no ill will, Wane."

Wane froze, his hand latching onto my arm tightly, like he needed me to hold him up. Horror and understanding dawned through his soul, edged with surprise. "Your voice..."

"Yes," the monster agreed, "I am the beast who was imprisoned beneath the Damned House."

Oh good, that place had a name. Of course it did. I couldn't think of anything more fitting.

"I thought I was hallucinating," Wane breathed, gripping my arm tight and looking like he'd seen a ghost. "Talking to myself, imagining the replies."

"You were my only companion in a thousand years of imprisonment," the monster replied, his dragons almost sad. "My only friend."

Emlyn took that moment to shear off two onyx dragon heads with a scythe of green magic. A roar filled his throat and every part of his body strained, bristling. Shit, he was seriously out of control.

"Emlyn," Wane breathed, darting forward and carrying me with him, seemingly unable to let go. "It's okay, he's a friend."

Emlyn curled his hands into tight fists. Panting, teeth bared, he dragged his power back into himself with a growl.

Discomfort and effort pierced his soul so strongly I felt its echo.

The second his magic was under control, I rushed across the carpet and broken furniture, both Wane and I reaching for him.

"Are you okay?" I demanded, staring into Emlyn's blue eyes, my fingers roaming his face, stroking his beard, his hair.

He didn't reply to me. He looked directly at the dragon-armed man and said, "If you touch a single one of my family, I'll eviscerate you."

He meant it, too.

"I will not touch them," Wane's friend promised, his dragons falling strangely still at his sides, spitting flames but almost ... relaxed. It was really, really fucking weird.

"Who are you?" I asked, just as Harvey and Kai barrelled into the room, Kai's snakes slinging through the air and Harvey fully shifted, trampling what was left of the furniture.

A lump rose in my throat as I watched tables splinter, an armchair sliced cleanly in half, the coffee table wrecked.

"Stop," Wane hissed at them, grabbing Harvey by the scruff of his giant neck. *"Stop it."*

Kai froze too, crimson eyes darting between all of us as he stalked to my left and loomed there like a deadly shadow.

"I am Typhon," the monster replied, his eyes straying to Wane as one of his dragon heads stroked his dark chest. Silvery marks spiderwebbed around the place a human's heart might be. "I came to warn my friend. The titan is free now. Everything he has planned for hundreds of years will come to pass."

"Which means what?" Kai demanded in a hiss, his hand sliding across my back to hook me closer. Wane's fingers slid off my wrist; I grabbed his hand instead and squeezed tightly.

"Every offspring of the gods will be devoured," Typhon replied in a suitably sombre voice, his dragons hissing sparks of flame in clear disapproval. "He'll consume their power and force the gods themselves to bow to his superior power. The age of the titans was millennia ago, but some still call it the golden age. The titan will bring back that age."

"He's going to kill the gods, isn't he?" Wane whispered, rearranging the bones in my hand with his death grip. "No one will be able to stop him, he'll lock us up again, torture *all* of us—"

Wane's terror snapped me out of my own misery, and I turned to him, blocking off his view of anything but me.

"Zivai, look at me. I promised you no one would hurt you again, and I meant it. He won't get to you again."

Wane sucked in a shuddery breath, his throat bobbing and eyes restless, frantic. Shadows thickened around his shoulders, a protective shroud.

"I will fight, if it comes to that," Typhon said, a hundred voices overlapping and making the statement eerie instead of reassuring. Hairs rose all down my arms.

"We all will," Emlyn agreed, wrangling his composure back together and stepping closer to us. We'd unconsciously huddled around Wane, their wings and fur brushing my arms.

"It's the child of Ares we should worry for," Typhon added, hovering strangely near the wall he'd melted through like a wallflower at a party.[1]

"Who?" Kai demanded, shooting the guy a hostile look.

"Your mate."

I jerked back. *Child of Ares.* "Um."

"I've put my foot in it," Typhon said, startling a burst of laughter from my chest when his dragons wrapped around his buff middle. Protective, defensive. "You didn't know."[2]

"Child of Ares," Emlyn murmured, stroking my arm as clever thoughts raced behind his eyes. "So that's who your grandfather is. Adhiti—Rhea—is *his* grandmother. If your mother is the daughter of Ares, that would make you his grandchild—and Rhea's great-great-grandchild."

Oh god, it added up. It was insane.

"My grandfather is *Ares?*" I demanded shrilly, gripping Wane's hand so hard I left marks. *"The god of war?* That Ares?"

"That one," Typhon agreed, clearly not understanding rhetorical questions.

"Oh god," I whispered, wrinkling my nose. "That means Zeus is my great-grandad. Gross."

Wane laughed, the sound startled from his chest, and I felt the terror lift from his soul. His hands still shook, and I knew memories stalked him, barely a step behind him, but he lifted his head and searched for Typhon over Emlyn's wings.

"Thank you for the warning. But what can we do to stay safe? The titan will catch us."

Typhon edged forward a step, a few dragon heads trembling. Shit, no wonder he wasn't acting fearsome and monstrous—he'd been locked up too, and for *far* longer than Wane. Cronus had broken him.

"Run," Typhon said fiercely, holding Wane's stare. "Hide forever. Never come back."

Run. Hide. Why was it all so damned familiar?

We'd spent ten years running and hiding, and that had ended with all of us shot dead by a man who was equally despicable. I couldn't do it again. I refused to let my family revert to that jumpy, terrified state, always looking over our shoulders, scanning roads twice before we dared to walk down them, searching new faces at markets because any of one them could be an assassin sent after us.

No.

Not again. *Never again.*

I ground my teeth, my wings ruffling. Emlyn shot me a curious look, but it was Kai who gave me a nod of understanding. I summoned a grateful smile. But we couldn't go solo like last time; we had to talk about it with the others, convince them somehow.

"So he just gets away with everything?" I breathed, and the room went so quiet my whisper was as loud as a shout.

I swallowed and tasted blood; I'd bitten the end of my tongue. "After everything he's done, everyone he's hurt, everyone he's *unmade,* he just gets away with it? He gets unlimited power and world domination? *No.*"

"You want revenge," Emlyn realised, soft with horror. "Haley, he'll kill you."

I sucked in a long breath, fighting the urge to argue. I'd fucked up so colossally in the past by not listening to my mates; I couldn't do it again. "It feels like deja vu, Em."

"I understand," Typhon said, as if I'd spoken to him. "May I sit?"

We all sort of froze. In the end, Wane had to nod and gesture for the dragon-armed man to take a seat in the remaining intact armchair. He sank into it with a groan, and I realised all at once that the silver marks on his chest were scars. Someone had tried to claw his heart out. Or had succeeded.

"You're thinking of Locke," Typhon murmured, looking from me to my mates. "I know the weight of a heinous father. The titan is mine."

"Cronus is *your father?*" Harvey blurted, jerking forward a step in shock, shifted and completely naked.

I jumped in front of him, shielding his body with mine. "No looking," I warned Typhon, and I must have looked scary because he covered his eyes with two long dragons. Huh. Cool. I had power.

"Cronus is my father," the monster—actually, I felt mean calling him that now, so let's just call him Wane's friend—agreed. "He never claimed me as such, and he imprisoned me long ago so I couldn't shame him. He moved me to the basement of the Damned House so I could—so—"

"You don't have to tell us," Wane said softly, walking around me to stand beside his friend. A deep ache of sympathy filled our bond. "I know how bad it was."

"It's relevant, so I will finish," Typhon replied in the same soft tone.

"Come on," I breathed to my mates. "I think we need to sit for this."

I sank onto the remaining sofa, trying not to remember sitting exactly here when we first got here, interrogating Wynvail.

My throat burned.

I grabbed a cushion and thrust it at Harvey, whispering, "Cover your dick."

"Why? It's pretty."

I huffed. "Because I don't like people seeing what's mine."

He pouted, his silver eyes big and wide, swimming with sadness.

"Yes, it's pretty," I sighed, earning a smile. "It's still mine."

He covered himself, sitting tall and proud beside me.

Typhon's dragons lowered from his eyes, black scales rubbing the silver scars on his chest. "The titan needed monsters. Ways to push his offspring and *their* offspring to their fullest potential." His dragons went tense, fangs bared and spitting fire. "He locked me up and made me father countless monsters. And then he sent them to be slaughtered in his trials. Fattening the offspring for him to devour."

A sick oily feeling went through my belly, and I swallowed hard. "I'm so sorry."

I hurt his children. I killed his babies.

I covered my mouth, bile rushing up my throat. If someone hurt my children, I'd explode every vein in their body in an instant, but Typhon just dipped his black head and said, "I hold no grudge against the offspring. They have no choice."

Em dwarfed my hand with his, warm and comforting, and a knot unwound from my chest.

"You said he's fattening up their power for him to devour," Em said to Typhon, his tone careful—the same way he spoke to us when we were mid-breakdown. "How does he plan to do that?"

"The usual way," Typhon replied.

Panic gripped my chest. I stared at Wane's friend, my heart loud in my ears. "He's really going to eat me. Just gobble me down like I'm a chipolata?"

"I don't know chipolata," Typhon replied with a furrow in his dark brow.

"It's a sausage," Harvey supplied helpfully.

"Ah," Typhon said, a hundred voices speaking at once. "Yes. Like a chipolata. He will devour me, too. And everyone alive who has a god or titan ancestor."

"So he'll eat everyone and—then what?" I demanded, taking my anger out on the wrong person. The need for revenge burned in my chest. "Rule *nothing?* There'll be no one left."

"He'll repopulate the world with whatever remains of humanity and rebuild the golden age. It was a time of peace. If you obeyed him," Typhon added bitterly, rising from the chair and looking unsure, glancing between Wane and us. His dragons shuddered.

"We don't have a chance of winning, child of Ares," he told me. "So run, far and fast. There's nothing he won't do for power. All of this—everything bad that has happened—" He waved a black, gleaming dragon at the room, at Wane, at my mates. "Is because of him. He saw you, before you ever discovered your mates. He saw you, and them, and everything you would be."

Typhon's face darkened, sadness and anger mixing in his harsh features as his voice grew louder, more resonant, more dragon voices joining the chorus. "That's why he helped Locke reach the Damned Realm that day. I'm sorry," he said quickly when Wane staggered back a step.

Pain cut through my chest; I covered my mouth as horror bled through my soul and into theirs. My mates had only died because of me.

"Why?" Emlyn demanded in a deep snarl. He squeezed my hand harder.

Typhon backed away from us towards the wall, a black sheen covering his skin—tar. I knew the look on his face, knew that itching need to run. "Death amplified your power."

"Power," I spat, shaking all over. "Everything comes back to *power.*"

Cronus helped Locke kill us. He held Wane captive for a century, and tortured him because he coveted his shadows. He tormented us, and sent us to die in the Labyrinth. He made Wynvail's existence a misery. All for *power.* Because he wanted to take over the world again.

"I want him dead," I breathed, glancing up at Typhon—and finding him already melting through the wall in a puddle of tar.

"Bye, then," I sighed, reaching out to clasp Wane's hand when he stumbled over to me, squeezing tight. His soul was as much a mess as mine, shock tangled with hurt and panic, poisoned by hatred and rage.

"Haley's right," Wane said after a moment, sucking in a laboured breath, his shadows thickening. "We can't hide this time. We need to set a trap—and kill him before he kills us."

CHAPTER 12

*S*omething was very badly wrong with me, but I was blaming it on trauma. Case in point: I'd just been told Cronus wanted to devour me, and the only reason we died was so he could fatten up my power. But my body *burned* when Wane and Emlyn began arguing, Wane pushing for offence, Em firmly defence. Eyes flashed with defiance and a spark of anger, and I swallowed, needing that intensity pinned on me. Fuck, they were so sexy when they were angry.

Wane threw up his hands when Em argued, and I shuddered, imagining them on my hips, holding me down while he filled me with shadows and cock, over and over until I screamed.

My need grew so badly that I whimpered and got to my feet, stopping their argument before it could get even more heated. My mouth went completely dry when they both turned to me, Emlyn's big chest heaving and Wane's shirt clinging to the fine lines of his body where it used to hug muscle. My mouth watered, and no amount of screaming at myself that *now really isn't the time* would make my body cool.

When Emlyn closed the distance and cupped my face, I

gasped, the touch *so fucking good* against my sensitive skin. Every part of me was sensitive, roaring with scalding sensation and pounding demand.

"Your eyes are dilated, Hales," he murmured, tucking a lock of hair behind my ear. "Fuck, you're burning up."

"I need you," I admitted, licking my dry bottom lip. "All of you. Please."

Wings and magic brushed against me from behind, Harvey's and Kai's touch a relief that made me quiver.

"Gently," Emlyn warned them, his blue eyes hardening. "Come here, beautiful girl. We'll give you what you need."

I couldn't hold in a whimper, heat scorching through my skin and sinking deeper, making sweat prick my face. My need was so vicious that the usual pound of desire became painful. I choked back a pitiful moan.

When Em sat on the sofa and pulled me onto his lap, I couldn't even focus on the broken furniture and the devastation it gave me. All I felt was the ruthless, burning demand in my pussy. I couldn't think, couldn't breathe. The second his cock was freed, I slammed down on it and exhaled hard in relief.

Yes, my soul breathed. *Finally.*

I knew logically it had only been a few hours since we'd had sex, but I rode them all, one by one, like I'd been apart from them for a thousand years.

It was only when the frenzy faded, and my temperature returned to normal, my pussy overflowing with cum, that the devastation I'd been outrunning caught up to me.

They'd completely trashed my living room while trying to protect me. All the pieces Wynvail picked out for me were ruined.

I pressed my face to Wane's shoulder and pretended to sleep while I cried.

CHAPTER 13

HARVEY

*T*ime was slipping away, and that used to mean nothing to me. Two weeks ago, I wouldn't have given a shit, but now we were five days away from the curse's deadline. Five days until some mystical bullshit would make me kill my mate. The only woman I'd ever loved. Hell, the only woman I'd ever *liked*. Before her, I'd been a dick and a user, only sticking around long enough to get my dick wet. Haley would have cut my dick off if I'd tried that with her in the beginning.

But it had always been more. With a bond in the mix and Wane's feelings obvious, his attachment to her instantaneous, there was no way I could use her like I used everyone else. I'd never believed in fairy tale romance shit, but everything about meeting Halwen was fate. Not the *bump into each other in the street and instant love* kind of fate. The kind that was forceful and gritty and undeniable.

If she hadn't been sent to hunt Wane, we'd never have met

her. I didn't give a shit that Cronus was pulling Locke's strings. Higher beings were the ones who measured and cut the strings of our lives. They were the ones who sent Haley to us, who made her every bit as sarcastic as me, as serious as Em, as sweet as Wane, and as volatile as Kai. She fit with every one of us, and she was the best damn part of all of us.

Now, I remembered every day we'd lived together, the thought of losing her, of killing her myself made me physically sick. Bile rose into my throat, but I pushed it back down, stroking my fingers over Haley's knuckles and wondering if we were idiots for leaving the house.

But we couldn't sit in the safe house and wait to murder each other. It had been agonising enough doing that yesterday after Typhon melted through the wall and left us.[1] We'd spent yesterday planning how to trap Cronus, and while we had a decent plan, it would be completely pointless if we killed each other before we could put it into action.

Which brought us to now, walking down the dubious, criminal Ulrich Crescent to meet an alchemist who was also dubious and criminal. But weren't we all? Fuck knows how many people I'd killed to protect my family. It had to be over twenty. Maybe over fifty. Haley's body count was higher; so was Kai's. I was in no position to judge.

"What are you thinking about?" Haley asked, squeezing my hand and peering up at me. Her stormy grey eyes sliced through my flesh and bone and right to my heart, making it skip.

"How goddamn sexy you are when you kill people," I replied, giving her a long, searing look from head to toe. Her boots were covered in dirt from trekking from the nearest rift, her black jeans so tight they were practically sprayed onto her thighs, and there was a slash in her distressed grey shirt that gave me a perfect glimpse of cleavage.

Noticing my attention, she dropped my hand so she could

press her boobs together, making my mouth water with more than a little glimpse. My cock hardened as I imagined sinking it between those perfect tits.

She laughed, mischievous and smug, but I grabbed her arm and dragged her against me, kissing the smile off her face so roughly, I tasted blood. Fuck. The taste made me almost feral, and I tilted her head with a grip on her chin so I could kiss her deeper, turning her into a gasping, moaning puddle. My beast was close enough that I could smell the arousal dripping from her pussy, and I wanted a taste of that, too.

"Harvey," Emlyn barked, straightening his new beanie hat —a silver that matched his wings and purchased from the same shop my gloves and Kai's scarf came from. I didn't know what gift she'd got Wane; he'd been secretive about it.

Haley let out a soft sound, her fingers curling in my jacket, and there wasn't a single word anyone could say to stop me kissing my mate.

"Now isn't the fucking time," Kai hissed. "Or did you forget we're on a deadline?"

"Emphasis on the dead," Wane murmured. He wasn't cursed to kill Haley like us, but it felt like a curse for him to watch us all die, leaving him alone. If Haley's curse mark didn't take him, too.

"They're right," Haley panted, drawing back from me.

But her pupils were dilated, so big they almost swallowed the bluish grey, and her hips rolled against mine.

"People will see," Emlyn pointed out as I bent and picked up Haley, her muscular thighs like fucking heaven in my hands. *Mine. All mine.*

No one would take her from me again. Not fucking ever. And if we were all going to die in five days, I was going to take every damn shot as happiness and pleasure I got.

"Then cover me," I replied to Emlyn.

I pressed a long kiss to my mate's forehead and searched the dingy street, finding a dark alleyway a few feet away. I headed right for it, loosing a deadly growl to send whatever critters hid within it running. Two rats and a demon woman with a rhino horn fled, the whites of their eyes showing.

"Hard," Haley breathed, sinking vicious fingers into my hair and gripping tight at the roots. I groaned, slamming my lips back into hers and pushing her against the wall. "I need it hard."

"Anything you want, Sugarplum," I replied, a little breathy, a little bestial.

It took two seconds to get her trousers and underwear dragged off—I had enough thought to not actually rip them—and to shove down my own, sinking into her before she could brace herself. I would never get tired of that little shudder she made when I first thrust into her. Or the sharp gasps or breathy cries she let out when I gave her what she asked for and made it hard and fast, rutting into her against the wall.

"We're all hard now, you bastard," Kai muttered.

I shot him an arrogant smile, sinking all the way inside our made and grinding deep until her eyes flew wide and her hands fluttered across my body.

"Gods," she cried. "Harvey, that's—too deep."

I kissed her, softly this time, and circled my hips again, tormenting her deep, deep inside. The others might have more girth, but my cock was the longest. Only I could make her body jerk and her breathing jump like this.

"It's just deep enough," I replied, holding her gaze and delighted when a deep ripple went through her inner walls.

I stopped torturing her and made the rest of my thrusts fast, hard enough to make her eyes roll back when I adjusted the angle so I hit a new spot.

She clamped down around me, making *my* eyes threaten

to roll back. I clenched my jaw, a muscle flickering in my cheek. Shit, she gripped me so damn well. If the world collapsed around us right now, at least we had this, at least we were connected.

"I love you," I groaned, fucking her as fast as my body would allow. "I love you so fucking much."

She whimpered in reply, and came so hard I had no choice but to follow her over the edge. Heat and pleasure surged through my body, my cock throbbing like crazy inside her, and every deep spasm of her pussy dragged a grunt from the back of my throat.

When the boiling pleasure faded to a warm glow, I rested my forehead against hers and panted to catch my breath. This woman was my whole damn world, and I'd be damned if a little fucking tattoo was going to make me hurt her. I'd cut it off my arm if I thought it would save her.

Her hands came up to frame my face, calloused and warm against my skin, and my heart fucking melted at the soft kiss she placed on my lips. "I love you more today than I ever have."

My emotions slashed from feral lust to hot satisfaction to emotional as fuck. I wanted to cry.

I love you more today than I ever have.

Me—the Harvey that was both the flirty, sarcastic bastard I'd been before and the feral beast Alphaven had made me into. She loved *that* me more than ever before? My heart thudded hard in my chest, a little flutter going through my belly.

"Are you done?" Emlyn asked, jealousy clear in his voice. "Or are you going to make Wane kill anyone else?"

I jerked in surprise, my head snapping around to stare at my twin. He stood in the mouth of the alley, nothing at all out of place about him except for the three bodies piled at his feet.

"Wane?" Haley breathed, her pussy clenching around my cock. Hard.

Was it weird I was almost proud of my brother for that? Everything he'd been through, and he drove our mate even crazier than he had before we died.

"He beat me to it," Kai muttered, his arms crossed over his chest as he kicked one of the corpse's hands.

I snorted, returning my attention to Haley as I slowly withdrew from her heat, sad as fuck that I had to part from her.

"You are so goddamn beautiful," I whispered to her, and the faint flutter in my stomach became full-on butterflies when a pink flush moved across her cheeks.

Emlyn took a pack of tissues from his back pocket as if he'd known we'd need to clean up in a rush. But I stopped him with a shake of my head.

"Actually, I'd like a tissue," Haley said when I set her feet on the ground, smug when she needed a few moments to steady herself.

"No, Sugarplum," I disagreed. "You're going to leave my cum exactly where it belongs. If it drips out of you, good. Everyone who smells you will know you're mine. And every drop you feel slide over your skin will remind you exactly who you belong to."

Her throat bobbed.

"You are mine," I growled, the sound throaty and full of my beast.

I gathered up Haley's trousers, made sure to brush off any dirt, and helped her back into them. She breathed rapidly the whole time, her skin heated as I fastened the zip and button on her jeans.

"And don't ever forget it," I added, unable to resist kissing her again. I made it soft and quick this time.

Haley licked her bottom lip. "I won't."

"Good girl." She practically melted when I pulled her close, my lips meeting her forehead.

I felt less feral now, no matter how fast the sex had been, and it seemed to be infectious because I felt Haley settle through the bond. She drew a deep breath, brushing stray pink hairs away from her face.

"You," she growled at me, her eyes flashing, "are spectacular."

I grinned.

"You," she said, turning to fix a narrow-eyed stare on my twin. "Are surprising as fuck. I like it."

Wane ducked his head, a smile curving his eyes.

"You," she huffed at Kai, stalking over to him. "Stop sulking. You can kill the next guy that leers at me."

Kai muttered unintelligibly, but accepted the kiss she placed on his cheek with zero complaint. I smirked. He was as weak for her as the rest of us, if not more.

"And *you*, Emlyn Johan," Haley went on, putting her hands on her hips. "Maybe you can enlighten me about where my underwear disappeared to."

He looked at the sky, his eyes roaming left, then right. "Aren't they still on the ground, Hales?"

I snorted. He was an awful liar. I closed the distance to lay another kiss in Haley's pink hair because I physically could not separate myself from her, and jumped when a shadow moved towards the little back street.

No, not a shadow. Just a woman with sharp, inky hair dressed head to toe in tactical black, only her face and hands a different shade—those were vivid purple. I groaned. Not this woman again.

"Why does it stink like sex in this alley?" she barked, her nose wrinkling.

"Oh, Harvey just fucked me against the wall," Haley replied brightly, grinning at her friend with zero shame. Gods, I loved this look on her—happiness and confidence. She should look like this every minute of every day. No worries, no stress.

Cronus needed to die.

"I didn't need to know that," Renna groaned.

"Twelve out of ten, and hot as fuck," Haley went on, preening. "My mate's exceptional in bed. Well, against the wall."

"I definitely did *not* need to know that."

Now, *I* was preening.

Kai rolled his eyes. "I'm a fifteen."

"I'm a twenty," Wane added confidently.

"I don't need a number," Emlyn said with a crooked little smile behind his beard.

Oooh, that was good. Power move.

"Wait, how the fuck did you find us, and what are you doing here?" Haley asked Renna, storming forward a step. We all hurried to flank her, surrounding her.

"Coincidence," Renna replied smoothly.

"You didn't … put a tracker in me. Did you?"

Wane and I exchanged a quick glance, our thoughts in sync. A sharp smile crossed my face, and I raised an eyebrow at Kai when he noticed us. He was quick to catch on, crimson eyes flashing.

"Only for emergencies," Renna replied calmly.

"How does it work?" I asked the woman, resting a hand on my mate's back, her feathers brushing my knuckles.

"I have a gemstone that works as a homing beacon. I can follow its pull towards the person it's linked to."

"Can it be duplicated?" Wane asked innocently.

Renna made a contemplative expression. "Depends what's in it for me."

Haley let out a throaty little growl that went straight to my cock. "Can you, for once in your lives, get your own friends and stop stealing mine?"

"No," Kai replied with a wink that made her breathing increase.

"You didn't answer my mate's other question," Emlyn pointed out, his spine straight and grey wings tense at his sides. "Why are you here, tracking Haley?"

Renna's grin deepened, sharpened. "We've found something. We might have a way to break your curse."

CHAPTER 14

HALWEN

*H*ope bubbled inside my chest right next to the rage and bloodthirst that drove me to get revenge on Cronus for torturing Wane and killing Wynvail. That fucker would pay, but first we'd break the curse.

The flight to Iarlon took too damn long. I was impatient to know what they'd learned at the palace, to know if it would save us—or break my heart when I learned it was unviable.

When we landed, I wasted no time, running up the stairs and into the palace, hurrying down pale hallways towards where Renna guided me—the sitting room where I first met Lucifer and Queen Lili.

Thankfully, Renna was unable to carry so many of us with her magic, so I wouldn't be throwing up all over the devil's fancy shoes today.

"Finally," Lucifer huffed when I burst through the door. His gaze went to Renna, his eyes deep red and impatient. "What took so long."

"You do *not* want to know," Renna replied, disgust twisting her face.

I snorted. Who'd have guessed she was a prude? Aww cute, the tips of her lilac ears were pink.

My eyes travelled around the room, and I jumped when I spotted another woman sitting primly on the sofa by the fire beside the queen. She looked supremely uncomfortable, and shot me a foul look as if I was to blame.

"Agatha Avonlea," I greeted in a cheerful voice I knew would piss off the grumpy old woman.

Her stare flattened. Her beautiful onyx face and shiny brown curls did not match her personality at all. "You know my name is Aggie."

"Just checking to see if you remembered me," I replied sweetly, and then figured out why she was here all at once. She was old—and if my instincts were right she was *old* old—and worked with the endless knowledge in Lucifer's library. "Did you find something to end my curse?"

"Doubtful," she muttered.

"Don't talk like that," Lili sighed, coming over to squeeze my hand. "It's the best hope we've found. Aggie had the idea, and it's brilliant, honestly."

Aggie ducked her brunette head, smiling. Fuck, I didn't know the woman *could* smile. Lili could charm anyone.

"With all this talk of gods and titans floating around," Aggie said, giving me a look that told me she'd heard of my involvement with said titans, "I thought it made sense to go directly to the source. Instead of fucking around with anyone who studied curses, we need to find someone who *is* a curse. We need to find the Arae."

I waited a moment to see if that would spark an inner knowledge. Nope. "Who?"

"They're spirits of curses," Emlyn murmured, skimming the edge of his wing down mine to reassure me—or himself.

"They were made *by* a curse, and they embody that curse. The Arae can also place curses on other people."

"And, in theory, remove them," Aggie added, giving Emlyn a sour look. Probably for stealing her thunder. "Let me see," she barked, getting off the sofa, surprisingly spry for someone who gave *older than Lucifer* energy.

She grabbed my arm before I could push up my sleeve, and did it herself, her wide lips pressing thin and eyes squinting as she scanned the geometric lines, circles, and arrows on my arm. "Nasty work."

"Why does everyone always say that?" I muttered.

"This circle here represents life, but yours is bisected," Aggie replied, tracing the mark. "This line should be longer, but it's cut off. All these signs point to death. The arrow pointing away from you says it'll be someone else's death. The two dots I'm not familiar with, but I presume it refers to your twin soul—the one you possess and the one your mates do."

"Twin soul," Harvey murmured, edging closer to frown at the mark on my arm, mostly concealed by the skulls and flowers I had Oren tattoo to mask the curse.

"Every mate is a twin soul. You have half, your mate has the other. With multiple mates, they all share the half, each possessing a piece," Aggie explained, releasing my arm. "I can interpret the curse, but I can't tell you how to break it. Not my specialty."

"I've never heard you admit to being less than perfect at something before," Lucifer remarked, striding forward for a look at my curse and halted by a wall of muscle.

"You can look at mine," Kai offered. I couldn't tell if he was being protective or territorial. Knowing Kai, probably both. "It's the exact same as Haley's."

"Don't hiss at the devil," Harvey whispered to him. "It's rude."

"And it could get us killed," Wane added, startling hard

when the door flew open and a scowling grizzly bear stormed into the room.

Well, he was a man, but he definitely had a grizzly soul with the deep slash of his brows, his unfriendly eyes, and the scowling face mostly hidden by a bushy beard. He didn't even blink at the rest of us, just fixed his attention on the king and queen of hell and barked, "We have a problem."

Wane's shadows thickened, his silver eyes widening with panic; I crossed the room to take his hand, squeezing hard and whispering, "You're safe, I'm with you."

But his teeth were gritted, his nostrils flaring, and shadows lashed around him. "My instincts are screaming," he said in a hoarse voice, like he was the one screaming.

Harvey reacted instantly, Kai and Emlyn following suit as we pressed close around him.

"What kind of problem?" Lucifer demanded, any friendliness hidden behind a hard mask, like he was ready to slaughter whatever the issue was. My interest piqued at the violent promise in his voice, and Kai snarled, his lip curled back from his teeth.

The look I shot him said, *what? I like dangerous men and he's* the devil. *I'm only looking.*

Then again, if *he* looked at anyone else, I might rip their guts out through their belly button, so I understood the glare.

"Aphrodite's here," the grizzly replied. "She's looking for someone called Halwen Vakhara."

What? My spine straightened. My heart galloped in my chest when Lucifer shot me a disbelieving look. I didn't understand that sentence either; it made absolutely zero sense that Aphrodite would be looking for *me*.

"Why?" Kai asked in a scary calm voice, already planning gruesome murder.

The grizzly bear turned, noticing us for the first time.

"She's sentenced to death. Something to do with treason, kidnap, murder, and breaking a seal."

I stopped hearing after *sentenced to death.*

CHAPTER 15

"She doesn't even have jurisdiction over Tartarus!" Lucifer yelled, his crimson eyes ablaze with anger on my behalf, which might have made me warm and fuzzy if I wasn't *sentenced to death*.

"Don't shoot me, I'm just the messenger," the grizzly bear who I'd learned was called Ceyx muttered, stalking over to the drinks cabinet and grabbing the bottle of whiskey. He didn't bother with a glass; I respected that. "She's in the reception room with Bernard but I can't imagine him holding her for—"

The door flew open a second time, tearing all the way off its hinges with a horrific shriek this time. It slammed to the floor, ruching the crimson rug under the sofas, and I flinched at the violent *boom*.

"Long," Ceyx finished with a scowl, coming over to stand beside Lili, like he expected the furious woman in the doorway to attack her.

My mates pressed tighter around me, Wane's shadows expanding but trembling, like fear made his grip weak.

The woman was clearly a goddess—an aura of power throbbed around her so oppressively that my breath caught and stuttered in my chest, and pressure filled my head until my ears popped. Her skin was rich umber, her brown-gold hair completely flawless, not a single hair out of place as she strode through the broken door and pinned unsettling eyes on me. She was too beautiful; my instincts bleated that something was wrong, something was unnatural.

I glanced away, unable to look into her light blue eyes for long.

"You," she seethed at me, "are a traitor to all gods, and to your own kind."

I froze in place, petrified like a single glance from her had turned me to stone.

"She's also under my protection, Aphrodite," Lucifer cut in, crossing the room to stand in front of me and my mates.

Aphrodite sneered, so furious and entitled that it took her beauty down a few notches and I could stand to look at her again. My heart stopped in my chest when I saw what was pinned to her lapel.

My voice came out hollow when I asked, "Where did you get that pin?"

Even the king and queen paused at the sound of my voice, at what I asked.

"That's not your business, traitor," Aphrodite replied, her voice sweet and high and perfect. That sneer was still on her face, though. She looked like she'd stepped in shit and sucked a lemon at the same time.

"That pin was stolen by my mate," I said, grief bruising my chest like a fist, "who was working for Cronus. How do *you* have it?"

"Your mate," Aphrodite replied in a low purr that made me colder, "never gave it to Cronus. He gave it to me. His lover."

It took a moment for the words to hit. For silence to ring inside my head.

"Bullshit," Harvey spat. "That psycho was so obsessed with Haley, he'd never even consider looking at anyone else."

"Positive about that, are you?" the smug goddess replied. "What about *before* he met her?"

My mate was dead. And this bitch had the nerve to claim him?

"Did you force your way into my palace just to make a scene?" Lucifer drawled. "If so, show yourself out. This is no place for drama."

Aphrodite's eerie blue eyes fixed on Lucifer. "Descendants of the gods are going missing. I see you've summoned your own spawn, so you must already know that some have been murdered."

"Don't bring me into this," Ceyx muttered. Which made him the devil's son. I didn't care.

He gave it to me. His lover.

Kai slipped his hand into mine and squeezed. I barely felt it.

"My mate is descended from a god," Emlyn said with barely concealed rage. He stood beside me, bristling, his hands curled into fists. "If what you're saying is true, she's in danger."

The goddess laughed, the sound both beautiful and poisonous. The aura of magic around her grew bigger, so oppressive that I recoiled as she took two steps closer, only stopping because of Lucifer's proximity.

"I don't doubt she's struck a bargain. Cronus must have promised you something for breaking the seal on Tartarus."

My ears rang. A lump rose in my throat.

"Promised me something," I echoed. "My mate *died* because of that seal, because of that titan." I bared my teeth, pain growing so sharp in my chest that every word hurt.

"To quote your monstrous mate," Aphrodite replied with a little smile, "*bullshit.*"

"My *monstrous* mate," I breathed, quiet filling my head.

Power trembled through me, a hundred heartbeats dominating my senses, the ones closest to me the strongest—my mates, Lucifer, Lili, Ceyx, Aggie and—where was Renna?

"Aphrodite, I'd like you to leave," Lucifer said coolly. "I won't tell you twice."

The goddess didn't look away from me, like I'd personally insulted her. "He's entirely feral, isn't he?" she taunted. "One little shove away from becoming a beast forever. I've never fucked a Feral," she mused.

"Shut your mouth," Lili warned, power spiking behind me like her magic was as out of control as mine.

"She's baiting you," Wane breathed, his shadows shuddering against my wings.

Her words were like a lit match thrown on kindling. "But if he's anything like the man who was made from his shadow, he'll be *spectacular.* There's nothing quite like the feeling of Wynvail's cock sliding into your pussy. Pity that he's dead now."

I was so still, so silent inside, it took me a moment to realise I'd attacked her.

Red light blasted from my curse marks, and I shot out of the protective grip of my mates far too easily, crossing the room in a blink. I latched onto the exhilarated beat of her heart, sinking my power into her and—a sharp-nailed hand closed around my throat.

"Maybe I'll take *all* your mates. Create my own little harem," she gloated, her pale eyes bright. She loved this— hurting me, watching me flinch with every blow her words landed. "Either way you, traitor, are sentenced to death by mutilation."

Sound and motion rushed around me. My mates yelled and snarled, Lucifer shouting, even Aggie spitting vitriol words at the goddess.

"This is my realm," Lucifer raged, dark magic erupting

around him, eerily still compared to Wane's shadows. "I won't allow you to march into my home and take a friend."

Aphrodite's fingers tightened around my throat. I didn't care, slamming more magic into her heart and trying—and failing—to crush the life out of her. Her other hand flexed, and a pang of alarm and panic went through each of my bonds as—as they were dragged forward four steps. Against their will.

"I just did," the goddess replied.

Three things happened at once.

Pearly magic shimmered around me, making my mates cry out in pain.

Wane threw his shadows as far as he could, wrapping them around Harvey, then Kai until they vanished out of sight. But he threw them away from himself, leaving him vulnerable, and Em was too far, too close to me, for more than a few tendrils to wrap around him.

Aphrodite's magic flared so brightly my eyes pricked and wept, and her pearly magic tore us out of Lucifer's castle. It was nauseating, similar to Renna's sifting magic, but blindingly bright. I couldn't see a single thing around me, but my mates' terror slashed through my soul. Kai's and Harvey's were the loudest; Wane and Em were muted, like a blanket had been thrown over our connection.

Full sensation blasted back into me when the pearly magic spat us out, and I crashed into an unyielding surface so hard that sparks flashed through my head. Aphrodite's magic must have muted Em's and Wane's mate bonds, because now they filled my chest so powerfully I thought my ribs would crack to fit them.

I panted, squinting my eyes open, reaching my hand out instinctively. I brushed a hot, trembling body, and relief had a small sound slipping out of me. My eyes landed on Emlyn first, as he wrenched me against him and held me with tight, shaking arms. Wane snagged my attention when he sucked in a jagged, shuddering breath and horror clanged through his soul like a bell struck.

I saw why a moment later: we were in a tiny stone room, each wall hewn from a single slab of brick except for the one across from us, where iron bars as thick as Em's arm ran from the ceiling to the floor.

Aphrodite had imprisoned us.

PART II
SUNDERED

CHAPTER 16

KAI

*L*ogically, I knew grabbing Lucifer by the lapels of his jacket and throwing him up against the wall wasn't the smartest choice. But my mate was gone, and I couldn't think straight.

"Bring her back!" I hissed in his face. *"Bring her back!"*

I waited for Emlyn to bark a warning at me, but the only sound was Harvey screaming and a familiar low, vicious thud that told me he'd punched the wall.

"If I could," Lucifer bit out, his eyes glowing crimson. "I would."

I matched his power with my own feral glow, my teeth bared.

He prised my fingers off his jacket with dark power, bending each one back until I gasped, tears springing to my eyes. *Fuck, no. I can't cry; if I start, I'll never stop.*

"You're the devil," I spat through gritted teeth, taking a step back when his power flared, sharper and more volatile than any shadow magic I'd seen before. Instincts bleated warnings at me, but my rose was gone and I didn't care to listen to them. "Bring her back."

"You heard him, lad," the older woman—the librarian?—snapped, grabbing my shoulder and not caring that magic erupted around me like a tornado. "He can't do anything, and fighting the devil won't bring them back."

Them.

The word rang through my head, over and over, until I was going to throw up. I spun, searching the room—Lucifer, Harvey, Lili, the bearded guy, and the librarian—that was it.

I staggered away, my hand pressed to my stomach as it caved in, pain worse than anything I'd felt in a hundred years kicking me in the gut.

"Aphrodite won't release them until we can provide undeniable proof that Cronus was behind his own escape," Lucifer explained, his voice quiet, like I was a wild animal he was afraid of spooking. "So we'll find it."

"We," Harvey repeated, something completely empty in his voice. A shudder went down my spine in a primal warning. "Why do you care?"

"You're demons, which makes you my people," Lucifer said carefully as the librarian tightened her grip on me and yanked me away from the devil, surprisingly strong for someone her age. Or maybe *because of* her age. "And your mate is both my employee and a friend. And most importantly, it's obvious that whatever's happening is bigger than you and Halwen—and it's building here in Hell, *my* kingdom. I'll do everything in my power to avoid another war. We're barely recovered from the last one. Some cities aren't even rebuilt yet; we can't survive another attack."

"A war," I echoed, scrubbing my face with shaky hands and wrenching away from the librarian's bony grip. "You think that's what this is? All this titan shit?"

"I do," he agreed, watching me warily.

"What the fuck has this got to do with my mate?" I demanded, stalking over to the spot where Aphrodite had stood, her hand around my mate's throat. Anger razed a path through me until my nostrils flared, my whole body quivering.

"It's all in those curses," the librarian muttered. "That's where this started, from what I can gather. You all died, came back to life cursed, and now this shit's happening."

"She's right," Queen Lili murmured. "Here, sit down," she said to Harvey.

"I don't want to sit," he replied in a frozen voice. "I want my mate."

Movement in the doorway had my head snapping up, a snake lashing out and slamming into the woman's chest hard enough to break her ribs. I realised too late that it was the purple woman—both enemy and ally. Haley's friend.

"Fuck!" Renna snarled, pressing her palm flat to her ribs and storming right for me. I didn't fight when she threw her fist into my stomach in retaliation. I didn't care. My mate was kidnapped by *a goddess*. Would I ever see her again? If the devil couldn't get her back...

I laughed, empty and low. Unsettling enough that Renna stepped back, giving me a strange look.

"You're too late," the queen murmured. "All of you."

I glanced up to see Renna had arrived with backup—a motley crew of powerful men and women, several of whom stalked right to the queen and scanned her for injuries. Their intensity reminded me of how we were with Haley, and my eyes stung.

I wanted my mate back. My hands shook harder, magic whirling around me in a vicious tangle.

"What happened?" a deep voice demanded.

What happened? A goddess took my mate, and kidnapped

Emlyn and Wane. Wane—who we'd just got back, who'd been through a living nightmare. What was happening to him right now? What if he was triggered? What if this broke him?

"Keep your shit together," the librarian barked at me, striding through the maelstrom of power around me and slapping my cheek.

I staggered back, clutching my face, my eyes wide. I'd just broken Renna's ribs with my power, but the librarian batted it away like it was nothing.

"That woman of yours needs you to think clearly, so pull yourself together so we can hunt them down, rescue your family, and kill that bitch."

"Aggie!" the queen gasped. "We're not killing Aphrodite."

Aggie muttered under her breath, giving me another hard look. Strangely, it reminded me of Emlyn, and helped me gain a fraction of composure.

I pulled my snakes back to me, forming a writhing shield over my body, and I strode across the room to grab Harvey's arms. He was trembling, his eyes staring into space, almost... empty.

"Fuck," I breathed, and dragged him into a brutal hug. "There's no force in any realm that can keep us away from our family. Yeah?"

"Yeah," he replied hollowly.

"You said we needed proof," Lili breathed, and I lifted my head to watch Lucifer nod. "I'll be back," she replied, and rushed out the door.

I returned my attention to Harvey, tightening my grip on him. "Stay with me."

He swallowed and nodded.

I took a ragged breath, aware all at once that *I* needed to be the strong one, to hold Harvey together. So I shoved all my volatile panic into a vault in my chest and slammed the door shut, locking it tight.

"That was Aphrodite," I said, facing Lucifer—and blinking at the other men around him. I vaguely recognised them from the days we'd lived in the palace before we went to find Adhiti —Lucifer's inner circle. The most powerful demons in Iarlon. In all of Hell. "The goddess of love?"

The big, bald guy beside Lucifer scoffed. "The goddess of spite and selfishness more like."

"She was one of the gods that fought against us in the war," Lucifer explained, watching Harvey and I like we were a bomb about to explode. "She sided with Zeus, and almost succeeded in wiping out all demons."

"And a whole host of other fucked up stuff," a scowling brunette man with thick-rimmed glasses muttered.

I took a slow breath, processing that. So Aphrodite had already started one war and lost. No wonder Lucifer was willing to help us.

"Aggie's right," I said, making the old librarian jolt and send me a sharp look. "We should kill her. If she doesn't give my family back, I'll make war look like a fucking fairy tale. So where did she take them?"

Lucifer sighed. "Olympus. Where even I'm not welcome without an invite."

I ground my teeth until they threatened to crack, shoving more rage into my inner vault. The floor shook under us, betraying my emotions.

"Fuck an invite," Harvey muttered, grabbing my shoulder and squeezing tight. "We don't need to go through the front; we need to break into the back door."

"Unless we bargain with her," Renna suggested, earning a sharp look from all of Lucifer's inner circle. "Exchange them for something she wants more."

"We're not handing her an object of power she can use to take us down," Cerny argued instantly, the only one of the new men I recognised—Haley's boss, the one who sent her to Alphaven.

"Not an object," Renna agreed, a calculating edge to her smile. "A person."

"She'll never agree to that," Lucifer shot down. "And I won't ask it of her. Aphrodite's out for blood."

"Who?" I asked, and was ignored.

"She's a goddess; she can handle it. Halwen can't."

Harvey flinched into me. "Stop it!" he yelled, so abruptly and raw that silence fell. "You don't know a damn thing about my mate," he snarled at them. "You don't know what she can handle, so don't you *dare* act like this is going to kill her. And what about my brothers? Do you think they'll be so easily murdered? We've been killed once before; death won't stop us. So shut your fucking mouths unless you have something actually goddamn useful to suggest."

I squeezed his arm. *Well said.*

The big, bald guy was nodding, his arms crossed over his chest. "Remember how fucked up we were when Lili was taken. But she handled it. Fuck, she broke herself and Is out."

"Not easily," a pretty, red-haired man muttered. "Any longer, and we might not have made it."

So their woman had been kidnapped; they should understand exactly why I needed Haley back, why my feral side threatened to rear its hissing head at any moment.

"We need to *ask* Hera, at least," Renna muttered, throwing a scowl at Lucifer that should have gotten her killed for her insubordination.

"Hera," I echoed. I might not have known a lot about gods, goddesses, and titans, but even I knew Hera. She was Zeus's wife, and one of the most powerful gods. If she'd help us, Aphrodite wouldn't stand a chance.

"We'll ask her," Lucifer agreed with a sigh, glancing up when Lili rushed back into the room.

"I might have something, but he—it won't be ready for another day at least. Probably two."

"My family is kidnapped!" Harvey snapped, his fingers biting into my shoulder, claws drawing blood. "We don't *have* two days."

"We'll find another way," I said calmly. "We'll convince Hera to help us murder Aphrodite—"

"It won't take much convincing," the bald man said under his breath.

"Let's use that as an incentive," the smaller, glasses-wearing one agreed.

"It might not work," Lucifer said, watching us sadly. "Even with her help, it might not be enough. That pin—"

"The pin I gave to Halwen, which is now in *Aphrodite's* hands," Cerny muttered, his sour expression only melting when the queen settled against his side. At the sight of their little touches, their closeness, my heart *screamed*, like it had been stabbed and now gushed blood.

My snakes shuddered violently, hungry for blood. *I want my mate.*

"It seems to indicate she's connected to Cronus in some way," Lucifer finished.

"That's a jump," Renna disagreed.

Harvey laughed, a low, animal sound that made my hairs stand on end. *"Everything* is connected to Cronus. We were killed because of him; we were captive in Alphaven because of him; we were sent into the fucking Labyrinth where we almost died because of him; and *he* was the bastard who had my twin locked up this whole time. He's a spider with a hundred legs, and there's *nothing* he doesn't touch."

"Harvey, calm down," I said, trying to summon Emlyn's tone—the firm, even one that always made me calmer.

But Harvey shook his head, tearing away from me, his

body shuddering and on the verge of a shift. I didn't know how to pull him back.

"You're the fucking devil," he snarled at Lucifer. "If you can't stand up to a goddess, what's the point of you?"

"That's enough," Queen Lili said softly—but dangerously soft. She left Cerny's side to stand with the devil, an unyielding expression crossing her face.

I reached for Harvey, but he evaded me; my fingertips brushed fur as it erupted from long claws and raced up his arms.

"If you can't fight a goddess, what makes you think you'd survive a titan? He's going to kill every single one of us, including all of you useless excuses for demons."

"Harvey!" I snapped, panic splintering my soul. "I'm sorry, he doesn't mean that," I hurried out, eyeing the king and queen warily, waiting for them to throw us in jail.

I'd grab Harvey and flee before I ever let them lock us up, but losing their support? It would be a final nail in each of our family's coffins. Fuck, how would we do it without them? I didn't even know where Olympus was. I was an archdemon; what if I ended up in Heaven by mistake and withered away before I could ever find my mate?

"Don't *apologise* for me," Harvey said with a sneering laugh. "Do you think you're in charge now Emlyn's gone? I bet you were just *waiting* for something like this to happen."

"What?" I laughed in disbelief.

Did he even hear himself?

The whites of Harvey's eyes showed as he was caught mid-shift. "You've always loved bossing us around, thinking you're better than the rest of us just because you're more powerful. Well, you're not, Malakai. You're just screwed in the head. You're not powerful; you're a fuck up and a thug. You'll never be like Emlyn. He's a man; you're just a knife."

"Tell me what you really think," I drawled, clenching my

jaw so I didn't lose my shit. I couldn't tell if I was going to rampage or break down in tears, and I'd be damned if I was shedding a single fucking teardrop in front of strangers.

Fur exploded across Harvey's body, ripping his clothes, and bones snapped as his beast form finally broke free. His sneer was the last part of him to vanish, and every fucking millisecond of that expression on his face gouged out a part of my heart.

I just stood there, staring as he trampled furniture and fled out the door, a vicious roar shaking the walls.

You're just screwed in the head. You're not powerful; you're a fuck up and a thug. You'll never be like Emlyn. He's a man; you're just a knife.

I swallowed the knot in my throat, not moving, not even breathing. He was right.

And what use was a knife in saving a rose?

CHAPTER 17

HALWEN

"*C*ocksucking motherfucker!" I hissed, snatching my hands back from the bars that trapped us in a cell fuck knows where. There were two lines burned across the middle of each of my palms, like I was a grilled piece of steak. I ground my jaw, breathing hard through my nose as tears built in my eyes.

"Let me see," Emlyn rumbled, but I curled my hands protectively to my chest, tears streaming down my cheeks now. It hurt *so damn much,* I couldn't think clearly. "Let me see your hands, mate," Em said gently now, holding his palms up for me to place mine into.

"It hurts," I said in a small voice, my bottom lip shuddering.

"Shhh," Emlyn murmured. "I know, I know, Hales. Wane, can you cover her burns with a shadow? It might help soothe the pain."

Em turned when he got no answer, and his shoulders sank.

Wane was pressed into the corner of the cell, his knees to

his chest. Only a swath of his face was visible, his bronze skin wan and sickly, his eyes unfocused as he stared at the floor. The rest of him was wrapped in shadows so thick I couldn't see his body.

"I'm okay," I choked out, tears rolling freely. "I'll be okay." I didn't care that the statements contradicted each other. "Can we just—can—"

My hands throbbed so badly I wanted to scream, but I just swallowed the sound and blinked more hot tears free.

"Anything you need," Emlyn murmured, brushing tears off my cheeks with his thumbs. "Just tell me, Hales."

"We need to sit with him. I'll be okay if we just sit with him."

I didn't feel the floor under me as I crossed the cell, didn't feel Em's arm as he supported my back. All I felt was the hot, throbbing agony in my palms. It was as loud and insistent as the heartbeats of my blood magic usually were, only now that was silent and dead, too.

"Is this just pain, or something else?" Emlyn asked when we sat, me between him and Wane.

"I don't know," I breathed, the dark cell blurring. "I don't care."

It didn't matter.

Emlyn pulled me into his arms, brushing his cheek over my hair before he kissed the top of my head. "I know you when you're in pain, Hales. You're loud, you swear a million times a minute, and you get angry. Not hopeless. I think there's something in the bars, some magic to keep us trapped, to stop us even trying to escape."

I shrugged, laying my head on Wane's shoulder. "Then it's working."

Because I knew we'd never get out.

"If I'd used my daggers, I could have killed her," I said

numbly. "Aphrodite. I could have killed her, but I used magic. I was stupid. And now we'll die here."

"We're not going to die, Halwen Vakhara," Emlyn said fiercely.

But he was just lying to himself.

THE WORLD WAS ENDING, LIFE WAS BLEAK AND NOT WORTH living, and I no longer wanted to exist—until, suddenly, I did.

"What the fuck?" I gasped, shaking my head as a dark cloud lifted from my mind, chest, and soul. This was ... weird. A second ago, I was fully prepared to be consumed by the dark abyss that was death, and now I was rolling my eyes at *the dark abyss that was death.*[1]

"Hales?" Emlyn asked in a rush, surging closer to me, his big hands on my shoulders. "Are you okay? What can I do? What do you need?"

"I'm fine," I replied, turning my head to brush a kiss to his clenched jaw before I hooked my arm around the empty darkness in the corner of the room, pulling Wane's body into mine. "It hurts like a bitch, but I'm alive. We're all alive."

A huge breath punched from Emlyn's chest, and he rubbed his face. "You sound like you again."

"Yeah, let's not touch the bars okay? They fuck with your head."

Not to mention my hands throbbed so viciously it was like being burned all over again with every second that passed.

"You should be lucky that's the only thing they're fucking with," a new voice remarked with twisted amusement.

I jerked to my feet, Emlyn right with me, and we subtly positioned ourselves in front of Wane as we faced the brunette stranger watching us through the bars. He was taller even than Emlyn, but slim where Em was broad, his hair short and slicked to his skull, and there was an ugliness to the slash of his mouth and the light in his green eyes.

A warning rang through my instincts, telling me I was unsafe and this man was dangerous. His smile as his bright eyes travelled down my body told me exactly what kind of danger he posed.

"Look at her like that again, and I'll rip your throat out," Em promised, lethally soft. When Em stopped growling, you knew you were fucked.

"Quiet, mincemeat," the stranger replied, his voice whip-sharp. A sense of foreboding unfurled in my stomach; I reached for Wane through the bond, relieved when he sucked in a sharp breath and reached back. "You're coming with me," the man told me, and my skin crawled when he met my eyes.

I drew both my daggers, the ring of volcanic steel settling my heartbeat a fraction, as if Kai was right here with me. *Cut him to shreds, my rose. We'll barbecue the slabs of his flesh and feed them to Harvey's beast.*

"Like fuck I'm going anywhere with you," I spat, tightening my grip on the pink hilts of my knives, plunging into the pool of my magic. I speared power through the clamour of heart-beats thumping around us—*so many, oh god, why were there so many?*—and shot it like an arrow at the leering man's heart.

I didn't slam into an ironclad shield so much as slip right off him like water off a duck's back. A tremor went through my hands, my stomach sloshing with fear. I couldn't touch him with my magic. And something about the brief feel I'd got of his heartbeat—too fast, too frantic, and *excited*—made me think he wasn't mortal.

Was he a god? I almost didn't want to think it but ... a titan?

I swallowed, stepping forward and pushing Em back with the hilt of my blades. "You're Cronus," I said, my pulse drum-ming in my ears, louder than everyone else's heartbeats.

The man laughed, his tan face crinkling like I'd told a joke. "Do you really think it would be that easy? That my brother would parade himself here for you to kill?" The smile fell, his face serious in an instant. He leaned closer, unnaturally long fingers wrapping around the bars of our cell. My breath hitched; the magic in the metal didn't affect him at all. "He's more clever than your tiny, useless mind can possibly imagine."

"So who are you?" Emlyn demanded, a dangerous light in his eyes when he matched my step forward. "Cronus's servant?"

"Cronus's servant," the man laughed, first quietly and then growing in volume until the cell was full of the sound, and it pressed on my chest until all the air was crushed out of my lungs. "I am his equal in every way, his brother in blood and strength, his—"

"No, Emlyn's right," Wane said suddenly, his voice raspy and hard. "You're his servant. I know who you are. You're Iapetus, the brother the titan sends to do his dirty work."

Wane got to his feet and wrapped his fingers around my wrist, needing the contact, but his voice didn't waver and silver eyes glared murderously at the man on the other side of the bars. "You're the one he risks when he won't risk himself, the one he sends after his enemies like a rabid dog."

"I am *the Piercer*," Iapetus roared, the bars crunching as he squeezed his hands into fists, glaring at Wane so furiously I had no doubt he would break the bars and try to kill him. Power rushed through me at the thought, crimson and incensed. "I am the titan of mortality and violent death. I ruled the world before you were even a speck of stardust, *pet*."

Wane flinched, his darkness trembling around him.

"The Piercer?" I sneered, waiting until blood-red magic washed down my arm and across my stomach before I took another step. My heart slammed against my ribs, but I needed the show of strength. The only way to stand up to assholes like this was to show no fear. They were intimidated by strength, by victims who fought back. "The Piece o' Shit more like."

Emlyn laughed abruptly, like I'd caught him off guard. Affection swelled in our bond, like a brush of sunshine, and I drew straighter, using it as strength—the true kind, not the kind I'd been faking all day.

"You'll pay for that remark, cunt," Iapetus snapped, spittle flying from his lips.

"Haley," Wane said weakly, his fingers tightening around my wrist. "He's a bad person. He's—like Locke."

I sucked in a breath through my nose.

"Say it, coward," Iapetus challenged, twisting the bars in his hands until they were a crumpled snarl of metal. "I have no shame for that word."

"Killer," Wane breathed, his shadows writhing, restless. "Rapist."

Iapetus grinned, like the words were badges of honour. "That word kills you, doesn't it pet?"

"Call my mate that name one more time," I breathed, my heart slowing, eerie calm washing over me. "I dare you."

"Will it truly kill you, I wonder," he went on, sneering at Wane, "when I take your mate's cunt? Will your heart cease beating when I make you watch as I break both her legs, so she can't even crawl away when I force myself upon her?"

Wane's shadows pulsed once, a deep thump of warning. "The only thing left of you will be a smear of blood."

Emlyn roared, tearing away from my side and slashing his arm through the air. Emerald power slammed into the bars so hard that the cell rattled and the walls shook around us like an earthquake gripped the ground. The bars didn't shatter, didn't fall apart when his magic sliced into the metal, but Iapetus's fingers were cut at the knuckle, and the dismembered tips tumbled to the floor of the cell with sick thuds.

But Iapetus laughed, flexing his hands in front of his face. Horror bled like ice water through me, making the magic in my curse marks stutter when flesh regrew from the bloody stumps until he was unharmed.

"Is that all you've got?" he taunted Em.

I stumbled back a step, but if Wane could be brave, I could be, too. I didn't know where my curse magic lived, didn't know why I'd woken up with it as well as two curse marks, but I gave it a silent command, refusing to let the power fade when there was a threat to my mates separated by only twisted iron.

It rose to my command, like it had been holding its breath waiting for me to call on it. I sucked in a sharp breath at the scope and *scale* of my power. I hadn't been this powerful in the arena in Alphaven, not even in the Labyrinth.

Well played, Cronus, I thought sourly. My magic was fattened for him to devour, exactly as planned.

"Don't even *look* at my mate," I hissed when the titan smirked at Wane, lifting my dagger and hoping he'd heard everything that happened in the Labyrinth. These knives had killed the Erinyes. Now they were god-killers.

Iapetus grinned, the smile too perfect for the vileness of his soul. I sent a tug to both Wane and Em, telling them to be ready as I gathered power. If I couldn't explode every blood vessel in his body, fine. It was time to find out if my curse magic could kill a titan, too.

I jerked forward when Iapetus leaned against the bars to taunt or threaten us again. I didn't allow his hideous words to echo through my head for a single second as I dove towards the gap in the twisted bars and aimed my knife for his heart.

He jumped back with a *tsk* before my blade could pierce him, safely out of range of my god-killing knives, but he hadn't accounted for Em and Wane. I let a little of my own rabidity show in a grin as Em's emerald magic scythed through the bars and slashed a deep, gouging wound across the titan's middle.

He split in two before I could ask if he was dead, and I guess that answered that question.

"Fuck," I gasped, letting out my breath and sheathing a knife so I could grab Wane, wrenching him tight against me. He was so cold, and trembling all over. His shadows pulsed and shook against me, furious, almost violent even when I kissed him.

"It's not enough," he seethed, his voice sending chills down my spine. "For what he threatened to do. It's not *enough.*"

"Calm down," Emlyn said firmly, grabbing us both in a squeezing hug, his magic settling now the threat was removed. "We're alright now."

I sighed with relief, still full of power but shaky, scared.

I flinched when a scraping sound came from the other side of the bars. Wane's breathing increased, his magic churning faster. Em just froze.

My strength waned as we stood there, imprisoned, watching the two halves of Iapetus pulling back together, his severed torso repairing at an alarming rate.

CHAPTER 18

I tensed my arm to throw my knife, but I couldn't lose my volcanic daggers. Emlyn must have been thinking the same thing I was—kill him now before he heals! —because his eyes flashed and he pulled away from us to send another vicious arc of magic through the bars. This time he severed an arm, but it didn't stop the mess of Iapetus's dismembered torso repairing until there was only a red seam where he'd been cut. And then his arm began to reattach, too.

"Fuck," Em grunted, hitting the titan with slash of magic after slash of magic, but as soon as he opened a wound, another healed.

It hit me then, as fear bloomed colder and worse than before, what the word *immortal* really meant. My mates were near-immortal, and could survive a lot, but *this?* This was unnatural. Fear froze my blood, my feet, until I couldn't move.

We didn't stand a chance.

He literally *couldn't die* and Cronus was even *more* powerful than Iapetus.

My hands shook, the dagger in my right hand trembling.

Don't you fucking dare, my rose. You stab that fucker in the eyes, the skull, the dick—whatever it takes to keep him down—and you get the fuck out of there and come back to me.

I inhaled a shaky breath and nodded, like Kai was really here talking to me.

"I was going to be nice," Iapetus snarled, pushing off the stone floor outside the cell and not seeming to care that his right foot was on the floor and his left arm hung by a single sinew. He looked right at me, violence in his green eyes. "But *now* I think I'll bleed you as I fuck you. Force you to come right as I snuff out your miserable existence."

Don't let the words stick. Don't think them. Don't even acknowledge them.

But I felt sick, and dirty, like an oily sheen covered my skin, and the horror made me shaky, my soul spiked with dark, primal fear.

Wane took my hand, lifting it to his mouth to feather a kiss on my knuckles, surprising me enough that I was slow to react when he brushed past me. He approached the bars, shadows thickening, lengthening until they trailed behind him, the train of a cloak made of pure, impenetrable darkness. I watched, too slow, too shaky.

When he lifted his hands, shadows poured out of him like a storm, and even frozen where I was, I saw Iapetus's eyes widen. He stumbled back, unease tightening his features.

"So it's true," he breathed, lifting his hands.

I flinched, movement slamming back into me with a suddenness that made my head spin. I stumbled across the cell for Wane, desperate to stop him, to protect him. Em right at my side, bristling with a constant growl.

But Iapetus hadn't raised his hands to attack. He bared his palms, like he was pleading for his life.

Wane's storm of inky shadows slammed into the titan like a battering ram, sending him skidding across the stone hallway outside our cell. It knocked him off his feet, drove him to the floor, and forced its way into his chest until darkness sprayed from his nose and mouth like vomit.

It was an unpleasant sight, but an evil satisfaction hummed in my chest. Iapetus deserved every bit of unpleasantness.

"I think I can push the bars," Wane breathed, his voice deep, enraged. Shadows roared around him like the waves of a stormy ocean, slamming into the bars once, twice, three times. I caught my breath in surprise when the metal dented and warped, Wane's darkness assaulting the gap until it was wide enough for someone to step through.

I fought to stop my body shaking, to get back in control. Iapetus just threatened to rape me, and so casually that it sliced beneath my skin and made my stomach twist.

"We'll need to be careful not to touch the bars," Emlyn said, a furrow between his brows as he watched Wane's shadows spray like a fountain from Iapetus's orifices. I didn't know how Wane had done it, how his power was strong enough to take out a titan when he'd been weak and healing only yesterday, but I didn't stick around to ask. The threats slid through my head, primal fear making me jerk into motion. There was an opening; we needed to get the hell out of here.

"He's not dead," Wane breathed, hesitating before he glanced at us. I wasn't sure what he expected to see, but relief spread through his silver eyes. "Iapetus. He's just weakened. I don't think I can kill him."

His grave stare drifted to the pink hilts of my long daggers, and I straightened with a sharp intake of breath. He couldn't kill him, but could I?

"The Furies said they were god-killers, not titan-killers," I pointed out, but I drew them anyway, their weight comforting.

"Quicker, Hales," Em urged, ushering me towards the warped gap in the bars.

I edged closer, my palms throbbing in warning, screaming not to get close, that my skin would burn away.

"I'll go first," Wane said urgently, giving me a hard look, his voice no longer deep and ominous but normal.

"Don't!" I panicked, racing after him as he wrapped himself in shadow and squeezed through the gap. "Wane? Are you hurt? Did it burn you? *Are you hurt?*"

A sob crawled up my throat. What if the burns were everywhere? What if the pain was too much and his body shut down? I'd just got him back, I couldn't—

"I'm okay," Wane said quickly, dropping the shadows around his hands and face so I could see him—on the other side of the bars. "I think the darkness shielded me."

Em blew out a relieved breath, scanning the austere stone hallway outside the cell. How long did we have before someone noticed Iapetus was taking too long to return?

"You next, Hales."

"I don't like this," I told him, but moved towards the gap in the bars anyway. Emlyn always went last whenever we needed to escape anywhere, like he thought he was the least important. I *hated* it. But only one of us could fit through the bars at once, so I edged into the gap, gasping when darkness wrapped me in a protective cocoon.

An instant weight fell off my shoulders. Fuck, I'd missed being wrapped up in these cool shadows, the velvet press of them around me. My eyes burned as I took step after step. I only knew I was out when the shadows peeled away, tendrils brushing the tears from my cheeks with a lingering touch.

"I missed you too, itzaia," Wane murmured, kissing my cheek as I approached him—and the weak titan on the ground. Whatever Wane's magic had done—and however the fuck it *had* done it—Iapetus stared at the ceiling with palpable anger, but he couldn't get to his feet, couldn't hurt us like he was obviously imagining.

I reluctantly pulled myself from Wane's arms and twirled my blades so they were gripped in my fists, blade downward. A better person might have hesitated, might have baulked at murdering a man who couldn't defend himself. But his threats rang in my mind, scarring me no matter how hard I tried to push them out of my head.

My body burned, violated even though he'd never set hands on me. He *wanted* to, and that was bad enough. So I swallowed the bile in my throat, and picked up my legs to take the last two steps to Iapetus.

With the skin crawling all down my body, I drove both points into his torso, one blade buried in his gut, and the other driving into his heart. I didn't know what my blades had become when they rebounded off the hippocampi in the Labyrinth, but now they sliced through bone and ribs like they were cobwebs.

"Thanks," Em murmured, even his soft voice making me jump and throw a shifty look over my shoulder. Shadows peeled away from his big body. He was out—we all were.

I tore my wavy daggers from the titan's body, giving him a long, hard look in his eyes—vacant, dull. But dead? I couldn't tell.

"He might still come back," I murmured, taking two steps back and startling when Wane wrapped his fingers around my wrist, his skin cool and dry—and thrumming with power. Mine was hot and clammy, heat burning through me that I couldn't explain.

"He's down for now," Wane replied quietly. "Come on, itzaia. Let's get out of here."

I pushed down the disgust and terror still crawling through my body, and met Wane's eyes. He'd survived Cronus and was here—strong, powerful. I could be strong, too.

"Which way?" I asked, looking at Emlyn for guidance.

He sighed, glancing in either direction. The corridor was

the same—a flat stretch of bleak stone with one cell on either side of the one we'd been condemned to. It was a tiny dungeon compared to the tunnel Wane had been locked in for a hundred years. I sent a wave of comfort through the bond, wishing I could hold his hand but too wary to drop a single weapon.

He wasn't okay—far from it—but he didn't let it show when Em chose a direction and led us away from the cells. And if Wane wouldn't break, neither could I.

"We'll be okay," I promised him, glancing up at his bronzed profile—stoic and harsh, like any softness had been chiselled away. I knew the truth though, felt it in the storm raging through his soul. The cell, the corridor, the confinement— he'd thought he would be locked up for another hundred years. Was that why his shadows were stronger? Because his fear had fed them?

"Keep up," Em barked quietly, leading us carefully around a bend in the corridor, his hands curled into fists like he planned to pummel his way to freedom.

Wane and I quickened our steps until I was close enough for Em's paper and ink scent to wrap around my lungs, easing a knot in my chest even if the paper was burnt and ink old. We'd get out. We'd escaped the cells with pitiful odds, after all. We'd be fine. Completely fine.

But my hands were shaking, and my mates could feel my panic through our bonds. Could Kai and Harvey sense it, too, or were we too far away? They'd find us—the bond was a beacon, calling them to me. But if they found us now, they could be caught, and that thought made me want to cry, scream, and burn this place down—in that order.

"Faster," Em growled, skidding around another corner. Was he following an animal instinct? Was the Feral side of him guiding him to freedom, like an animal's senses guided them to water? Or was he guessing?

Oh gods, please don't let him be guessing.

Panic flared, crimson light splashing my shirt—my curse was glowing. I gasped when it poured power into me, responding to my fear even though there wasn't a visible threat. Why was my magic so much stronger here? It made no sense.

We flew around the next corner so fast I had to snap my wings out to stop myself falling. Wane's shoes squeaked on the tiled stone floor. Columns lined the corridor on either side of us, carved with beautiful figures and draped with pink tulips. This place was too pretty to be a prison, nothing like the ominous darkness of the Damned House. It sent a shiver down my spine.

"Fuck!" Em roared, grey feathers flapping and his hands snapping out to catch the wall on either side of him.

I dug my heels in to stop momentum slamming me into Em's back, and Wane staggered to a halt beside me, breathing fast, his panic spiralling so out of control that it escaped his calm mask.

Beyond Emlyn, the pretty tiled floor dropped away like a giant had hacked it off, and on the other side was a sheer drop so high that even my stomach twisted up despite the wings on my back. I'd never flown from this high up before.

"Em," I breathed, stepping away from Wane and sheathing a dagger so I could latch onto the back of my mate's shirt and haul him back from the edge. My heart thudded, every beat hitting my ribs.

Emlyn's nostrils flared with rough, panting breaths like a spooked horse, his skin bleached with fear when he took slow, careful steps backward. Scared that even that tiny movement would send him back over the edge.

Like it was furious we'd escaped the perilous fall, a vicious wind howled outside, its greedy fingers tearing at our clothes, wings, and hair. A small, frantic sound escaped as I threw trembling arms around Em and tore him away from the edge, my whole body like jelly.

His wings snapped out for balance as we backed up, and I could barely breathe until Wane grabbed each of us in a bruising grip. We were on solid ground. We didn't fall.

"We could fly," I breathed. "Right?"

"From that height, Hales? With that wind? It would rip us out of the sky."

I knew that, but I didn't want to hear it. My stomach churned, hands shaky. I dredged some positivity from the black pit in my stomach, and said, "We'll find another way."

"Going somewhere?" a sweet voice asked, not quite able to hide her sneer.

We spun as one, Wane and Em on either side of me, magic rising instantly—Em sent an arc of devastating power. It ricocheted off the solid walls, but Aphrodite sidestepped it like it was nothing, holding up her hand—with my bone pin clutched in her dark fingers. Wane's shadows met a solid wall of air, fracturing apart on impact. He winced, clutching his chest, and my rage grew big enough to swallow the world.

He gave it to me. His lover.

His lover? Wynvail had touched *this* thing? This sneering, spiteful, poisonous goddess?

I'd kill her.

Magic flashed from both my curses this time, but instead of looking intimidated, Aphrodite's eyes glimmered with amusement. She wore another beautiful dress, her hair perfectly styled and makeup flawless. It couldn't hide the rotting thing inside her.

"There's no way out," she gloated. "You must think I'm especially stupid if I'd put your cell near an exit. This way out is obviously a trap. I'm actually impressed you didn't fall into it." She made a thoughtful noise, her eyes travelling over

Emlyn's body like a physical touch. "Maybe you're valuable, after all."

"I belong to myself and my mate," Em warned, sending another destructive arc of magic. It did nothing, didn't even *touch* her. "No one else."

Aphrodite tilted her head, brown-gold hair falling over her shoulder like a swath of purest silk. I wanted to rip it out of her scalp until she bled. "I wouldn't be so sure of that, Emlyn Johahn."

"Don't speak his name," I breathed, taking a step forward and bringing so much magic with me that I should have blasted her apart. But she was *a goddess,* and even though their magic had faded from immortal grace to limited power in the war, she was still a deadly threat. And armed with the bone pin that had fried my bones, prickled my eyeballs, and made the tip of my tongue burn ... she was untouchable.

If it had amplified my ordinary power to that level, what the hell had it done to a goddess?

"What name?" she asked, all innocence as she blinked at me. "Emlyn Johahn? Or do you mean Wynvail Locke?"

It was like she'd slammed a *rage* button inside me. Power and murder took possession of my body, and I flew across the hallway before I could stop myself. I'd choke the name from her lips, rip her fucking tongue out and make her eat it so she could never *never* speak my dead mate's name—

My nose crunched, bones breaking, when I slammed into her shield. *Fucking fucker!*

My curse's magic might have been amplified, but it was nothing compared to hers. Even digging my fingernails into the solid shield, even gnashing my canine teeth into it and carving the claws on my wings through it, I didn't even *scratch* her shield.

"*Was* it that name?" Aphrodite asked coyly, just *begging* to be ripped into teeny, tiny gory pieces. She tapped her full bottom lip with a long fingernail. "Or is it *Wane* Locke? You really should be more specific, Halwen."

Wane went still behind me, his soul frozen but throbbing with pain. Trauma bled through him like ink through water, and I felt his fear—the old fear that had haunted him for ten years. It would never go away, would never stop stalking him.

But I could kill the bitch who triggered him on purpose.

I roared, my teeth bared and dagger raised, and hurtled myself into her shield, the wavy blade of my knife lighting crimson as I drove it into the invisible wall between us, over and over and over.

That pin wasn't hers. Wynvail won it from me through cleverness and cunning and stealth. It was *his*. Not hers. Never hers.

"Give it back," I spoke through my teeth, only distantly aware of shadows blacker than night slamming into the shield where I clawed at it, trying to weaken it with me. Hairs rose all down my arms as so much power built in this tiny corridor that it shook the floor below us. I tasted the acid bite of it on my tongue; it burned. "Give it back."

"Are you done?" Aphrodite drawled, her gaze flat and her perfect mouth pursed with annoyance. She needed to be screaming in pain, begging for mercy. Instead, she was *irritated.*

"With you?" I seethed, my heart clamouring in my chest. Power drowned out my own heartbeat. "Never."

"This is tedious," she sighed, and waved her hand. The pin caught the light, the flowers carved into it both beautiful and devastating. The dagger Wyn gave me had been carved with flowers, too. I wanted him back. I wanted my hateful, spiteful, cruel mate back so badly it killed me.

I slammed my teeth into the shield again, but before I could draw back for another attempt, magic gripped my arms, stilled my hands, and forced my legs immobile. Light bled from around the beautiful, twisted goddess.

No!

I tried to fight, tried to carve through her power until all that remained were ribbons, but her magic swallowed me in light before I could do a single bit of damage. She ripped me away from that corridor and threw me through the blinding tunnel of light.

When I fell out the other side, I had to grab the wall to stop my body slamming into the floor. My head spun, blood rushed violently through my head, and I groaned.

It took me a moment to lift my head, to see Em and Wane slumped on the ground in this new cell. It took another moment for a solid glass window to snag my attention. There wasn't a sheer drop on the other side of it, but a shining golden palace built into the side of a mountain.

Oh, gods. No wonder my magic was stronger here, and no wonder Aphrodite was so powerful. We were at the seat of the gods. We were in Mount Olympus.

CHAPTER 19

HARVEY

I grabbed my head in both hands and squeezed, a dark, throaty sound pouring from me as I fought to stay in two-legged form. I'd barely wrangled control from my beast, and I only managed *that* because the rage had faded, leaving horror and sharp, breakable fear behind.

The things I said to Kai...

He'd never forgive me, and I deserved that.

Worthless waste of space, my uncle's voice snarled from my memory. *What good are you? You're a whore and a hole—that's your only value.*

I flinched, pressing tighter on my head, my magic spiking and spiralling out of control. What if he was right? I was a useless mate; Haley was kidnapped right in front of me. I was a useless brother; Em and Wane were stolen with her. And what I'd said to Kai, the sickening way I'd treated him when he'd done nothing but support me? I was a heinous, hideous person.

We'd *just* got Wane back, just freed him from that prison under the Damned House, and I couldn't even protect him for one week. Now he was gone, and suffering, and terrified —I could feel it, like a lance through my chest, screaming at me that my twin was in danger, he was scared, he needed me.

And where was I? Sat on the roof of the palace, being a worthless piece of shit like my father always said I was. He always said I'd amount to nothing, that I should be ashamed to be so weak, and he was right.

Whenever I'd cried, it led to boots breaking bones and fists drawing blood, brutal hits breaking my nose, others snapping my fingerbones, knowing full well I'd heal from the injuries. It didn't matter whatever Locke and his brother did to me, because the marks vanished. So they hurt me without restraint.

I curled my hands into shaking fists in my hair, tempted to turn them on myself as if it would appease the vicious universe, like my pain would balance the way I'd hurt Kai with my poison tongue.

Everything about you is poison, boy. There's something fucked up in your head. You're a defect, a mistake. You should thank *me for touching you like that.*

I flinched, the memory so sharp I could *see* the basement, smell its blood and damp scent, feel the press of walls and skin against me, pain biting into me.

I screamed, the roar coming from deep, deep in my chest, and the leash nearly tore off my destructive magic. If I released it, I'd obliterate all Iarlon.

Don't act like you're special. Wane's suffering is far worse than yours.

Those words were my own, and they were true. I hadn't been caged in a room, tortured by a titan for a hundred years. I'd fought and battled and broken, over and over, but I'd had

Kai and Em nearby even if I hadn't recognised them as my brothers, my family.

Wane had suffered *alone.*

Tears poured from my eyes like scorching lava, and I couldn't get them to stop.

Weak. Pathetically weak. You'd never survive outside this basement, Harvey. Keeping you here is merciful.

I shook my head, screaming louder, not caring that I was on the palace roof and people could hear me. Not caring that the capital spread out around me, full of demons and spirits and life.

I wasn't here; I was in that basement under the gilded manor with pain clawing through me over and over, the rattle of a belt buckle like a razor to my nerves and Wane's gasping cries worse, always worse. I couldn't handle it. I needed him here, needed to know he was safe, needed to protect him.

Like you protected him when Aphrodite stole him?

Worthless, useless—

"Harvey," Kai barked, ripping me out of the memory with a rough hand on my shoulder.

"I can't—I can't do this," I sobbed, hating myself for crying but unable to stop. The lilac city blurred in my vision, twisted and pale. My breaths came faster, sharper, shorter.

"You're not alone," Kai swore fiercely, his bruising grip on my shoulders keeping me grounded. It should have made everything worse, should have reminded me of crueller hands on my body, but somehow it—didn't. But I couldn't catch a breath, couldn't stop my head spinning. "I'm right here with you, and I'll eviscerate every single bastard who tries to fuck with you. Yeah?"

I tried to gasp out an agreement, but I couldn't. My head spun, my cries awful and wheezing. *Weak. Useless.*

"We'll get our family back," Kai swore in a throaty hiss, prising my hands out of my hair and dragging me into the world's roughest hug. "I know you're scared shitless, and so am I. But we'll find them."

I squeezed my eyes shut, shaking hard when he crushed me closer, arms locking mine at my sides. The pressure, the weight ... it helped me suck in a gasp, then another.

"Wane—"

"Is with Haley, and Em," Kai finished. "They'll kill anyone who so much as looks at him wrong. Even a goddess won't stand a chance if she threatens Wane; you know Haley."

I did know her, and I knew she was panicking and afraid, too. I felt her in my chest, muffled and distant but there. Scared.

My mate should *never* be scared; I should have provided for her, kept her safe, kept her happy. Not miserable and petrified. I was a pathetic excuse for a mate.

"What if—she—locks him—"

"We won't lose him again," Kai snarled, like all I was doing was voicing his own worries. "Not a fucking chance after we've been separated a hundred years. It's different this time, Harv. We know where he is, and he's not alone. It won't happen again."

But I couldn't believe that, and I couldn't stop shaking, and I couldn't stop hearing my abusers' voices. I couldn't *breathe.*

"Why are you—here? Should—hate me—"

Kai scoffed. "You're my family. I don't hate you; as if I fucking could."

"I hurt you."

"Yeah," he agreed. "And I've hurt you over the years. We say hurtful shit when we're scared; we lash out, that's just us. I'm not gonna walk away from you, and I'm sure as shit not leaving you to have a panic attack on the devil's roof."

I choked on a laugh, tears squeezing out of my closed eyelids. "Devil's roof."

"This is a bird thing, isn't it?" he asked, squeezing my

shoulder. "Are you gonna hang your ass over the edge and shit on people who walk past?"

I opened my eyes to slant a glare at him. "Fuck off."

"Just as soon as you fuck off," he replied, the retort familiar.

I swallowed, realising at once that my breathing was under my control again. Not easy—far from that—but my chest expanded with a breath again.

"I didn't mean what I said, Kai. Any of it. Those words were—they were for me. Only for me."

Kai grabbed the back of my skull and shook my head until my glare deepened. "Fuck that shit. You don't deserve that any more than I do. It's not your fault they were taken; we're up against *a goddess* and we don't know anything about her power, her weakness, or who the fuck she's working with. This isn't on you. Yeah?"

I swallowed, my eyes burning viciously. "Seems like it is."

"Yeah, well, that's because your head's fucking with you. It's lying, Harvey. Don't listen to that shit."

"Has anyone ever told you that you swear too much?" I asked, swallowing the lump in my throat.

"Mother Hen every two seconds," he replied, making me laugh at his name for Emlyn. When the laugh fell from my lips, he hauled me back into a hug. "We're getting them back, whatever it takes. And I could never hate you, so don't worry about that. You know I'll get you back for what you said anyway."

"The usual way?" I asked, my voice hoarse.

He tugged on a feather, making me hiss. "Nah, I think I'll mix it up this time. Instead of handing your ass to you, I'll keep it a mystery. You'll never know when I'll strike."

I snorted. "You give away every move you make. You think you can surprise me?"

"Your ass will be beaten before you can say, *please, big, strong Kai, don't bruise my pretty face.*"

"Was the high voice necessary?"

"Very." He whipped off his scarf and dragged it roughly down my face, wiping my tears. And taking off the top layer of my skin, probably. "You okay?"

"No," I laughed, shoving his hand—and his scarf—away. "But I'll be fine."

"Then come off the roof," he replied, tying the scarf back around his neck. "Renna thinks she can use that tracking stone to get us into Mount Olympus."

CHAPTER 20

HALWEN

I glanced at my arms again, checking my flesh was still attached. Yup, still there. But I burned so hot that it should have blackened and peeled away, a furnace inside me.

Sweat dripped off the end of my nose; I wiped my face on my sleeve, panting through my teeth. I might have thought Aphrodite had fucked with me if I hadn't felt the exact same thing yesterday morning before Typhon melted through our wall and gave us an ominous warning. Shame the dragon-armed guy didn't warn us about psycho gods as well as the titan; we might have escaped this cell.

Then again, the bitch kidnapped us from *Lucifer's palace* so maybe nothing would have stopped her. The fact that she outmatched the devil was scary as fuck.

I clenched my teeth against a whine, squirming where I sat with my back against the wall, my legs stretched in front of me.

Em was still passed out from whatever Aphrodite did when she transported us, but he was breathing and his heartbeat was strong; I tuned into it with my blood magic at all times. All my magic was returned now, my body gradually recovering from Aphrodite's bullshit. Wane had woken up long enough to lay his head in my lap and cling to me, fighting the power I sensed ravaging him.

I knew why I wasn't passed out. Aphrodite was trying to mess with my head. This was *so* much worse than being unconscious with them, and panic spiked itself through my chest like a permanent wound. *You win this round, bitchface.*

I tested my burned fingers with small movements, holding my breath in anticipation of another sharp flash of pain. When it didn't come, I exhaled in rough relief, scraping my palm down my face. My fingers had healed, and my nose was no longer broken, but nothing would stop the heat razing its way through my whole body. It wasn't helped at all by Wane's head in my lap and the soft breaths puffing over my stomach.

I wasn't stupid; I knew this was arousal, but I also knew it wasn't natural. Was there such a thing as a horny curse? Because I was seriously starting to think I'd been struck with one.

I peeled the shirt from where it was glued to my chest, trying not to wake Wane. Whatever dark magic coursed through them, they needed to sleep it off. And that was without all the exertion Wane's shadows must have taken from him. How the hell did he take down a titan?

His magic was far more powerful than I'd seen it before, close to invincible. Only the bone pin had kept Aphrodite conscious; if we could get it off her, she was screwed. And hopefully, her buddy Cronus would be screwed too. It was obvious they were working together.

Cronus ... was he the reason Wane's shadows were amplified? Volatile?

He'd thrown me in the Labyrinth to fatten up my magic for him to devour like a roast pig. Had he done the same to Wane? Pushed him to the limit of his ability so he could take his shadows for himself?

And why the fuck had he tried to cut them away and not just eaten Wane like he devoured his sons eons ago?

My skull hurt trying to fit so many questions inside it, and I was too hot, too sweaty, and too pained to make any sense of them. My nose and fingers didn't hurt anymore, but a knot tightened in my lower belly, gripping so vicious that my nostrils flared.

When had this started? I tried to remember when I'd begun feeling hot, but my head was too much a mess. I whined when the next cramp scythed brutally through my pelvis. Like the worst kind of period pain, a ten out of ten on the agony scale.

I shifted, trying to curl around myself and clutch my belly, and Wane came awake with a gasp.

"Shit," he breathed, scrambling up and reaching for me the second he was sitting. Panic sharpened his sleepy silver eyes. "Where's the pain, itzaia?"

I shook my head, tears squeezing out of my eyes. "Stomach. I don't—know why—"

"Shh," he soothed, his fingers soothing gently over my abdomen. "I'm here, Haley, it's going to be alright."

My body locked with the next cramp, a cry escaping my clenched teeth. I was so hot it felt like the air rippled above my skin, and I screwed my eyes shut as it flared hotter.

"I think—I might know what this is," Wane said, pulling me into his arms, my back to his chest, and settling against the wall. "I just don't understand why."

The kiss he laid on my shoulder was so tender it hurt.

"I need you to find Em in the mate bond and give him a tug. You're going to need both of us. Okay, Haley?"

I swallowed and nodded, keeping my eyes shut as he pulled me back until I was laid against him, my head on his shoulder. I felt through the fire and pain for the place I was bound to Em and yanked on the thread, desperation making me pull harder than normal.

Emlyn came awake with a ferocious growl, protection and warning laced in his voice. My bottom lip wobbled.

"Hales?" he breathed, the rustle of clothes telling me he'd rushed across the cell. "Haley, darling, what's wrong?"

"Hurts," I said through gritted teeth, curling around myself when another cramp struck. This couldn't be as simple as my period coming, right? If it was, it was the worst one I'd had in my entire (one hundred and) twenty-seven years.

"She's cramping really hard here," Wane said gently, feathering his fingers over my lower belly. "I can feel the contractions."

"Your cycle was never this bad before," Em murmured, taking my face in his hands and pressing a kiss to my forehead, not seeming to care that I was a sweaty mess.[1] "Is it worse because you—died?"

I opened my eyes at the falter in his voice, fighting the heaviness of my eyelids. The pain grew the tiniest bit more bearable when Wane's fingers massaged firm circles over the worst area, allowing my jaw to unclench.

"Fuck, it hurts," I rasped, pressing my cheek into Em's hand and breathing in short, fast breaths.

"I can—feel you really clearly," Wane said, his voice almost careful. "I can feel what you need, itzaia, and I think—"

"What?" Emlyn demanded before I could speak, a muscle fluttering in his cheek above his thick beard. "*What*, Wane?"

"I think she's entered a mating cycle somehow."

I shook my head. No chance. Stygian demons didn't have mating cycles, or if they did I'd literally never heard of it. Some demons didn't have periods every month; they had a vicious, painful heat once a year where their body demanded they fuck like crazy and make babies. It was a base, biological demand and it was violent and torture. I shut out the pang in my chest at the thought of babies.

"That makes no sense," Em muttered, his voice rough with worry. "Her cycle is monthly, not yearly."

My cheeks might have heated at them so casually discussing my period, but one) my cheeks were already enflamed and two) it wasn't some shameful thing I had to keep secret. Sure, I hated having periods, but they were just part of having a vagina. I hadn't realised quite how much attention Em paid to mine before, though. It explained how my bloody clothes ended up in the laundry and where all the cloths and rags came from, though.

"Love you," I panted, clenching my hands into fists when another cramp rose.

"I love you more than anything in the world," Emlyn replied seriously, stroking tears off my cheeks when pain bit deep into my abdomen. Wane tried to massage the pain away, but it only barely worked.

"She needs to mate, Em," Wane murmured.

"Here?" Emlyn scowled at the cell, from the solid walls to the window overlooking Mount Olympus. I saw the moment he figured out where we were; his blue eyes widened, a hitch of panic going through his soul.

"I think—you're crazy," I told Wane, reaching for his soul. "But I want the pain to stop. How do we fix it?"

"Yesterday morning," Em said before Wane could speak. "You were needy and aroused, even though we'd all been together the night before."

"With me that morning, too," Wane mused. "I think your body's been trying to tell you something for a long time. And we can figure out why later—if it's got something to do with your god ancestor or Rhea or something on your demon side."

I clenched my jaw when pain washed over me again, my body locking this time.

"I can't bear this," Wane breathed, fingers making quick work of the fastenings of my trousers and slipping inside. He groaned, and my hips bucked at the sound. When he drew his fingers out they were slicked with so much arousal it dripped from the tips. "Still doubt me?" he asked Em.

Emlyn blinked, a thousand emotions chasing across his face. "Is—is that why we struggled—"

"Stop," I said through gritted teeth. I didn't want to follow that dark path of thought, didn't want to taste the hope if it was true.

But I wasn't the only one who'd felt the lack for those ten years, and I wasn't the only one crushed by disappointment every time my body sabotaged us. Because it needed a mating cycle...? Then why bleed monthly? Ugh, I hated my body.

"Questions later," Wane agreed, pushing my trousers down my hips, Emlyn kneeling to unfasten my boots and pull the fabric off me completely. "Don't fuck about with foreplay."

"Since when were you this mouthy?" Emlyn asked, a flicker of amusement in his blue eyes until another whimper of pain escaped me. "I'm here, I'm here, Hales."

I still clung to denial that Wane was wrong—right up until Emlyn sank all the way to the hilt inside me, his cock stretching me so fiercely that the burn replaced the painful twist in my stomach. Relief was instant, like Em's cock was imbued with a healing tonic, and it spread further with every slam of his hips into mine.

I melted into Wane with a deep breath, covering his hand with mine. I squeezed, trying to swallow my panic at what this meant.

"It's okay," Wane breathed against my ear. "We've got you. Whatever happens, we'll be okay."

I shuddered when Em's hands slid under my ass and lifted

me, hitting deeper but with enough skill that all I felt was blinding pleasure and no discomfort. A loud groan tore from the back of my throat, my breathing coming faster when Wane's free hand dipped down and drew slow circles on my clit. I was so desperately wet that the noises we made were obscene, but when Wane's lips found the side of my neck, suctioning to my weak spot, I forgot every bit of embarrassment.

"That's our good girl," Emlyn murmured, driving into me faster, making goosebumps cover my body in a rush of cold that fought the scalding heat inside my body. "I can feel you getting close. So tight around me."

I bit my lip, my eyes screwing shut when the stimulation on my clit and Em's purposeful strokes combined to send me so high my toes curled.

"You need to come inside," Wane said, husky with arousal.

Emlyn groaned, his hips moving frantically now. He sought my lips, kissing me in a rush that sent another rush of shivers through my body. I reached up to clasp the back of his head, keeping him close as I melted into the hot kiss, my hips stuttering up to meet his.

"Shit," I gasped, pleasure coiling so suddenly, so dangerously, in the exact same place that pain had ravaged only minutes earlier. "I—"

Wane's fingers moved rapidly, assaulting me with pleasure, and I came so suddenly, so hard, that my cry filled the cell, echoing back to me. I swallowed Em's ragged sigh, the last of the pain fading when his cock throbbed inside me and filled me with cum.

Wane's fingers didn't slow when I shuddered and slumped into him, and I whined. "You need another, itzaia. We need to make sure you don't lose a single drop of cum, okay?"

My head spun. I was hot and sweaty, but dazed by pleasure instead of pain. I just nodded.

My heart slammed in my chest when Wane slid out from behind me, settling me against the wall in his place.

"Hold her hips up," he told Em, who shot him a sharp growl.

"I know, I'm not an amateur."

Wane held up his hands. My gaze fixed there, remembering the way those fingers felt on my pussy. Em choked out a sound when my pussy throbbed around his cock, and quickly withdrew from my heat.

The second he drew back, Wane was there, lifting my hips with two thick shadows so he could thrust into me. I kept my eyes fixed obsessively on his face, watching his mouth slacken, his eyes glaze over. I sighed in relief, whatever tension had returned to my body bleeding out of me now. This was what I needed—my mates inside me. I needed Kai and Harvey and—

No. Don't go down that road, Haley.

"Eyes on me, itzaia," Wane rasped, leaning down for a rough kiss. "Don't take your eyes off me, okay?"

I nodded, a deep shudder making my hips tremble against his when shadows stroked every spot of weakness inside me, his cock driving in purposeful strokes.

His lips moved against mine, both tender and possessive. I opened my mouth to whimper when his cock grazed an especially sensitive spot inside me, and Wane drew my tongue into his mouth and sucked it, pushing me so close to the edge that my back arched.

My hips slammed up into his and my orgasm crashed through me, stars filling my vision until all I saw was shadows and starlight.

When he released my mouth, he breathed, "You are so beautiful when you come. You're a gift, Haley." His shadows pulled my hips until they were flush to his body and he ground his cock deep inside me, forcing a grunt from my lips.

"I want you to come so hard now that your pussy grips my cock and you can feel your name scarred into me."

"Ah—"

His thumb found my clit, smothering every nerve ending in sharp, blissful sensation until my whole body shook, my legs trembling around him.

"Come with me," Wane breathed, drawing all the way out so he could plunge back inside, his shadows swirling and teasing with every inch. I didn't think I could follow him over the edge, but then he groaned loudly, his hips jerking against mine. His thumb grew frantic on my clit, and my eyes flew wide, my mouth dropped open, and a slow, all-consuming climax rippled from my toes all the way up my body. My pussy clamped down around his cock, milking with frantic pulses, drawing the sexiest, throatiest sounds I'd ever heard from my mate.

"Shit," Wane grunted, a shiver running through him as he lifted me against his chest with hands and shadows. His eyes were heady lidded as he settled us in the corner, his cock still inside me. "Holy shit."

Emlyn laughed softly, his cock tucked back into his pants, but there was something soft and smug about his expression when he pressed close to me and ran his fingers through my hair, gently working through the tangles.

I had so many questions, so many anxieties, but I kept them at bay for now and let a blanket of calm cover me, allowing a full breath into my lungs for the first time in hours. My stomach had stopped cramping, proving Wane's theory correct. *Don't think about it yet.*

"Um—" I blurted when *something* grew inside me, Wane's cock thickening near my entrance. "Wane?"

He brushed a kiss to my forehead, arms settling around me. "We can't lose a drop, itzaia. I don't know how your instincts will react. So I'll make sure it all stays where it belongs."

"What *is* that?" I breathed, the base of his cock swelling even further, until it was almost uncomfortable, and then it started to feel strangely good, and then it—oh, gods—my eyes crossed.

"It's a knot," he replied, feathering kisses down the side of my face. "A shadow knot. I've never seen a real one before, but I know enough about them to shape my shadows into one. It's supposed to feel intense."

"Hng," I agreed, grabbing his shoulders and digging my fingernails in. "Wane—"

It was too much, an assault on all my senses. I was going to kill him.

"Shh," Emlyn breathed, stroking down my back with his big, warm hands until I sighed and melted into Wane. "That's our perfect mate. Take his knot like a good girl."

I bit my lip so hard it bled, and drew pricks of blood from Wane's shoulders, too, the knot so swollen that it teased so many nerve endings all at once. I squirmed—and cried out when the knot shifted inside me, slamming me into a sudden climax.

This was insane. If they wanted me to climax so many times that my pussy swallowed every drop of cum, how many more times would I have to come?

CHAPTER 21

*S*even. That's how many more orgasms they coaxed from my oversensitive pussy, reducing me to a shuddering, sweat-slicked mess with permanent cross-eye.[1] I dropped into a deep sleep for long, long hours after we cleaned up, as much as we could when we were locked up in Mount Olympus.

When I woke up, at least I wasn't boiling hot and desperate for cock. But I flinched when a familiar voice snapped, "Look at you, such a fucking whore."

I sucked in a breath, hurt blooming through my chest as I searched the room for the source of the voice. Em and Wane were still sleeping, all of us pressed into the corner. But that voice...

"Wyn?" I whispered, getting to my feet and approaching the door.

"You're such a selfish bitch," he snapped, and I spun, searching for him. His voice was here, in the cell with us, but I couldn't see him.

Was this ... his ghost?

"You crossed that threshold, condemned me to death, and here you are screwing your mates instead of grieving me."

"I—I'm sorry," I breathed, my chest cut through with shards of pain. "There's something fucked up with my body, I couldn't help it, it *hurt*— "

He scoffed, and I spun again, searching for him, aching to see him. My bottom lip wobbled.

"Where are you? Wyn, *please*. I—I miss you. I shouldn't, you're a complete dick, but I do."

"Sure you do," he replied with heavy scathing, his voice hitting my skin like the lashes of a whip. "You miss me so much you didn't even bother to save me. You're selfish. Heartless. I gave *everything* to keep those thankless mates of yours alive. And then I saved you from the cave collapse *and* kept your useless hide safe in the Labyrinth. You should all be dead. *I* should be alive."

"Why are you saying this?" I asked, a hot rush of tears slicking my cheeks, burning my eyes.

"Hales?" Emlyn pushed to his feet, shaking out his wings as he approached me. "What's wrong?"

I swallowed hard, fresh tears veiling my eyes. "Can't you hear him?"

"I can't hear anyone," he gently answered, pulling me into an all-consuming hug, both arms and wings wrapped around me. My breath hitched in a sob, and I recoiled when Wynvail's voice lashed the air again.

"You're happy I'm dead, aren't you? It gives you more time to focus on your perfect mates, instead of the villain. What was it you called me? A monster? Congrats, honey, you got everything you wanted."

"I didn't," I cried against Emlyn's chest, my throat so tight it hurt. "I'm not happy, I'm fucking miserable—"

"Shh," Em soothed, his arms tightening until I was flush with his big body.

"Haley?" Wane asked, a note of alarm in his voice. Cool velvet pressed against my back, shadows moulding to my body in a matching hug to Em's feathers.

"It's Wynvail's g-ghost," I choked out, a cry smothering my voice until it was a pathetic squeak. "He hates me."

"You could have saved me," he sneered. "You're a pitiful excuse for a mate."

My knees almost buckled; my hand shot up to clutch my chest as a sharp ache cracked through my soul. He was right. I should have noticed something was wrong, should have known he was too quiet, too serious. I remembered the Damned House in unforgiving clarity; he'd been reserved, watchful, and when Wane lashed out at him he stood there and taken it. I should have known something was wrong then. A real mate would have, but not me. A pitiful excuse for a mate.

"It can't be his ghost, itzaia," Wane said so gently. "Even if he had a spirit despite being made by Cronus, it would be drawn into Hell. It wouldn't be here in Olympus."

"Maybe, if he was mythical instead of demon," Em murmured, "he might go to the underworld."

The resting place of gods and monsters. What did that make Wynvail? He was formed from shadows and sunlight— from archdemon magic. But he'd been shaped and brought to life by a titan, like so many gods in the past. What did that make him? I didn't know.

"I hate you," Wynvail sneered, driving another knife into my heart. I breathed through clenched teeth, fighting to get my tears under control.

"I hate you, too," I whispered like a confession, a declaration. I scrubbed the tears from my cheeks and rested my head on Em's wide shoulder, letting his scent fill my lungs and smooth the sharpest edge of my grief.

"It's not real," a new voice called—through the thick wall to our left.

I jumped, air catching in the back of my throat. Wane rushed from my back and approached the wall; I wiped the next wave of tears from my eyes to watch him.

"Hello?"

My bottom lip shook. How familiar must this be to him? Calling through walls to his fellow captives. Was this how he and Typhon became friends? Deja vu threatened to shake me, and I hadn't even been locked up under the Damned House.

"Who have they caught now?" a caustic voice bit out—female, American, and ... young. Fuck, she sounded really young. The shock was enough for me to pull my shit together, hug Em in thanks, and approach the wall too.

"My name's Wane," my mate replied to the girl, his tone completely changing—soft, tender, and worried. I fell so deep in love with him right then, as if I wasn't already head over heels. "I'm here with my brother Emlyn and my mate, Haley. We were captured by Aphrodite. How did you get here?"

The girl sighed, and when she spoke I tried to place her age. Sixteen? Fifteen? Younger? She had a natural bite of sarcasm that made her seem older, but I knew that bravado; I'd worn it most of my life.

"Hephaestus grabbed me out of my bed. Fucking perv. Apparently I aided a psycho titan in overthrowing the current regime and a whole lot of other bullshit."

"The same reasons we were," I murmured, a deep sigh punching out of me. I stared at the solid white wall.

"If you ask me, they're a little too quick to throw suspicions around. Usually means someone's covering up something."

"Should we tell her what's happening?" I whispered to my mates, softening all over again at the blazing anger on Emlyn's face. We were all on board with being furious that Aphrodite had locked up a kid. Hephaestus was her husband and dog's body if I remembered my myths correctly. He was devoted to her and would do anything she said, apparently including kidnapping a girl from her bed.

Emlyn shrugged, but Wane nodded, his brows a dark slash over his eyes and his shadows all but receded.

"There's a titan—Cronus—who used to rule this place, but he was dethroned by his sons eons ago," I told her, keeping my voice low but strong enough that it would carry to her.

"Zeus, Hades, and Poseidon," Emlyn put in, his arms crossed over his chest. "They locked him in Tartarus, where he stayed for millennia. But he manipulated us into breaking the seal, and now he's free."

There was quiet for a long moment, and I bit my lip, waiting for her to laugh or scoff.

"Yeah, that makes sense," she said eventually. "I kept having these screwed up dreams. And then the guy from my dreams turned up in my foster home, which is fucked up enough. But then he got really pushy about using my magic, said I needed to be stronger."

I sighed, shaking my head in disgust.

"To cut a long story short," the girl said, her voice louder— did she move closer to the wall? "He kidnapped me, put me through 'trials' and I killed him. I thought I got away with it until that god dick kidnapped me."

"Sounds familiar," I said dryly. "Are you okay?"

She laughed, a rough bark of sound. "Sure, I'm *amazing.*"

"She's like a mini you," Wane whispered, stroking down my arm to clasp my hand.

I debated how to reply, but if she was a mini me, she'd appreciate two things above all else—the truth, and revenge.

"It's almost 100% certain that the god who kidnapped you, and the bitch who grabbed us are working for Cronus; that's why I'm sentenced to death. He wants me dead for two reasons—he's trying to take over the world and devouring me will give him more magic; and there's a prophecy tattooed on my back that says I can kill him. So I'm going to kill him. He'll pay for everything he's done to me—and to you."

The girl was quiet for so long that Em, Wane, and I glanced at each other.

"The air's full of magic," she said eventually. "It fucks with your head, makes you see and hear things that aren't here."

"Thanks," I said, a smile creeping across my face. I understood the exchange of information for information. If she'd grown up in foster care, we were more alike than I realised, and just telling me *that* much was significant. "That's good to know. I'm Haley."

"Verena," she replied.

"We'll get you out of here, Verena," Emlyn promised in a rush, like the words had been desperate to escape for minutes. I stroked his back, feathers skimming my knuckles.

"Doubt it," she replied, "but thanks for the sentiment. My death's scheduled for tomorrow."

I went as stiff as an arrow. Without a single word, my mates and I were in agreement.

"We'll get you out of here," Em repeated firmly. "Non-negotiable. You'll be safely returned home to your family by tomorrow night. I swear."

Verena laughed hollowly. "What home? What family?"

"You have no one?" Wane breathed, a flash of determination brightening his soul, followed by aching sadness and fierce protectiveness.

"Nope," she agreed blithely. I knew that tone, knew it was casual to mask a deep and endless hurt.

"You do now," Wane vowed.

Verena snorted. "Whatever. And good luck getting out of here. I've tried. A lot."

I eyed the solid door keeping us locked in, letting my rage

spread through me, blood magic roaring in my ears until all I heard was heartbeats and then Emlyn's soft voice asking, "How old are you?"

"How is that your fucking business?"

A tiny smile tugged up one side of my mouth. Oh yeah, she was a mini me alright.

"We're not bonding, we're not gonna be best prison buddies, so whatever delusion you've got in your head, forget it."

Wane said, "We were moved into this room because we broke out of our first cell, and then weakened a titan so badly he couldn't move from where I threw him to the floor. We came so close to escaping that Aphrodite had to use a magical object to catch us."

A shiver went down my spine at the way Wane retold our failure—like he was proud to have gotten so far in the first place.

"I'm thirteen," she sighed. "Happy?"

Thirteen. Jesus.

"Far from it, Verena," Emlyn growled. "But we'll get you out."

"Whatever," she muttered, but all I heard was her age echoing around my head, over and over.

Power erupted from my curses so brightly and viciously that Em and Wane were pushed back, and I stalked to the door. I curled my fingers into fists and slammed both into the solid wood, a sharp breath whistling through my teeth when pain bloomed in my fingers. I punched the door over and over, my magic casting a blood-red glow on my fingers, on the wood.

It should have splintered. But no matter how hard I hit it, it didn't so much as rattle in its frame. Even when I drew a dagger and the blade lit up crimson, it didn't nick the wood.

Fuck!

I flexed my hands, swearing at the soreness, but I'd heal. I gave Em and Wane a glance loaded with dread.

"Let me try," Wane offered, something different about him —in his posture and the way he walked and—his eyes. His irises weren't silver but as black as ink.

Darkness erupted from him like when it had slammed through Iapetus's chest and incapacitated the titan, and the hairs stood on end all down my arms, fine hairs lifting on the back of my neck, too.

But when the ocean of darkness slammed into the door, it did nothing.

"Shit," Wane breathed.

"Told you," Verena said through the wall between cells. "There's no way out. We're all fucked."

I hated to admit it, but the kid was right.

CHAPTER 22

KAI

"*D*oes your crown have cows on it?" I blurted, staring at the woman—the goddess—standing by the window in one of the palace's highest rooms. Not quite a tower, but tall enough to give a view of the whole city, buildings stained purple by the setting sun. My family had been missing a whole day, and it killed me.

"Cows are far nobler creatures than you, Malakai Virex," the woman replied dryly, turning to face me. I shielded my eyes at the bright glow of her godly grace, so severe that I couldn't see a single one of her features until she turned the gleam down. "And this is a circlet, not a crown."

"Still sure you wouldn't prefer a crown?" Lucifer asked from where he leant against the doorframe, a dark eyebrow raised as he watched the goddess.

Hera shot him a narrow-eyed look. I could see all of her now, and I wasn't sure what I'd expected a goddess to look like but it wasn't ... this. She was beautiful and regal, sure, but her chestnut hair was pulled into a messy bun and her caramel skin was lined, her face carved with tiredness. She wasn't dressed in a fancy, flowy dress but a pair of white linen trousers and a silver blouse.

She looked like a lawyer more than anything, and that made me itchy. Anything with the word *law* in it didn't suit me well.

"As convenient as that might be for all of you," Hera replied, lifting her head, showing some of that godliness, "I'm still processing the last war."

When her husband had died. Apparently, he was a cheating scumbag and she hated him, but it still must have hurt to lose him. Kinda awkward that she was now staying with the people who murdered him, but life was complicated and who was I to judge?

I checked on Harvey, standing silently beside me, his turbulent eyes fixed on Hera and a new hollowness in his expression.

"I know who you boys are," Hera said, her attention drifting from the devil to Harvey and I. "But I don't know why you're here."

"Aphrodite kidnapped our mate and our brothers," Harvey said, an aching emptiness in his voice. He cleared his throat and added, "We need your help getting them back."

Hera turned away, staring out the window again. "No."

I lunged forward a step before I even realised I'd moved into the austere stone room. *"Excuse me?"*

"I said no." She half turned to give me a thin-lipped glance, her curved eyes narrowed. "I fought in one war; that's enough for this century."

I paused at the reminder of how old, how immortal, this woman was. Not the sort of woman you ordered around without being smited. But Em, Haley, and Wane were missing. *Stolen.* And a dangerous mix of panic and rage built in my chest, my tattoos beginning to swirl in constricting circles around my arms and throat.

"If you don't help us—"

Hera laughed. "What? You'll loose those snakes on me? I can see them, you know? There's little you can do that will surprise me."

I sucked on a tooth so I didn't shout and scream at a goddess—at the queen of gods, for fuck's sake.

"Please," Harvey breathed, his voice so raw that I grabbed his arm and squeezed, an arrow shooting through my chest at the sight of desperate tears lining his eyes. "Whatever you want, whatever price you ask, we'll pay it. Just *please*. Haley didn't do anything wrong. Aphrodite made up all these bullshit accusations because she's obviously working with Cronus—"

Hera stiffened and shot Lucifer a look. The devil nodded.

"That escalated faster than I expected," Hera muttered, her shoulders tightening in her blouse. "No doubt my heinous father is the reason Aphrodite was able to usurp me so soon after Zeus's death."

There was pain in her voice, sharp and vast, just beneath her anger. I knew how that felt, and it was strange to identify with a goddess. Maybe grief made us all equals—god, demon, human, animal. Loss fucking sucked, no matter your species.

"Help us," Harvey rasped, flicking a tear off his sharp cheek before it could fall. "We'll give you whatever you want, but we need a way into Olympus."

Because Renna's stone had confirmed everything we feared—Aphrodite had taken our family to the home of the gods, a place half in the mythical realm, half in Heaven. I didn't know if it would weaken me like Heaven did, but I would risk anything to get my rose back. But Olympus was armed to the teeth and shielded even worse than Lucifer expected; Renna went to scope it out and returned paler than before, shaking her head.

"Please," Harvey begged when the goddess was silent. "My mate is sentenced to death, and she did *nothing* wrong. Cronus tricked her, he tricked all of us. She just—she *just* lost her mate. Cronus killed him. My brother Wane was locked up and —and tortured by Cronus for a hundred years, and now he's —he's kidnapped again, and they don't deserve *any* of this. Please."

I squeezed his arm, my nostrils flaring as I fought back emotions. Fuck. If Hera wouldn't help us ... I didn't know what we'd do. Olympus was locked tight with shields powered by *gods*. Nothing we had would go up against that. Lucifer and Lili were the king and queen of Hell, but they were *demons*. Not gods.

They'd die.

Haley, Wane, Em—they'd *die*. And we'd be stuck here, powerless.

"Fine," Hera muttered, straightening her crown—sorry, *circlet*—on her head.[1] "But you two are coming with me and doing the talking. I'll get you in the front door, but I'm not involving myself in another war."

Air punched out of my lungs like I'd been kicked in the stomach. "Thank you," I said profusely. "We owe you one, seriously."

I knew I was telling a god I owed her a favour, but fuck it. If this helped us get to Haley, it was worth the cost.

Hera narrowed her eyes, contemplating me. "You're a strange one, Malakai. A common criminal with a heart of honour."

Was that a compliment or an insult? I frowned.

"There will be war either way," Lucifer remarked, and I turned to find his gaze fixed on Hera. "Whether you claim the throne or don't. It's coming. Cronus is determined to restore the golden age, and you can sense it as much as I can. That's why you're really here, isn't it?" He took a step into the room, shadows trickling from his shoulders and down his back despite his calm, sympathetic voice. "You're grieving, and Aphrodite stole the throne from under you, but—you were scarred by Cronus before, the first time he rose to power."

Shit. All the blood drained from Hera's face. The light around her dimmed. I knew that panic, had seen thousands of times in Harvey and Wane.

"Drop it," I warned the devil, my voice hard.

"You're here to hide from him," Lucifer went on, gentle as if a soft tone made the words any easier to hear. "I can't imagine the things he did to you, Hera. I'm sorry. But he *will* reclaim his former glory unless someone stops him."

"It doesn't have to be me," she said coldly, turning back to the window. "Let someone else fight my father."

"Your father," I murmured, my mind racing. "If that bastard is your sperm donor, Typhon's your brother right?"

Hera spun, stray chestnut hairs escaping her bun. "Typhon?"

"Cronus had him locked up under the house where my brother was captive," Harvey said, his voice upset and furious all at once. "He's Wane's friend. He warned us that Cronus wants to—to kill my mate." He glanced at me. "Our mate. He wants to devour her. And Typhon, too."

"Like he consumed us," Hera breathed, her hand to her throat. She looked at Lucifer, steel entering her expression. "I won't make promises, Lucifer. I'll lend you my power if I'm able, but nothing more."

"Thank you," the devil breathed, sounding more than a little relieved. "We'll round up whatever gods are left on our side. You won't be alone."

Hera laughed, shaking her head, her face full of scepticism

even as her godly glow brightened. "We're not what we once were. Not enough to defeat a titan."

"Didn't you take him down with tricks and cleverness before?" I asked, stiffening when her attention settled on me, her glow stabbing my eyes until they watered. "We're not crazy powerful, my family and I, but we're savvy bastards. If there's a way to trick him, we'll think of it. I *will* kill him, without a fucking doubt."

"Stop swearing at the goddess," Harvey hissed,

Hera straightened her circlet, looking between Harvey and I. "You're serious about killing him."

"Deadly," I confirmed.

Harvey nodded, taking a deep breath and standing straighter.

"You do know he's a titan older than most other beings in the known universe?" she asked, frowning a little as she crossed the room, her posture sharper, straighter, and something clearing in her eyes. The scent of magic hit me, sharp enough to make my nose burn.

"We do," Harvey said firmly.

Hera nodded, looking between us. "You've got nerve, and a strange well of kindness. This might just work."

"It will," Lucifer agreed, so confident there was zero chance he wasn't faking it.

"And if Aphrodite kills me?" Hera gave the devil a flat look. "Do you have a plan for that, too, Lucifer?"

If the goddess killed Hera, the rest of us were screwed. I glanced at Harvey, finding him already watching me.

"Whatever it takes," he said, and held out his hand.

I clasped it and squeezed hard. "Whatever it takes."

If we died trying to rescue our family, well … they were sentenced to death anyway. At least we'd all be together.

CHAPTER 23

HARVEY

*J*ust don't have a mental breakdown, I coached myself, *just don't breakdown and everything will be fine.*

Easier said than done, with golden gates towering twenty feet above us and a godly city spread out on the other side, half hanging off a massive cliff. We'd reached Olympus by climbing a peak in Greece, but facing the city, all my hairs and feathers standing on end and power thrumming through the air, tingling the back of my tongue, there was no way we were still on Earth.

My arms burned when Hera set her warm brown hands to the gates. My nose tingled, my sore eyes stinging as magic crackled through the air like a the air before a storm.

"Fuck," I muttered, rubbing my face and reaching for Haley through the bond. She was close—far closer than when we were in Hell—and the feral beast in me settled. She was ... soft. Sleeping. Em and Wane must have been with her, too, because there was no way she'd be asleep without them. Her calm bled into me, soothing my ragged soul until I could drag in a full breath.

"Kai?" I brushed him with my wing, peering at my brother as he stood as rigid as iron beside me. "You okay?"

"Fine," he bit out, his jaw clenched and red eyes glowing.

"You're a shit liar," I told him.

He slanted a glare in my direction. "Takes one to know one, asshole. Can you feel her?" When I nodded, he said, "Me, too. She's here."

At least we knew Renna's tracking stone worked. I'd be more confident about this rescue plan if Lucifer was here with us, but he'd disappeared with a cryptic remark about having to take care of something. It was either a weapon to take out Cronus or a sneaky fuck with his queen. Not that I could blame him.

Gods, I missed my mate. I needed her back in my arms, where I could keep her safe and fight off every goddess and titan on the damned planet.

"Yes!" Hera hissed, and magic spiked in the air until my whole face stung, my hand prickling where I gripped the hilt of a dagger. "Almost—got it!"

I staggered back when a wave of power blasted from the gold gates, setting my teeth rattling and prickling all the way to the tips of my wings.

"My fucking eyeballs," Kai snarled, grabbing my shoulder and squeezing to steady me, his pale jaw clenched. It hadn't escaped my notice that he kept touching me ever since the others were kidnapped. Like he was scared I'd be taken, too. Or I was the only thing keeping him grounded.

"The gates are open," Hera said, like we couldn't see that right in front of us. She turned to give us a tense look, her long cloak glowing in the soft wind and her eyes heavy with reproach—and unease. "Go, quickly. I'll shatter them while you're rescuing your family; the way will be open when you flee Olympus."

I tucked my wings in tight, sucking in a deep breath and trying not to let the towering buildings intimidate me. There was something otherworldly about this place, all pale stone and columns with domes covered in delicate carvings. Unearthly clouds hovered around them, pearly and peach and perfectly, eerily fluffy.

"Let's go kill a goddess," Kai muttered, letting go of me and curling his hands into fists as he strode through the gap in the gates Hera had opened.

Kill a goddess. *Yes,* the feral part of me purred. *Anyone who hurt our family deserves to die, and die screaming.* My heartbeat quickened as I passed through the gates and started up the pale, winding path to the city above us.

"Wait," Hera called when we'd taken five steps.

I turned, Kai frowning beside me, and found the queen of gods hurrying after us. She tugged out the tie in her hair so it spilled around her shoulders, her circlet shining brighter, fiercely gold.

"For telling Lucifer to stop pressing me about my father, I'll come with you," she said, and before either Kai or I could react, she stalked ahead of us up the steep path, her back straight and blinding light flashing around her.

The light was a warning and declaration, and my pulse thumped even faster.

Let's go kill a goddess.

CHAPTER 24

*H*era stormed through the city and up to the impressive castle that cast its many-towered shadow over the mountain. There were four guards at the immense golden doors of the castle who made a token effort to stop her, but Hera dialled up her grace, shining so brightly that I couldn't stand to look at her, and they stepped aside.

Wordless, she marched through the vast halls of the castle, the blush pink ceilings so tall that every sound echoed back to us, distorted and long.

I shot Kai a look; he matched it with a quiet laugh of agreement. This place was too pristine, too perfect. Everything was either pure white, pearly pink, or gilded. And why did it smell of violets and roses? Wasn't that taking the whole *godly realm* thing a step too far? I swore I could even hear the far-off tinkle of angelic voices singing.

Kai leaned close to whisper, "It's missing some bloodstains."

I grinned. "We can fix that."

"Don't even think about it," Hera muttered six steps ahead

of us, turning to raise a brown eyebrow at us. "Don't start trouble; we're here for one reason."

Hera was here to bargain with Aphrodite. We were here to kill her and reclaim our family. The queen of gods didn't need to know that, though.

"We'll keep violence as a last resort," Kai lied, so convincing that even I believed him.

Hera's mouth thinned but she nodded. "The king's room is down this hall. If I know Aphrodite, she'll be on Zeus's throne."

Her eyes tightened, grief pinching them.

"I'll introduce you," she added, turning back around and walking faster, her shoes clipping the perfect white floor. "Then you can plead your case. Don't try to lie; most gods can taste falsehood."

Of course they could. A shiver went down my spine.

How far out of our depth were we? We were only demons, and sure archdemons were so rare most people thought we didn't exist, but we weren't gods or titans. How the fuck were we supposed to stand up to legitimate *myths*?

My stomach twisted when Hera pushed open a set of high double doors, the gold-veined marble carved all over with scenes I was too stressed to interpret. Aphrodite had kidnapped my family, and if we fucked this up there wouldn't be second chances. She'd execute my mate.

What if we were too late?

I jumped when Kai knocked his shoulder into mine.

"Breathe. We've got a goddess as backup."

But Hera didn't know Haley, Em, and Wane. She didn't love them like we did. She wouldn't fight for them.

I dragged a breath down my throat when the doors opened with a creak so high pitched it was almost musical, and Hera strode into the room, her clothes somehow flowing into a deep violet dress that trailed behind her and the circlet around her temple glowing so bright I couldn't look at it.

The room was as tall as the hallways and the ceiling came to a sharp point above us, making it seem bigger and more imposing than it was. Straight forward, the far wall was cluttered with gold and silver windows that reflected a spectral pattern on the pale floor. Intentional shards of light fell around the glass throne set under the windows, and they lit the dark-skinned woman seated upon it in gleaming metallics.

Panic stopped my heart as we followed Hera deeper into the room, but it was rage that resumed pumping it, and that dark, hateful emotion spread through my whole body like flowing lava. I took a deeper breath, my back straightening, hands curling into fists. Beside me, the air shuddered with Kai's magic as he fought to keep his composure.

We weren't supposed to be here parlaying for our family's lives. We were the brash, thoughtless ones who acted first and asked questions later. We needed Emlyn and Haley to keep their cool and bargain. No one would say Kai and Harvey and *diplomacy* in the same breath. We were going to screw this up.

"No violence," I breathed to Kai, whose nostrils flared as he stared at Aphrodite. "Kai."

"Fine," he bit out, but he didn't tear his eyes away from the goddess, and my stomach knotted when they glowed as red as blood.

"Hera," Aphrodite purred in greeting, sitting casually on the throne and watching us approach like a cat might watch a mouse near its claws. Cold shot through my whole body when she smiled; my beast tucked its tail and lowered its ears, pleading with me to run.

If Aphrodite, a goddess made my blood icy, what would it be like to face Cronus, a titan?

Movement caught my peripheral, a dark smear against the pale pearl of the king's room, and a clang of warning went through my chest. I snapped my hand out and grabbed the back of Kai's shirt, stopping him from launching himself at the goddess just in time.

Aphrodite noticed. Her smile grew, like she'd just *love* us to attack her.

"You brought the two strays I missed, I see," she remarked to Hera with a smile laced with arrogance—and violence. "Much obliged."

"They're here to campaign for their loved ones' freedom," Hera replied with more than a little bite. She straightened to her full height, and if I wasn't going completely mad, she grew a few inches, too. "The ones you stole and sentenced to death *without* a trial. Curious. Was there a reason you decided to skip the judicial process?"

"Zeus was never fond of trials, and neither am I. Is there a reason you take offence with my leadership, Hera?" Aphrodite replied in the same tone, her smile unwavering.

Hera had warned us not to fight Aphrodite, but she looked more than willing to kill her herself. "I'm not here for me." She took a step back with visible effort, her tawny face carved of stone. The single glance she flicked at us ordered us to speak.

I swallowed and spoke before Kai could blow this for us.

"Halwen didn't choose to free Cronus," I said, goosebumps lifting all over my body at the hollow echo my voice made around the room. The hall was empty except for us, which struck me as strange. Wouldn't someone as vain as Aphrodite want an audience? "We were lied to, and tricked by Wynvail."

"Wynvail," Aphrodite repeated slowly, a light in her eyes that I didn't like one bit. "And why would *he* want Cronus freed?"

"He didn't have a choice." I felt a little sick saying it out loud, but I forged on, my eyes fixed on a point on the goddess's shoulder because I couldn't stand to look her in the eye. If I did, I'd lose it. I'd try to kill her. "Cronus *created*

Wynvail from bits of me and Wane. The only reason he existed was so Cronus could use him to break his prison. I don't know how, I'm not a magic expert, but Wynvail lured us to a house in the Damned Realm on the titan's orders, and the second we left, it—it freed Cronus. And killed Wynvail."

"Haley didn't choose to do it, she had no clue," Kai added tightly, inked hands curled into fists at his sides. "Trust me, I'm fucking thrilled that bastard died, but it damn near *killed* Haley when Cronus killed Wynvail. He unmade him, turned him to dust like he'd never existed. If we'd known it would kill Wynvail and free Cronus, we'd have stayed in that house for the rest of our lives. This wasn't a choice we made. This was all Cronus tricking us. She's *innocent.*"

"And Emlyn and Wane had nothing to do with it either," I added, biting back every threat I wanted to snarl at the poisoned goddess of love and beauty who sat on her throne *still smiling.* "We're all pawns in Cronus's game," I breathed, remembering Typhon's words. "We're demons up against a titan; we don't stand a chance."

A little laugh came through Aphrodite's nose, her round eyes flattening with annoyance. "Do you truly expect me to believe that? Out of all the people in Hell, Cronus just happened to single you *out?*" She shook her head, perfect brown curls swaying with the movement. "I've never heard a more ridiculous tale. What's more likely is Cronus offered you untold power, and you agreed to free him to get it. What's your next command? To kill me? I have no doubt he wants Mount Olympus, and I'm the one in his way."

"What?" Kai blurted, his magic throbbing in a dark warning. "You can't be serious."

She didn't believe us?

"We're not working for Cronus," I said fiercely, fighting back anger. "We certainly didn't want him free. He's going to kill our mate for her power; he threw us in the Labyrinth and almost killed all of us just so he can steal her magic."

Aphrodite gave Hera a dry look. "Why did you waste your time with this? They're such obvious liars."

"*You're* the liar," Kai seethed. I lurched at him to grab him, to cover his mouth with my hand, to stop him condemning us all to death, but he shook me off. There was a manic glint in his red eyes. He was panicking, whatever calm had held him together in Iarlon disintegrating. "You got that pin because you're Cronus's best buddy. You're fucking *thrilled* he's free, you're just good at hiding it. What did he promise *you*, Aphrodite? You've got your throne and your mountain, so what else do you want? Earth? Heaven? Hell? All of it?"

"Malakai," Hera warned, stalking closer.

"I can promise you one thing," Kai went on, staring directly at the goddess on the throne. "Cronus is the type to stab you in the back the second you stop being useful to him, so I'd watch out if I were you. You're right—*you* are the one in his way. So why would he keep you around?"

Aphrodite rose from her throne, and my heart skipped at the power that rippled from her, a soft, far-reaching glow. "So not only did you free the titans, now you're threatening the queen of gods?"

"I never threatened Hera," Kai replied with a smirk.

Hera laughed. She probably shouldn't have, but she did.

"You know what my father is capable of," she said, recovering quickly as she gave Aphrodite a no-nonsense look. "You know everything he did. He devoured my brothers; he almost killed me. Please, Aphrodite. End this insanity. Align with the right side."

Aphrodite tilted her head, staring at Hera with thinly veiled hatred—and jealousy. It burned inside her, consumed her, and she did a poor job hiding it. "You expect me to believe a single word out of your deceitful mouth? You helped those spiteful little ants kill Zeus!"

A wave of power struck me so brutally that I staggered back a step, gasping for breath. Silver-pink magic filled the room like daylight, certain and inescapable. We needed to get out of here, run while Aphrodite was distracted and find our family while we had the chance.

But when I lifted my foot to take a step, Aphrodite's dark hand lashed out and my foot slammed back into the floor. I froze.

The doors opened with a musical creak, and guards in polished silver flowed around us.

"These men conspired to kill me. Lock them on the western side."

I yanked on the feral magic inside me, willing my body to shift, but it ignored me, and the guards grabbed me so easily. *Pathetic. You can't do a single thing right, you waste of space.*

"You're so smug, standing there by my husband's throne," Hera breathed.

Oh, shit.

Even the guard dragging me paused, like he felt the pulse of rage and wicked power go through the room. I wished I could turn my head to see Kai, but even my head was immobilised.

"You're right that I helped the demons defeat him. He was paranoid, *irrational*. So obsessed with losing his power that he couldn't see how foolishly he was acting. It makes me wonder who nurtured those irrational thoughts, because it certainly wasn't me. And look at *you*, sitting on his throne, alive with power even though the rest of us survive on the scraps that remain."

Was that why she'd looked so ungodly in the palace in Hell? Her power had faded?

"How long has Cronus been planning his rise to power?

And how long have you been helping him, you treasonous shrew?"

The grip of magic on my body slackened, and I used my sudden movement to elbow the guard in the stomach. *Why? Oh gods, whyyyy?* He was dressed in silver armour—why the fuck did I think I could hurt him? Pain blazed through my elbow and shot up my arm like a lightning bolt, and I grunted. But he let me get free anyway, stumbling back in surprise as he watched the fight unfold between the queen of gods and the pretender to the throne.

"*Me* treasonous?" Aphrodite laughed, her steps echoing around the room as she came closer. That laugh was as sharp as a whip's crack and every bit as dangerous.

"You," Hera agreed, her voice deeper, darker. "It's convenient that Zeus's paranoid grasp for power led to his death, and here you sat in his throne. I know you orchestrated his death."

I turned to free Kai—and sucked in a sharp breath when I found the guard who'd restrained him fleeing out the door. Kai rubbed his arm, his teeth gritted and murder in his red eyes, hatred in his flared nostrils. There was a mean streak in Kai that I'd only ever seen in Alphaven, but I was seeing it again now. He'd tear Aphrodite apart—*if* he had the power to go up against her. Which he didn't. None of us did.

"I need you at my side," I bit out in a whisper, grabbing his arm where he'd rubbed it and hoping it hurt. Hoping it would clear his furious mind. "Not smeared across the floor because Aphrodite murdered you."

"Fuck," he bit out, teeth bared. Power thrashed around him, but he gritted his teeth and spat, "Fuck."

It was a surrender, that curse. An assurance he wouldn't leave me alone.

"I challenge you," Hera announced, and Kai and I froze.

This wasn't part of the plan. How would this help Haley, Wane, and Em?

But one glance at Hera told me she'd forgotten all about freeing my family. She'd fallen into the dark pit of rage and grief that must have been eating her up for months.

Aphrodite's smile this time was slow blooming and confident. Her skin shone with a golden light, brighter than Hera's. Far brighter. "I accept. Sunrise tomorrow, at the arena behind the castle."

Hera matched her smile, her teeth bared. "I'll be there. And I'll be taking the boys."

Aphrodite shrugged. She didn't care about us now; she'd got a far bigger prize than us.

This whole thing had gone completely to shit. I glared at Hera as she guided us out the door of the king's room. We were no closer to saving our family than before.

CHAPTER 25

HALWEN

*S*omething was happening, and something big. The air sizzled with magic I sensed even locked into this room, with solid walls on most sides of us. I approached the window, my heart fluttering in dread and anticipation. Wane had been staring out the solid glass pane for hours, reassuring himself that he wasn't back in Cronus's captivity. I suspected the window was the only thing keeping him from going mad.

"What's out there?" I asked, brushing his shoulder with my wing, a subtle reminder that he wasn't locked up alone this time.

Wane's scarred throat bobbed, a few of his shadows thinning so I could see more of him. He had his arms wrapped around himself, and my heart *ached* at the sight of him trying so hard to hold himself together.

"Nothing," he sighed. "It's the same mountains and buildings it's been all night."

But something had shifted, and it was powerful enough to

wake us all up simultaneously. I eyed the picturesque city with suspicion.[1] The clouds were too perfect out there, too pearly and perfectly pastel. The buildings were all delicate columns and pretty domes, the windows all arches cut into the ivory stone, stained peach by the dawn light. Even the trees and greenery that speckled the landscape were impeccably preened, not a leaf out of place. And still something made my skin crawl.

"What if—he's here?" Emlyn asked quietly, filling the space on Wane's other side and settling a hand on his hunched shoulder.

"Then we kill the bastard," Wane hissed, his jaw clenching with rage but panic slashing through his soul, spilling over until he shook.

I wrapped my arm around him, pulling him into my side and sending a rush of support through our bond. I wouldn't let Cronus anywhere near him, and deep down he knew that. But fear was a manipulative bitch, and she tricked us into forgetting truth and trusting lies.

I scanned the mount again,[2] searching the wide parks and clean streets and the spires and arches of the castle I could just about make out to our left.

"There are no people," I realised with a gasp. That was what unsettled me, what sent a rush of cold down my spine. "Where are the people?"

The streets were empty. Silent.

"Shit," Em breathed, pressing closer to the window. "You're right; this is Olympus, it should be crawling with offspring of the gods."

Wane's throat bobbed. "What if—he ate them?"

It sounded insane hearing it out loud, but that was a legitimate worry, wasn't it? Cronus *eating* them like people were just different flavoured Skittles. "But where are the other gods?"

"In hiding?" Em suggested.

"Or devoured, too," Wane muttered, pressing closer to me.

I shuddered, a definite wave of power going through me this time, and Wane and Em reacted like they felt it, too.

"Aphrodite or Cronus?" I asked, chewing my bottom lip and trying so hard to stay calm. But being locked up in the home of the gods wasn't exactly conducive to keeping my cool.

I was literally imprisoned in Mount Olympus while Aphrodite waited to execute me at her leisure. Or ... while she waited for Cronus to arrive to devour me. Was that what had happened to the residents of Olympus, too?

And how long had it been since we met Verena? How long did she have left until her execution? My chest cinched tight.

"Both?" Wane replied, grabbing my hand and squeezing tight. I rubbed my thumb over his knuckles, at a loss for how to soothe him. My power did nothing on the door—or the walls *or* window. I tried. Hours of all three of us trying to make any sort of dent in it had failed, too. I was starting to believe Verena was right, and there really was no way out of this prison.

I double and triple checked I still had my weapons. For whatever reason, Aphrodite wasn't intimidated by them. I guess she hadn't heard they were now god-killers. *She* was right at the top of my list of gods to murder as soon as I got free. If I ever got free.

"Hales," Em began, but he froze when a low, piercing horn came from outside—loud enough to reach through the thick window, loud enough to make my breathing hitch and my magic erupt with warning.

"What the fuck was that?" I shrieked, squeezing Wane's hand harder.

Emlyn had gone still, his blue eyes fixed on the city outside but his gaze distant, like he wasn't really seeing it. "It's a summons," he said, swallowing hard and glancing reluctantly at me and Wane. "It means there's either a trial or a challenge."

I sucked in a breath, trying and failing to fight the tremor in my hands, not wanting my mate to feel it.

We'd run out of time. Verena would be killed. A fucking *kid* slaughtered so pointlessly, all to fuel a madman's appetite for power.

Or ... was this *my* trial? Would I be sentenced by a crooked goddess and murdered for doing absolutely nothing.

Either way, Emlyn was right. Cronus was here.

CHAPTER 26

KAI

*H*era wasn't *completely* insane, just three quarters of the way there. She hadn't slept since we left the castle, when she'd stormed across Olympus to a villa on the edge of the mountain that was worth more money than I'd ever seen in my life. Not that Mount Olympus had estate agents; if you wanted a house, you could probably kill the current occupants and take it.

We'd stayed up all night coming up with plan after plan for how to maximise her challenge at dawn, throwing out idea after idea until we had something that might work. It certainly helped that the only other people in the city were Aphrodite and her guards. Hera was fuming at the absence of her people, but we had more immediate problems.

"She'll be focused on me," Hera said for the sixtieth time since we'd settled on a plan of action. She reminded me eerily of Haley when she buckled on vambraces, sword sheaths, and settled tough leather armour over her dress. Were my mate and this god related? I could see it; both disarming but hot-headed, deadly, and full of magic. "She won't be looking at you. While I fight her, you need to—"

Hera erupted into a blaze of light and wrath when someone kicked in the front door to her house. Shit. We were under attack.

I drew a long dagger, calling up my snakes until the air shimmered with them. But when their tongues flicked out to taste the air, one of the scents was familiar. I reached out and grabbed Harvey's shoulder before he could shift.

"It's Renna," I said, squinting through the vicious light filling the atrium, Hera's godly glow at full power. "And the killer panda."

Tali bared her sharp teeth at me and snapped her jaws. That sound made my skin itch, the instinctive urge to fight, to kill crushing my chest, my gut. *You're not in the arena now, get your shit together Malakai.*

"What are you doing here?" I asked, keeping as much bite out of my words as possible.

These are Haley's friends. They'll help us get her, Wane, and Em back.

"And how did you find us?" Hera pressed, dialling down her grace so we could stand to look at her.

Renna grinned, her teeth white against dark purple lips. "I can find anyone I've met."

I narrowed my eyes. She better not have made a tracking stone for me, too. She flicked her eyes to Hera and smirked. Ah. She'd tracked Hera.

Tali rumbled a growl, shoving Renna with her big head.

"Alright, keep your fur on," Renna huffed. "So what's the plan? We're on a bit of a deadline."

"Because Hera challenged Aphrodite in a fight to the death," Harvey muttered.

Renna's mouth fell open. "No. Not that, but … fuck. We're

all panicking because Poseidon's daughter is missing and he's losing his absolute shit. We've got about twenty minutes of Luc and Lili stalling him before he marches on Olympus and turns it to rubble in revenge. He's a little protective."

Tali made a low sound.

"Yeah, *over*protective," Renna agreed. "So can we hurry this thing along?"

"Remember what I told you," Hera said sombrely, her stare heavy on me and Harvey.

The guards were bespelled, in love with Aphrodite even if they were terrified of her. There wasn't much they wouldn't do if she asked. We had to make sure she didn't get a chance to ask, and take out the guards while the goddess was fighting Hera. I didn't let myself think about what we'd do if Aphrodite killed Hera and ordered all her guards to capture us. Or kill us.

I didn't know if I was strong enough to take down a god's guards, but I was crazy enough to try.

None of us brought up what we'd do if Cronus showed his ugly face. We all knew we were fucked.

A loud, low horn blast cut off whatever Hera had been about to say next, and a hiss built in the back of my throat, instinct warning me to *run* when the horn was echoed by a deep tremor of magic.

"It's time," Hera proclaimed with unnecessary dramatics.

I sucked in a breath and reached through my soul for my rose, her panic like a red flag to a bull. My nostrils flared. I angled my head at Harvey and he fell in beside me when I moved to the door, impatiently ushering Renna and Tali back outside.

"Best of luck," I told Hera when she followed, rising a few feet off the ground.

Oh. Goddesses could fly. Right. Of course they could.[1]

The sun rose all across Olympus, painting the pale buildings with pink and peachy orange. This place was too damn pretty for the poison sitting on its throne.

"Good luck to you too, Malakai," Hera replied, and rose higher, flying away from us—towards the giant coliseum built into the edge of Olympus behind the castle.

I took a slow breath, trying to steady myself but pissed off all over again at the floral sweetness in the air. It was like they perfumed this place, trying to cover the rotting stench at its core.

"So what's the plan?" Renna asked, following our lead as Harvey and I strode down the street towards the castle.[2]

I walked faster, my breath short. "Knock out the guards, break in through the white door at the base of the second tower, suffocate the guards there because they'll never back down. Then Harvey will shift and clear the path while I—we— take the third staircase up to the tower cells, threaten the matron there into removing the shields, and get our family out of the cell we tracked them down to last night."

I paused, giving Renna and Tali a hard look. "Any questions?"

CHAPTER 27

HALWEN

*S*o much magic filled the air now that I choked on it, coughing as it burned the back of my throat. It singed my nose too, and made my eyeballs tingle. I *knew* that power, and I knew exactly who possessed it—who stole it. That was the bone pin Wynvail stole from *me*. The one Aphrodite now had. I needed answers. I needed to know how she got it, because her explanation—*your mate never gave it to Cronus. He gave it to me. His lover*—made my whole soul shrivel.

"Who is *that?*" Wane breathed, jerking forward so suddenly his nose hit the glass.

I scanned the city, and my heart skipped when I saw a woman floating above the rooftops, her brown hair streaming behind her. She wore a dress but leather was layered over her arms, shoulders, and chest.

"She's armoured," I murmured. "Cronus's backup?"

"We're completely screwed," Verena muttered next door, the first thing she'd said in hours.

Emlyn took that as a cue to run at the door like a battering ram, driving his shoulder into the solid wood with a growl.

"Em!" I exclaimed, running to stop him before he hurt himself again. "It won't budge."

"I'm not waiting here for them to kill us," he growled and tore away from me, ramming his shoulder into the door again. It didn't even rattle in its frame.

"It won't work, you'll just hurt yourself," Wane breathed, launching after Em when he lunged again.

But before Emlyn could collide with the door it—swung open.

Wait, what?

I dug my fingers into Em's big arm as my heart palpitated. I was ready to jump in front of him if that's what it took to save him. We were locked up because of me and my inherited god powers; I wasn't going to let a single person hurt my mates because of that.

Shadows whipped into a cyclone around us, expanding as they swarmed the door. Wane's magic was stronger, denser, than even before. So full of power that I felt it against my skin, a tingle raising goosebumps.

It surged towards the door, dangerous enough to suffocate, but golden light fractured the cloud of darkness like veins of lightning, and Wane's breath hitched in a sob that cracked my heart in two. The darkness dropped in an instant, dispersing as Wane rushed from my side as fast as an arrow.

"Need some help?" a dry, amused voice asked, and now I was crying too as Harvey appeared in the doorway, golden light pooled in his right palm. He was in control—he wasn't Feral at all in this moment, and that made my bottom lip wobble viciously.

"You found us," I choked out.

"Always, Sugarplum," Harvey said gently, hugging Wane so tightly his fingers turned white. "Let's get the fuck out of here. This place gives me the creeps."

A twisted, feminine cry of pain echoed up the hallway outside, and I jumped, my heart kicking into overdrive.

"What the fuck is that?" Emlyn demanded, grabbing my hand in a death grip.

"Just Kai torturing the matron," Harvey replied casually, still hugging his twin. "She wouldn't remove the shields, so he got creative."

Kai was here—they were *all* here. My heart soared, a lump swelling in my throat.

"Are the shields down on all the cells?" I asked.

"All of them," Harvey confirmed, scanning me from head to toe and raking over my soul in the bond, feeling every sore spot and weakness.

I squeezed his arm and leaned up to kiss his cheek as I brushed past him and through the door, reassuring him I'd be okay.

Emlyn refused to be parted from my side even when I strode down the hall to the next cell door. I still didn't know how to use my curse marks' magic, but I didn't have to.

"How's your shoulder?" I asked Em.

"Strong enough," he replied with a narrow-eyed determination. "Move back from the door, Verena."

"Thought you'd forgotten about me," her reply came, as sharp as a viper's fang. And then: "I'm out of the way."

Emlyn brought my hand to his lips, fanning a kiss across my knuckles before he let go and threw his entire body weight into the door.

This time, it flew open so hard it rebounded off the wall. Fuck! I rushed forward, forgetting how to breathe until I caught the solid door and stopped it slamming into Em's face.

My hands hurt like a bitch but my mate wasn't bleeding or unconscious so that was a win.

"Oh, what the *fuck?*" Verena demanded, her voice harsh and biting. I didn't know what I'd expected, but it wasn't a red-haired teenager with freckles, cute pigtail braids, and an adorable pouting mouth. She was short as fuck, but maybe that was because she was thirteen, and dressed in beaten up jeans, a Led Zeppelin shirt, and ragged black Converse. "I thought you were *adults.*"

"I'm a hundred and forty four years old, thank you very much," Emlyn rumbled, striding over to her. "Now come on, we're getting you out."

CHAPTER 28

"Who's she?" Kai demanded when we reached him, his eyes going past us and fixing on Verena. She was hard to miss with her blazing red hair and tough-bitch attitude.

"This is Verena," I replied, not quite able to take my eyes off the woman he'd tied to a chair and bound in so many snakes that there were pale bands all over her body where blood couldn't flow. There was a fat white stripe across her throat; her watery green eyes bulged, her mouth open on sharp, choking breaths.

"We're keeping her," Em added firmly.

"Who's *this?*" I asked Kai with a raised eyebrow, descending the final step onto the landing where Kai had bound the woman. There was a little desk where she'd obviously been stationed, probably to watch over prisoners like us. Kai had trashed it, and thrown all her files and knickknacks to the floor. Possibly to scare her. Probably for kicks.

"This is Sofia," Kai said cheerfully, his stare intense as it ran over me, then Wane, and finally Emlyn. "She just brought down the shields for us. Very nice of her."

I rolled my eyes at his coyness and stalked over to him, linking my hands behind his inked neck and dragging him down for a kiss. The noise Kai made when I kissed him was definitely not PG, and highly inappropriate considering there was a kid behind us. I quickly pulled away, giving him a warning look.

"Thank you for getting us out."

A certain wildness in him softened, the fine edge of madness leaving his eyes. "Any time, my rose." He kissed my cheek and let go, his attention snapping to Verena when she made a gagging noise. "Got something to say, Verona?"

"Verena," she hissed, glaring heatedly.

"I know," he replied flippantly, his arm sliding across my back. "Just wanted to annoy you."

A weight fell off my shoulders at his easy acceptance of her. None of us had spoken about it, but Em was right. She was a foster kid with zero family, and now she was embroiled in this Cronus bullshit. We were keeping her. At least until we found her a safer place than with us.

"Let's go," Emlyn barked. "Before Aphrodite notices we're gone."

Cold went through me at the thought of her catching us. Again.

"We should be ready to fight," Wane warned, shadows flickering at his shoulders. "She probably already knows we're out."

"Not necessarily," Harvey disagreed, brushing his brother's shoulder with a tawny wing. "We didn't come alone."

I gave Harvey a sharp look. "Why do I have a bad feeling about this?"

Emlyn nodded, his wings tightening.

"Nothing to worry about," Harvey replied flippantly, ushering us to a wide staircase and taking the steps two at a time. "Just Hera challenging Aphrodite in a fight to the death that could cause a cataclysm so big it wipes out all of Earth."

"Harvey, what the *fuck?*" Kai shouted behind us. "Where did this cataclysm shit come from?"

"Do you have any idea how much magic the gods have?" Harvey replied, sprinting across a stone landing and down another staircase. I followed, my heart racing fast—afraid, but exhilarated to have my family back together, too.

"He's right," Emlyn agreed behind us. "Bad things happen when the gods fight."

"How bad? Tiny little earthquake bad? Or end of the world bad?" Kai demanded, his voice sharp with panic. "Harvey's exaggerating, right?"

"End of the world shit tracks with everything else the gods have done," Verena remarked dourly. "Wait, what is *that?*"

I spun at the breathy tone of her voice, and a strange protective rage filled me at the sight of her terrified face, her freckles standing out darkly on her cheeks.

Em and Wane reached her first, peering out the stone arch that had caught her attention. Wane's sharp intake of breath had me moving faster, catching the toe of my boot on a step and almost smacking teeth-first into the stone. Harvey caught me before I could smack into the wall, and my gaze shot out the window, past the arch of a wall and over a domed rooftop. From this angle we could see down into a perfectly circular coliseum, eerily similar to the arena in Alphaven but without the dramatic flames.

There were no people on the stone benches, either, no hungry spectators. Just two women in the centre of a plume of dust and magic—and hovering in the air above them, a black vortex that made my heart skip one, two, three beats. In the heart of the swirling blackness was a ring of light, and then a darker circle. An eye.

"He's here," Wane breathed, grabbing my hand in a desperate grip.

"We're all dead," Verena laughed, gripping the edge of the window with white-knuckles hands.

"We need to leave," Emlyn growled. *"Now."*

I began to turn, but the vortex pulsed, the eye *blinked*, and when the blackness shot to the floor of the coliseum, I couldn't look away. It happened so fast, I would have missed it if I'd blinked. Dark magic formed a column that slammed into the arena floor, and then like something out of a supernatural horror film it resolved into the shape of an enormous man.

Cronus was here.

Really, really here.

And when he turned in our direction, like he knew we were watching us, I struggled to breathe.

"Run!"

CHAPTER 29

WANE

*T*he sweet, floral scent of Olympus filled all my senses when Harvey barrelled into the door at the base of the palace tower, bursting it open with a resounding *boom*. The scent was sickly, too sweet and cloying in my lungs. I wanted to run as far away from this place as possible; it was every bit as insidious as the Damned House even without mould and blood on the walls. And there was no doubt the titan had heard the door slam open.

"Faster," Emlyn barked behind us, ushering Haley, Kai, and Verena out the door and down the steep cobbled road outside. I kept close to my brother, my heart hammering my ribcage so frantically I felt it in my throat. The titan was here. He'd find me and force me to my knees and tear me apart until my heart stopped beating. Then he'd bring me back all over again so he could force me to watch him kill my family.

Haley squeezed my hand hard enough that I gasped, ripped from memories and back to the present.

"Stay with me," she breathed, running so fast her pink hair flew behind her like a ribbon, her face flushed with exertion and storm-grey eyes wide with terror. That fear cleared my own panic until rage filled its place. Rage was good; I could use that.

"I'm here, itzaia," I promised, squeezing her hand back and scanning the steep road we fled down. At the bottom, it led to another avenue that curved out of sight, the buildings ancient and pale, bricks carved from enormous chunks of stone. And empty—every building was empty.

Where is everyone?

A tremor ripped the ground from under my feet, and I cried out in surprise. My breathing cut off. I threw out my hands to catch myself before I broke my nose on the ground.

Haley's hand was torn from mine, but she leapt across the ground, throwing her wings and arms around me to stop my fall. A thin breath rasped up my throat as she steadied me, but a grunt of pain had my head snapping up. I scanned the steep road, terrified the titan had stolen someone while we were distracted but—Kai was still here, his hand locked around Verena's upper arm; Harvey had shifted into his beast form and bared his teeth at nothing in particular; and Emlyn was on the ground, wincing as he pushed back to his feet.

"Em," Haley breathed, releasing me when the ground steadied under us, and rushing across the road. "Are you okay?"

"Fine," he muttered, catching her face in his big hand. "Just a bruised ass. Nothing fatal."

Kai snorted at the same time Verena did, and I smiled even if I was scared to death.

"We need to keep moving," I urged. "Where's the exit from this place?"

"At the base of the main road," Kai replied, sobering as we

resumed walking even faster. The air crackled with magic, adding an acidic bite to its sweetness until my nose burned and my lungs tingled. "We'll be able to see it around this corner."

"How far?" Haley asked, drawing her wavy daggers, her fingers bone white around the pink hilts.

"Five minutes," Kai replied tensely, scanning the street the same way I was, waiting for the titan to jump out of the sky and snatch us up. "Maybe ten."

"Fuck!" Emlyn growled. "We don't have ten minutes. Haley, grab Kai. I'll grab Verena and—"

"And me and Harvey are fucked," I pointed out, a lump in my throat.

Emlyn's blue eyes flashed. He shot me a stern look as we rushed across the bottom of the street, following Kai's sense of direction. "You think we'd leave you behind? Not a single damn chance of it."

My chest warmed. My eyes stung. I nodded.

The titan was here; he'd kill me, lock me back up, and resurrect me to kill me all over again, but my family was here, too. They'd stop him. Haley wouldn't let him hurt me. She didn't make empty promises.

I ran through every reassuring word she'd told me to settle the frantic edge of my panic.

"Kai, get over here," Haley barked, stopping so suddenly at the bottom of the road that we all froze with her. "Em, grab Verena. Verena, don't fight, this shit is life or death. Wane, ride Harvey. Run as fast as you can. Yeah?"

Harvey rumbled his assent, and I nodded. Shit, this might work.

Climbing onto my brother's huge, furry back wasn't easy, but with the help of a few shadows, I scrambled up onto him and dug my hands into his fur, settling my weight and bracing myself so—

He shot off without warning, and I screamed, throwing my body low over his back.

"You could've given me some warning," I quipped.

His rumbling reply seemed to remind me that we were in immediate danger and didn't have time to piss about. He was right.

I tilted my head back, searching the skies above us and—was the sky darker than it had been a few seconds ago? It had been a perfect cloudless blue, but now it edged closer to storm grey. My heart sprinted; I speared my soul through my bond with Haley and exhaled a rough breath when I found no pain, only urgent fear.

Haley flew above us, her dark wings carving gracefully through the air and Kai clasped to her body. She was too high for me to see, but I swore she glanced down and met my gaze, and the sharpest edge of my terror eased. She was right there; she was safe. He hadn't killed her.

Emlyn flew beside her, Verena clutched in his arms, her face drawn with fear and red hair whipping around her face. She was too young to be facing anyone as evil as the titan; she didn't deserve this. None of us did.

I dropped my head back to Harvey's neck when his body shook with a deep noise, and I realised what he'd seen: the gate was ahead of us, massive and golden and—ripped off its hinges?

Had the titan done that? He loved destruction, loved to take things apart until they were broken beyond repair.

Fear closed my airways until I could only gasp, but I clenched my hands into fists of Harvey's fur and kept my gaze fixed on the open gates. Salvation. I focused on the wind tearing at my hair, raking claws through my clothes, trying to knock me off Harvey's back; wind meant fresh air, and air meant freedom. I wasn't locked up. My family found me again, freed me again.

Haley sent a rush of reassurance down the bond, and I nodded as if she'd spoken. They would always come for me. I was safe now. No matter what happened, the titan would never take me away from them again or—

Harvey pulled up so suddenly I screamed a curse, knocked violently out of my seat. I hung by a single hand clenched in his fur, my breathing sawing in my lungs and fingers clenched so tightly pain shot through my joints.

The toes of my shoes scraped the ground. I slipped another inch.

No!

We were so close to freedom, I had to stay on, I couldn't fall or—

The tuft of black fur ripped from my grip and I was thrown to the ground, landing so hard my teeth sliced the inside of my lip, filling my mouth with blood. A bad omen. My hands shook when I saw why Harvey skidded to a stop; directly in front of us, a black blur of dark magic spiralled down from the sky like a tornado.

Shadows. *My* shadows.

I flinched so hard I whimpered when that stolen magic drove into the cobblestones of Olympus, and cracks raced through the buildings on either side of us.

My own shadows fled when the blackness pulled back, revealing *him* beside a tall, regal woman with warm caramel skin and brown hair. We were close enough to see his smile when a tendril of dark magic struck, piercing her heart, and she crumpled to the floor at his feet. Her eyes lay open. Sightless.

Oh gods, she was—a goddess.

He'd killed *a goddess.*

Harvey rumbled a warning, backing up swiftly and nudging me behind his huge body. My feet were entirely numb as I stumbled back a step.

I jumped violently, gasping when something slammed into the ground beside me—more titans, more monsters, more—Haley. It was *Haley*.

I shuddered, my teeth clacking together. A tear burned my eye, streaking down my cheek. Haley was here; I was safe. I was safe.

"No," Kai hissed, lurching out of her arms with an expression of raw horror. "Hera!"

So that goddess was our backup, and she was in a broken heap at the titan's feet, and now—*oh gods, no*—

Haley threw herself in front of me, her body alight with crimson rage as the titan rose and expanded, becoming something *more* as he loomed twenty feet tall, his entire body made of a still, stagnant evil.

I covered my mouth with my hands when he lifted his powerful leg and stomped on the goddess until her bones broke and crushed to shards. She didn't even cry out.

Terror made me sick. My whole body was cold, weak. We needed to run. I tried to say it—*run!*—but my mouth wouldn't form words.

Emlyn dropped from the sky and grabbed me, holding Verena in one arm and me in the other.

"Run!" he ordered, like he saw the weak plea I tried to shout, his command deep and throaty and enough to send Harvey into motion.

But the gates were blocked by the titan's mammoth form and—and Kai and Haley weren't running.

"I brought her here," Kai hissed, fury in his voice and the air shimmering around him.

"We can't fight a titan," Haley warned, pulling at his arm. "Please, my night."

Emlyn rose into the sky with brutal wingbeats, clutching Verena and I in a brutal grip, but he hovered, refusing to leave the rest of our family. As much as instincts howled at me to flee, I wouldn't leave them either.

"Oh shit, oh shit," Verena whispered like a chant.

"Shhh," Emlyn soothed absently, a constant growl filling his voice, vibrating his chest against me.

Motion caught my eye and I whipped my head towards it, throwing my hand up on instinct to build a hasty wall of shadows around us. I gasped when my magic slammed into Aphrodite, the goddess's eyes blazing with—excitement. Not rage. *Excitement.* She was enjoying this.

"Pathetic," she remarked, but she was less interested in us than the broken body of Hera at the titan's feet. He didn't have a face, but some of the blackness split in the semblance of a grin as he drove his foot into Hera's body again.

Evil—he was pure evil.

When Haley grabbed Kai and shot back into the sky, I could breathe again. But being airborne wasn't much comfort when the titan was twenty feet tall and so close it made my stomach clench.

"All gods are pathetic," the titan chuckled, his voice gravelly and rough.

I recoiled so hard that Emlyn nearly dropped me, angling us away with rapid wing beats. I knew my shaking made me harder to hold onto, but I couldn't get my body to stop. What if he dropped me? Would the titan crush me to bones and blood too?

Aphrodite laughed, hovering in the air through some fell power. "So true."

I kept an eye on her, shadows writhing inside me, ready to knock her aside if she came at us. But instead it was Haley who shot through the sky towards us like a dark-winged bullet. My heart settled to have her close again.

"We need to fly over the walls," she yelled. "Fuck the gate; just get out of here."

Emlyn nodded, following her command without question.

"Harvey," I choked out, scanning the ground for a dark streak of fur. My heart resumed beating when I found him racing away from the titan. Good. Anywhere but near *him* was good. Being close to the titan would only cause unbearable pain and death.

"Oh god," Verena blurted. "Is he going to—?"

I snapped my head back to face the titan right as his dark hand shot out and plucked Aphrodite from the air.

She laughed, thinking it was a game.

My heart raced, my hands shaking; I grabbed Emlyn's thick arm and held on tight.

The titan's face split, that awful darkness parting as he lifted Aphrodite and tipped the goddess into his mouth.

His jaws snapped shut.

He'd devoured her.

CHAPTER 30

HALWEN

*H*e ate her. He really fucking ate her.

I slashed my wings through the air and spun away, flapping like crazy. He could grab us next, grab *any* of my family. Maybe we were safer on the ground—no, he'd trample us like he trampled Hera. My arms shook, gripping Kai so tightly it had to hurt. He held me just as viciously, his eyes fixed on the nightmare over my shoulder as I flew as fast as I physically could.

Where was Harvey? Where were the others? I struggled for breath.

"There!" Kai yelled over the sudden wind hammering at us, making it harder to stay in the air. "He's with your friends."

My friends? What? I didn't know wh—I saw them. Kai was right. Harvey was racing across the ground with Renna on one side of him and Tali's massive red panda on the other. *Thank fuck.* I could breathe again.

"What the hell is *that?*" Kai demanded, his panic slamming

into my soul over and over, like a violent ocean crashing into helpless cliffs.

Wind tore at me, too similar to when we were in the Labyrinth. I tried to follow his line of sight as I flew across Olympus, aiming my shaking body towards the tall walls around the city. I didn't know why I thought a wall between us and a titan would help, but I fixated on the idea of getting out of the city and I couldn't stop now.

Cold bloomed through me like ice fractals on a window when I finally spotted what had unsettled Kai. A plume of inky smoke as big as a city roared towards us from outside Olympus, and on its heels flowed an endless sea of silvery white fog. Magic. Vast enough to belong to more gods—or titans.

The magic was so immense that Olympus shook with a horrible wrenching groan, and the fragile buildings fell apart below us like they'd been ripped at their seams. It took all my willpower to stop my wings faltering when even spires and domes toppled from their heights, crashing into the ground with such echoing, violent *booms* that I flinched.[1]

"Oh shit," I breathed, gripping Kai so tightly he grunted when a giant wave of Caribbean blue water roared at Olympus from the other direction, like two natural disasters had conspired to wipe the city off the map.

I spun, scanning the mountains around us, hoping I was just being paranoid but—no, *fuck,* there was more. Light blazed from the tops of the mountains, racing down into the city like sunlight shaped into a weapon. Trapping us in a triangle of magic so powerful that the whole city trembled and crackled, the air tingling my skin.

"It's a guy!" Kai yelled, startling so hard I nearly dropped him. "The water's *a guy!*"

I scrambled to adjust my hold, lightheaded with visceral

panic. I couldn't drop him. Kai wouldn't survive a drop this big.

"Look," Kai urged.

Carefully, I turned to face Cronus, looking beyond him at the dark storm, the silvery fog, and the tsunami. Fuck, Kai was right. There was a man with long white hair in the heart of the water, riding a wave deadly enough to cause a tsunami. If that wave struck, even in the air it would be fatal.

"There's no way that's Poseidon," I said faintly, my head spinning. "Right?"

"Is he good or bad?" Kai asked, scanning the city with an intensity that usually scared people.

"I don't know, but Harvey, Tali, and Renna are running *towards* him so maybe they know something we don't."

I had to trust Harvey.

Besides, we were trapped with no way out, hemmed in by magic on all sides; flying to Poseidon was only as dangerous as flying into the blinding glow behind us.

A low tremor of warning went through me like an injection of cold, but I flew us closer to the wall. I kept as much distance from the darkness and ocean as I could, and I jumped when both magics slammed into Cronus like a punch to the gut. So Poseidon was good.

Cronus didn't even falter as he was pummelled by magic; his horrible featureless face cracked open again. My stomach twisted.

Did Poseidon know I un-cursed two of his hippocampi? Had he come to help because he owed me? I tried to remember the overgrown seahorses' exact words, but my head was too muddied with fear to recall them. My mates' panic clamoured in my chest, making my movements jittery as I flapped my wings, scanning the stormy sky for Emlyn.

He was unsettlingly far away, his grey wings propelling him around the inky storm and towards the western city walls like we'd had the same thought. Even from a distance, I saw Wane and Verena in his arms, and a tiny knot unfurled in my chest. Okay. Em had them; they were safe. Wane was safe. Cronus didn't have him.

Not holding back now, I flew full-out for the wall, keeping an eye on Harvey. I felt feral myself, desperate to scream for Harvey and my friends to turn around and run *away* from the natural disasters converging on Olympus. But I was too afraid to draw Cronus's attention. Was it just me, or was the titan growing even taller, his reach spreading further?

"Faster, Haley," Kai urged, his hands quivering where he gripped me.

"I'm trying," I bit out, wind battering me from all directions, whipped up from the giant ocean wave that rammed the walls.

"Oh gods," I gasped, watching cracks erupt through the solid stone, racing through the long wall around the gate in either direction, forming branches of fissures until—the whole thing collapsed.

So much for being safer on the other side of the wall.

"We fly over the sea and keep going," Kai shouted over the wind, his eyes wild. "Renna can get us back to Hell."

Right. Good. I could do that. I swivelled my head, searching for Em, Wane, and Verena. We all needed to fly in the same direction, but fuck knows how Renna, Tali, and Harvey would meet up with us and—

"*No!*" I screamed when Cronus's giant arm flung up and he swatted Emlyn, Wane, and Verena out of the air. Like they were an annoying fly and not my whole goddamn world.

"Fuck, *fuck!*" Kai snarled, his breath catching.

Emlyn spun out of control, his grey wings twisting, arching, frantically trying to catch air.

And failing.

My stomach clenched. *Move!* I growled at myself, and launched into flight.

I shot back the way we'd come, swerving and diving and flying faster than I ever had before, even with Kai's added weight. I barely saw the flattened buildings or the rubble that used to be walls. All I saw were my mates and a fucking *kid* falling to their deaths.

I can't do it again.

Not after watching them get shot by Locke. Not after Wynvail collapsing to dust in my arms. I couldn't do it again.

I won't survive this.

Harvey roared so loudly that the sound penetrated the wind lashing us. I fought to fly faster, further. It was useless; even streaking across the city, the storm battered me back until I sobbed, useless.

"They'll be fine," Kai chanted, his arms trembling where they locked around me. "They'll be fine."

But Cronus had knocked them out of the sky and now they free-fell into the enormous cloud of black, black magic spilling through the streets of Olympus until it was almost entirely under shadow.

My eyes burned, a tear racing down my cheek and over my wobbling bottom lip. I flew until I felt my wings buckle, and still I refused to stop.

"They'll be fine," Kai said weakly as I fought my way across the city, my muscles dangerously strained after the Labyrinth.

But my mates had vanished into the dark storm, and I couldn't see them. I dropped fast into our mate bonds and couldn't tell if it was just my panic or was numbness spreading through my soul. Exactly like it did when I lost Wynvail. Nothing good ever happened inside a cloud of magic that black, that powerful. The wielder was a titan; they had to be.

The dark storm, the cloud of silver, and the blinding light behind us—all of them had to be titans. Cronus's backup.

We were all dead. Verena was right.

It was happening again. I'd be forced to watch my mates die, one by one. I couldn't fly fast enough, couldn't reach that fell storm, couldn't dig them out of it or save them.

I was helpless, useless. Again.

"I'm sorry," I sobbed, blinking a hot wave of tears down my cheeks. "I'm so sorry, Kai."

"*None* of this is your fault," he hissed, but his voice was ragged, rough. His magic trembled around him, snakes brushing my feathers when my wings faltered. His magic was the only thing keeping us in the air, stopping us crashing into the collapsed villa below where bones would snap and lives would be lost.

It was too close—death.

We both flinched when a deep, resonant voice roared through the air, so loud and otherworldly it made my eardrums shake.

"*Where is my daughter?*"

A chilling, rattling noise came from Cronus when he parted his awful featureless face, his maw split in a slash.

It took me a moment to realise he was laughing.

"*Where is she?*" Poseidon roared, water stilling around him until it hovered in a lethal riptide. The kind that looked harmless but pulled you to your death.

I flew away from him and closer to the dark, churning cloud, tears burning my eyes as I scanned for any sign or remnant of my mates. What if this titan had unmade them like Cronus unmade Wynvail? What if there was nothing left of the men I loved? What if—

"Shit," Kai laughed, shock like a firework in his soul. "They're there! The cloud thing just put them on the road. They're alive, my rose. They're alive."

My throat tightened, hope like a noose around my chest as I scanned the ground, searching the wreckage of gods' houses and once-beautiful parks and—they really were there. My bottom lip caved in. A sob burned my throat, but it emerged as a soft scream. I couldn't tear my eyes away as Em snapped his wings out at his sides for balance as he wavered on his feet, Wane and Verena still clutched to his big chest.

I flew as fast as I physically could, swerving and dropping until I escaped the wind around the ruined walls, and caught a current to glide to the ground.

I landed clumsily, a broken face only prevented by Kai's snakes anchoring us to the ground. The second I was steady, I set him down and took off running, my heart in my throat and breaths wheezing.

"Wane! Em!"

My voice cracked. I sounded broken.

They turned as we raced towards them, frustration mounting when we had to swerve fallen debris, too slow, *too slow.* Emlyn opened his arms right as I jumped at him, throwing my arm out to hook Wane into a rough hug too. My limbs jellified with relief and terror. My eyes burned as tears streaked my face.

"What happened?" I demanded, my voice squeakier than usual.

"The black fog is Lucifer," Wane said, rubbing my back and strangely calm.

I started so violently that my whole body shook. *"What?"*

My head spun. The storm wasn't a titan. It was *Lucifer.* Our ally. Okay. Okay, everything was okay.[2]

"He caught us before we could hit the ground," Em continued, folding a wing around me. "He said more backup is on its way, but we need to get out of here before Cronus can—"

"Eat me," I finished in a flat voice. "Got it."

I clung to my mates harder. They weren't murdered. They

were still here, still with me. I was exhausted, at my limit of being terrified I'd lost them. *No more. Please no more.*

I needed Harvey. Now.

"It's Poseidon, isn't it?" Wane asked, rubbing my back harder, like he knew I needed the touch. He craned his neck to see the deadly still wave and the man floating atop it, roaring in Cronus's menacing face. Was this Cronus's true form, this thing of darkness and flashes like lightning? "Did he come because he owes you?"

"He came because Cronus kidnapped his daughter," Kai muttered. "Renna said something about it this morning."

"We can use them as a distraction," Wane said, silver eyes shifting back to Cronus, always returning to the titan. And I knew his calm was just a mask; I felt his terror. "We need to go, but not that way. The queen just came over the mountains; we need to escape that way."

The queen...

The blinding light racing into the city like a spear of Heaven. That was *Lili?*

Holy shit, my friends were cool.

"We need Harvey," I said, clearing my throat when it came out thick. I dove through my soul to the place I was bound to Harvey and gave him a rough tug, urging him to find me, to join us.

Please, please, please...

"What's the silver shit?" Kai asked, slashing his hand in front of us and building a serpentine shield around us.

"Spirits," Emlyn muttered, a growl threaded through his voice. "Verena! Get over here. Now."

She hovered a few feet away from us, her arms wrapped around her middle and her face turned up to the clash of titan, shadow, and storm in the sky. She looked small and scared and alone. She didn't even glare at Emlyn's bossy tone; she just slumped over to us.

"What do you mean spirits?" I asked, hooking the kid into a hug. She looked like she needed one, and if she was anything like me at that age, she'd be too proud to ask for one. She shook with tiny, barely perceptive tremors. "They can't leave Hell. Can they?" I pressed when no one spoke.

Kai shrugged. "He's Lucifer. He can do what he wants. Now if everyone's in one piece, we need to get Harvey and get the fuck out of here."

I liked that plan. I turned to scan the city, the whole thing flattened, domes lying on the ground, cracked in pieces with columns shattered beside them, walls in rubble around us. Harvey was massive, and Tali wasn't much smaller. They should have stuck out, should have been easy to spot. My heart skipped a beat. I didn't see them at all.

I trusted Renna, and Tali was the closest thing I had to a best friend, but it was *my* job to keep Harvey safe. I needed to find him now. I couldn't leave his safety in anyone else's hands.

"Duck!" Verena yelled, so sharp and piercing that I only hesitated for a second. When she dropped to the ground and covered her head, I followed suit, my mates all doing the same thing.

The second we were down, a plume of magic erupted across Olympus, so powerful that the whole mountain shook under us. Shit, they were going to bring the whole thing down. We needed to get back in the sky, but not without Harvey.

I pressed my face to the dusty ground, magic sizzling over my back, raking through my wings and burning into all the sensitive places I couldn't protect. I kept my head ducked until the oppressive cloud lifted and I could suck down a breath without lining my lungs with pure, electric power.

"It's the queen," Wane breathed, and I lifted my head to see what he was talking about.

Blinding light slammed into Cronus in a severing line, knocking him out of the city and past the collapsed wall. I sucked in a sharp breath as another rush of magic crackled over me.

The cruel sensitivity in my wings made me cry harder, tears flowing fast. Kai threw himself over my back, flattening me to the ground. I grunted at his added weight, but I was so touched by him shielding me that I didn't complain. Even if he was a stupid bastard who needed to protect himself as much as me.

"Let's go," Emlyn barked when no more flashes of magic crackled over us. "Wane, do you have enough strength to shield us?"

"Maybe," Wane replied, pushing off the ground and brushing off the little stones embedded in his arms. "I might—"

He cut off with a visceral shudder when Cronus laughed again, his horrible face cracked open.

"Hales, is the queen descended from a goddess?" Emlyn asked suddenly, and my heart thrummed faster.

"I don't know," I admitted. I didn't know much about my new friends. "But—I know Lucifer is."

"He's going to devour him," Wane rasped, his body shaking hard, shadows spitting from his hands. "And he'll consume Poseidon, too."

"Where the fuck is Harvey?" I growled, fear making me sick. I helped Verena to her feet, my panic reflected on her freckled face. "We're not leaving him."

Come closer, Cronus taunted, so suddenly and intensely loud that I clutched my head. Kai grabbed my face and brushed away the blood that ran from my nose, ignoring his own pain with his teeth clenched and rage glowing in his eyes. *Closer, little gods.*

"*Where is Zara?*" Poseidon roared, the ocean he'd brought

with him no longer still. It drove into Cronus with a deadly crash, shaking the foundations of the mountain. Water hit the ground around the titan, so volatile that it frothed and thrashed and raced into the ruined city.

We were going to be swept away.

My heart drummed faster. I felt faint.

Frantic, I pushed Verena and Wane to Emlyn and then I grabbed Kai and leapt into the air.

My wings strained, aching so badly I clenched my jaw against the effort, but they held out enough to carry us to the top of a fallen dome. It was only six feet high but it was enough to escape the sudden waves below. I glued my eyes to Emlyn as he flew up to us, Wane under one arm and Verena under the other.

My bottom lip wobbled without mercy. I didn't know what I'd do without him.

"I know," he murmured when he landed beside me, standing on the top of the dome and ignoring the ocean that surged through Olympus so he could set Wane and Verena down, ducking close to me. His lips were warm on my cheek, a comfort that went far beyond words.

"Where have you taken my daughter?" Poseidon screamed, completely beyond reason, almost mad with rage. And fear—there was no denying that was fear in his voice. My heart gripped with sympathy. I'd be fucking terrified if something like Cronus stole my kid.

She'll be put to excellent use, Cronus replied in his resonant, all-consuming voice. My breath hitched, warmth running down the sides of my face. Oh great, now my ears were bleeding.

"Where?" Poseidon raged, slamming into Cronus on the top of an impossibly high wave, so much magic in the blow that the ground shook. I tensed, prepared to grab my family if the dome fell.

She's right here, Cronus purred and—snatched Poseidon right off the top of his wave, shoving the god into his awful, gaping mouth.

For a second I just froze. Horrified.

"Go!" I yelled, snapping back to life. "Kai—use your snakes, figure out a way to fly. I'm going to get Harvey."

"Like *fuck* you're going alone," he hissed, so guttural that cold warning travelled down my body.

I spun towards him, but Lucifer's inky cloud soared suddenly, filling the spaces around Cronus. My stomach turned. Cronus was just playing with them, taunting them close so he could consume them.

"Don't!" I yelled at Lucifer, staggering forward a dangerous step on the pale dome like I could stop him.

He'd helped me, housed me, given me the means to find my mates, and I couldn't just stand here and watch him get devoured by a power-hungry[3] psychopath.

The second Lucifer became a friend, he became one of my people. And I didn't leave my people behind.

"Em, get Verena out of here. Kai, find Harvey. Wane—" I turned to him, taking his face in both my hands and trying not to notice how dirty and bloody the back of my hands were. "Do you trust me?"

"There isn't a single part of me that doesn't," he replied, his throat bobbing like he already knew what I was going to say.

I kissed the space between his dark brows, lingering. "He wants your shadows, maybe more than he wants to devour all the children of the gods."

"Bait him," Wane agreed before I had to ask. "Use me. Wherever you go, I go, itzaia."

My throat swelled; I nodded.

We were killed by Cassander Locke because we were all together, all in one convenient location. But splitting up? Maybe some of us would survive.

"I love you," I told him, then turned to face Em and Kai, making eye contact. "I love you all so much I can't breathe. Remember what Adhiti said, what *Rhea—his wife—*said. I can kill him. I'll be alright."

It was a sad attempt to convince them and reassure myself, all rolled into one.

"I'll get her to safety and come back for you," Emlyn promised, dragging me close for a long, heated kiss. I held onto him, tracing his tongue, memorising the shape of his mouth, the curves of his lips. Would this be the last time I kissed him?

No. Don't be defeatist, bitch. You've got this. You're the great-great-granddaughter of a titan. The daughter of a man who refused to give up when life dealt him shit hand after shit hand. Dad hadn't broken. He'd been brave. I would be, too.

"No," Kai said when I turned to him, his voice guttural and eyes flared with panic. "Don't kiss me; I don't want your goodbye."

"It's not goodbye," I argued softly, sliding my hands into his ashen red hair. "You think you can get rid of me that easily? No chance, Malakai Virex."

For all his refusal, it was Kai who grabbed the lapels of my jacket and wrenched me against his body, crushing my mouth and kissing me like the world was ending around us. It certainly looked like it was.

He drew back and met my eyes in a dangerous glare. "Who do you belong to?"

My heart skipped a beat. I swallowed and said, "You. Always you."

He flicked his tongue against his dry lips and demanded, "And who do I belong to?"

"Me," I rasped. "You're mine."

"And don't fucking forget it," he snarled, kissing me again. It was over far too fast. My stomach twisted into knots.

I'd see them again, wouldn't I?

"Come back to me, or I'll hunt you down wherever you end up."

"Probably the shady part of Hell where the worst spirits go," I said, trying for lightness. The croak in my voice ruined it.

"I know the area," he replied, his jaw clenching. "I better not see you there. Ever."

I tried to smile. "Likewise."

He nodded once, sharp, and reached for my waist, drawing both my volcanic daggers. He placed them in my palms and lifted each hand, pressing a kiss to my knuckles. "Kill him."

"I will," I promised.

"And you," Kai snarled at Wane.

"I'll protect her with my life," Wane vowed, his long chestnut hair batted by the wind. Silver eyes blazed with seriousness—and readiness to do just that. The thought of him laying down his life for me made me physically ill.

"Not what I was going to say, fuckhead," Kai snapped, grabbing the back of Wane's head and wrenching him across the dome until their foreheads touched. "Be careful; stay safe. We can't lose you again. You're too important to lose. Got it."

Wane's eyes were wide, surprised. He nodded. He looked close to crying. "Got it."

"Fuckhead isn't even a word," Verena murmured, watching our goodbyes with a terrified look on her face. "I can fight," she blurted, like she'd been desperate to say it for long minutes.

"I bet you can," I agreed, rubbing my face free of tears, dust, and blood and giving her a hard look. "But not here and now. I'm the one prophesied to kill him, and I'm not letting you go up against a titan."

I held out my arms for Wane; he stepped into them without question, his back straight and head high. Ready to do whatever he had to, even if it meant baiting the titan who terrified him. His strength stole all my breath from me.

"Go to Lucifer's palace. We'll meet up there," I said, and before anyone could stop me, I tightened my arms around Wane and dropped off the edge of the dome, catching a swell of wind.

Flying toward Cronus like I had a death wish.

CHAPTER 31

KAI

I couldn't let her down. My rose was relying on me, and Harvey was, too. Where was the giant, furry bastard? He couldn't have vanished; the whole city had collapsed, there was a clear view all the way to the edge of the mountain. So where the fuck—

My knees buckled when Cronus laughed, his nightmarish voice cracking my skull apart with pain, and I staggered around with a ragged gasp when my mate's voice tore across the city.

"Focus," I breathed to myself, my whole body shaking with the urge to run to her. But I had a job to do, and my mate wouldn't be able to function if Harvey was in danger. The second I found him, we could both help her.

It felt like I ripped out a part of myself when I turned away from Haley, searching the collapsed city. There was only rubble all around me. Fuck, there was only *rubble* and where was Harvey? What if I couldn't find him? What if he was—

"Don't even think it, asshole," I snarled at myself, my tongue flicking out and tasting ashes. Ugh.

I set off in a random direction, sending out small scouting corn snakes to scour the ground for any hint of Harvey.

With every minute that passed, I lost more hope, and grew more frantic until—

Bright golden light slashed through a collapsed wall to my left. I jerked towards it, my heart faltering when Cronus laughed again, his awful voice stabbing my skull until my whole head pounded and blood trickled from my ears. Great. My brain was melting to gore. That was the last thing I needed.

But that golden light—I *knew* that light. I'd seen it shatter whole villages. I knew it had once ruined an entire city. That was Harveil's power.

I didn't dare glance back at Cronus. I threw myself around the side of a wrecked library and ran as hard and fast as I could, unerringly aiming for that bright slash of power. The light died out, but I kept running, pushing myself so hard that my breathing wheezed and a half dozen sore points throbbed on my body.

What the fuck was up with my elbow? Holy *shit* it hurt, and I couldn't even remember what I'd done to it. My wrist and thigh, too.[1]

Dust kicked up around me, when I skidded, grabbing a fallen column so I didn't slam into the ground. Haley would still love me if my face was mashed, but I was a vain bastard and a broken nose was about all my vanity would accept. My rose deserved someone in possession of a full set of teeth.

"Harvey!" I yelled, racing down what was once a road but now had craters blasted out of it, and what survived was strewn with pale bricks and gilded debris. Another hole tore through the ground a few metres away, too close to comfort. The entire street shuddered under me.

Fucking hell, what had Cronus even done to this place? Mount Olympus was ripping itself apart beneath us.

"Harvey!"

I sent out more snakes, gritting my teeth as I grazed the bottom of the usually endless pit of magic inside me. I'd drawn too much this past week, with little time to rebuild my reserves. I'd never run out of power before, not even locked up in Alphaven's tunnels, but I was dangerously close now.

Light split a toppled library ahead of me, and relief drove a rough breath from my lungs. Thank *fuck*. I corrected my course and leapt over holes in the ground, pushing my body to exhaustion until I found him.

"Harv—" I croaked, unable to finish his name. I bent over, bracing myself on my knees. Fuck, I needed to work out more. I bet the safe house had a personal gym, as well as the training room. "The—fuck—been?"

Harvey had his jaws locked around a giant chunk of stone; he tossed it aside and peered down at me, working his jaw like it was stiff.

"There are cells under the city," Renna barked, striding around the pile of rubble Harvey was dismantling, with Tali at her back. Both were covered in dust. Tali's mouth and chest was streaked with blood. I couldn't help but remember my mate telling me her friend ate people, so I gave the giant red panda a friendly *don't eat me, thank you very much* smile.

"So?" I demanded carefully, straightening my posture. "How is that our problem?"

"They're full of gods and people of Olympus," Renna explained like I was stupid as she grabbed a chunk of mortar and threw it aside. "With them, we might stand a chance of getting off the mount alive."

"Great pep talk," I drawled, but I grabbed a stone and heaved it aside, scanning Harvey to make sure he was in one piece. "The faster we get this done, the faster we get back to Haley. She needs us."

Harvey froze, deadly magic flickering across his fur like smoke.

"She needs godly backup even more," Renna argued, her voice sharp and biting. An eerie red power pooled in her hand, chilling my blood, and she somehow moved a chunk of mortar bigger than my torso.

Harvey snarled, his giant head swivelling, searching the shattered streets. *Where is my mate? Is she hurt?*

"She's with Wane," I said hesitantly, catching my breath enough to shove aside a broken pillar. Shit, there was a grate under here. "They went to kill Cronus."

Harvey erupted with sunlight so bright I had to shade my eyes. When the deadly gleam faded, there was nothing left of the grate *or* the library; it was obliterated.

"If you killed everyone inside, we're fucked," Renna hissed, Tali echoing her remark with a low growl.

Harvey didn't reply; he took off down the street, running so fast that he blurred. Driven by pure panic, following the mating bond to Haley.

"Good luck," I told Tali and Renna and raced after Harvey, weaving around obstacles and giant pits in the ground, struggling to stay on my feet when more holes ripped through the streets as Cronus's magic devoured Olympus.

"Hey!" Renna yelled behind me. "What the fuck?"

Did she really expect me to waste time on strangers when my mate was fighting a fucking *titan*? Panic made my legs weak as I ran, following the dark furry mass of Harvey's beast form and barely even flinching when vicious slices of sunlight arced from him and through the buildings around us, venting his rage and fear.

I climbed a perilous mountain of rubble blocking off the path, but I nearly slipped when Cronus roared in pain. The sound stabbed so deep in my skull that my legs gave out. I clutched my head, my teeth gritted and impact shooting up my knees.

Haley, I hissed at myself, a reminder that this pain was nothing. Losing her would be unbearable. So I pulled myself up and scaled the rubble pile, needing a vantage point of the whole ruined city so I could find—

There you are.

I could breathe again when I found her, pink hair lashing the air in a devastating wind as she flew twenty feet above Olympus. Her daggers were raised to the titan who loomed over her, the volcanic metal glowing crimson, and pride beat in my chest at the sight of her driving them towards the bastard's eyes.

Kill him, my rose. Make him regret every second of suffering he gave us.

I grabbed a fistful of power from my depleted reserves and built a tower of invisible cobras, bolstering me into the sky. I was too far to reach Haley, too far for her to even notice me, but with a half-thought, my magic carried me across the rubble towards her.

"Keep pressing," I breathed when Cronus knocked her knives aside, as if she could hear me.

Where was Wane? I scanned the skies—and found him collapsed on the ground.

My stomach pitched. I forgot how to breathe.

No. Fuck, no.

I hurled myself across the city, carried on the scaly backs of my snakes. But movement drew my eye; Harvey was already streaking across the ruined city to his brother. So I swallowed my dread and kept pushing across the city to our mate. Renna was right;she needed backup.

I threw together a hasty plan to distract Cronus so Haley could kill him once and for all, but there was no guarantee it would work. Where was Lucifer? She'd gone to save the devil, but I didn't see him anywhere. Didn't see any gods, actually. Poseidon had vanished too.

Fuck, were we on our own?

Hurry up, Renna, Tali. We're gonna need those imprisoned gods pretty fucking sharpish.

Cronus laughed when Haley's wings dropped her lower; she slashed her daggers across his stomach until inky magic parted and his guts spilled flickers of light and blood. *Kill him,* I chanted in my head as I raced faster towards her, still too fucking far away. *Kill him.*

But even from here, I saw the titan's wound close, not even a scar visible as proof that she'd hurt him. My hands started to shake. I pushed my magic faster, pushed to breaking point.

Ice pumped through my veins instead of blood, panic making my heart race so fast I felt every beat against my ribs. Wind whipped past me, grabbing me like it was sabotaging me.

"I'm coming," I promised Haley even if she couldn't hear me.

Six metres away. Close enough to shout, but I didn't dare distract her.

Five metres. I rose higher in the air, gathering the last dregs power, planning to hit Cronus with every bit of venom I had. It wouldn't kill a titan but it might weaken him and that was all Haley needed.

Four metres. Haley made another blow, jamming her wavy dagger into his hip, severing a brutal hole.

Three metres. Cronus's hand snapped up so fast that I blinked, and he had Haley in his massive hand. I couldn't even scream a warning.

My heart stopped as his awful voice echoed across the city. *I'll have this meal tenderised.*

"Haley!" I screamed, wishing I had wings, my body fucking

useless as I pushed my magic to my limit, the empty pit of my power taunting me. There were no more snakes, no more magic.

More! I need more!

Two metres. Too far, too fucking slow. Cronus reared his hand back and threw her.

I dragged inner claws across my well of power, summoning anything, any hint of power. I tore and pulled until I felt a snap, and every snake and scale keeping me in the air fell apart.

"Harvey!" I screamed at the ground, begging for him to do something, anything, to save her.

I dropped faster than I could stop myself, but it didn't matter when my rose fell like a meteor from far, far higher, trailing crimson light and devastating magic.

The impact of my mate hitting Olympus sent shockwaves so far that I heard shouts and cries in the distance. A force slammed into me, until I fell even faster, the world a blur.

I wrenched at whatever power I had left to slow my fall, but magic slipped through my hands like sand. Snakes fled around me, vanishing into nothing, snuffed out of existence, and I had nothing left to save me, nothing to—

"Fuck!" I screamed when I slammed into something hard, unyielding, and—furry? "You—son of a—bitch," I panted, and slid down Harvey's side on weak legs. I was hurt but I was alive. I could save her, I could. "I fucking love you, you bastard. Have I told you that?"

I wavered on my feet, my knees weak, but I grabbed his giant head and pressed a loud kiss to his forehead. I should have been dead, but he caught me.

But no one caught my rose.

My mate's body splayed on the ground twenty feet away, her wings at awkward angles, but she was moving, wasn't she? Was she groaning, or was I deluding myself?

All exhilaration and relief drained from me, and I stumbled back into Harvey's shoulder. My heart thudded slowly, heavily in my chest, the beat irregular.

"Is she...?"

Numbness spread through my soul until I was full of ice. I didn't know how to exist without her.

But I'd seen her move, hadn't I? I'd heard her groan, hadn't I?

Harvey lunged forward with a haunting cry, nearly sending me to my ass, but any words I might have snapped at him died on my tongue when I realised a shadow cast over us —and over Haley. Cronus walked towards her, his giant foot raised to crush her, to kill her like he did Hera.

A wordless scream poured up my throat. *No. This wasn't happening. No!*

I launched across the road, too weak and my body too fucked to walk in a straight line, but Harvey raced for her. I choked on relief. He'd get her, he'd—

He'd die right with her.

Cronus's foot drove down towards them, and a sob twisted my throat as I staggered as fast as I could to my mate, knowing she was dead and refusing to stay alive without her again. *Never again.*

Harvey screamed a bestial cry, skidding across the last bit of distance between them to shield her prone form with his body.

I wasn't breathing right, wasn't functioning. Cronus's foot blacked them out entirely, until I couldn't see either of them, and a sob choked off the last of my air.

Never again.

I threw myself into that void of light, my pained body slamming into Harvey's. I moulded myself around both of them, hands shaking, death wrapping like arms around me.

At least I wasn't alone. This was better than dying in

Alphaven, trying to kill my family, not remembering the lives we'd lived together. At least I was dying as myself. With the ones I loved.

Blackness pressed around us, choking all life from the world, but my whole being jolted when light tore through the darkness. For a second I thought it was the white light at the end of the tunnel. But I could still feel my body; I wiggled my fingers just to check. Yup. Still alive.

Harvey—it had to be. But ... this light was moon-white not sun-gold.

Run, Harvey growled, his body shaking against me.

"What the fuck *is* that?" I hissed, stumbling to my feet and pulling Haley up with me. Harvey shielded us, a broken growl in the back of his throat.

Haley came to life all at. once, and one sob was followed by another until I couldn't choke them back. She scrambled to her feet, wobbly but alive, gasping, shaking. And wiping the tears from my face. She was touching me. *Alive.*

A voice cut through the silence, too far away for me to hear, but Haley jerked forward a step, a small sound in her throat. I reached for her frantically, but I was still drained, still in pain and weaker than I'd ever been before.

Haley shook her head, tears sliding down her ash-covered face, and then she tore away from me and down the broken street.

Back into danger.

CHAPTER 32

HALWEN

*O*ne second, Cronus was bleeding with my dagger
buried in his thigh, the next his leg was swinging
through the air. His foot slammed into me and sent me
careening through the air and—Wane!

I slammed my wings out, beating backwards to stop my
fall, and frantically scanned the ground, my heart drumming
in my throat. He'd been just below me, wrapped in shadows as
he went for Cronus's ankles, but I couldn't see his darkness
anymore. Pain throbbed through my chest, each pulse as
sharp as a spear. He'd been struck.

"Wane!" I yelled, my ears straining for a reply.

Please, please...

Silence.

Where was Lucifer? He'd been just beside me, flying on a
swell of dark magic and—

"I'll move your mate to safety," he said urgently, appearing
at my side and making my jump. His tawny face was drawn

and a shade paler than usual. "You can kill Cronus, Halwen. Use your magic."

I nodded. Right. Easy. Just kill a titan. No problem.

"If Wane's hurt," I breathed, giving the devil a vicious glare, "I'll end you."

If I wasn't mistaken, he gave my daggers—my god-killers —a wide berth as his inky magic carried him to the ground. To Wane.

"Get your spirits to surround this bastard," I yelled down to him, my heart skipping when a silver swarm of the dead appeared as if they heard my command. Lucifer must have held them back until now, but cold spread through me, sapping my energy as they swarmed.

Hopefully draining Cronus too.

I shook with the instinctive need to go to Wane, but I clenched my teeth and flew higher. He'd be fine with Lucifer. And he'd be a hell of a lot better when his abuser was dead at our feet.

Cronus laughed, the sound carving through my skull, down my throat, and into my chest.

Laugh all you want, asshole, you're dead.

"Shit." I flung myself out of the way when the titan's hand sliced down through the air, scattering the spirits. Oh, that wasn't a good sign.

I flew out of the path of his hand—and realised too fucking late that he wasn't making a grab for me.

Lucifer.

"No!" I flew hard, plummeting towards the devil, terror cutting off my air and making my wings tremble as I cut through the air, my arm outstretched in front of me. "Take my hand!"

Shadow magic shot the King of Hell into the sky away from Cronus's hand, and I exhaled a selfish breath of relief when the titan's attention followed him, drifting away from my unmoving mate. *He's fine, Wane's fine. He's just—conserving energy. Yeah. That's it.*

A feminine scream shattered the sky as I hovered in the air, power knocking the breath from my lungs and making my head pound harder.

Fuck, what was *that?*

I twisted, keeping Wane in my field of vision and marking Cronus's whereabouts at the same time I searched for this new—oh. Shit. Queen Lili.

Sympathy and pain arrowed through my chest. I knew that panic, knew that rage.

Wane was safely out of Cronus's sights for now—but Lucifer wasn't. And Lili loved him every bit as much as I loved my mates.

I better go to a nice place when I die for this, I thought, and shot up through the sky, slashing my daggers at every part of Cronus I passed, opening weeping slices that closed like paper cuts.

I better be made a damn saint.

Cronus's hand snapped out again, and Lucifer dropped in a plume of darkness, evading his grasp. But my heart skipped when I realised what was going to happen, what Lucifer couldn't see because he was too close to Cronus. The first swipe had been a distraction. Bait.

As fast as lightning, Cronus snatched the devil out of the sky with his other hand, and crushed him in his fist until the darkness faded to wisps around him. Panic made me unsteady at that obvious sign of Lucifer's weakness.

Lili howled in rage—and blind terror. Bright magic filled the city. Pure power hung around the city, nearly dropping me from the sky. My heart pounding, I slashed at Cronus over and over.

If the king of gods didn't stand a chance against Cronus, what made me think I did? Stupid—so fucking stupid.

But that didn't stop me lunging through the air, pumping my wings fast to reach Lucifer. The wind drove me back, and I screamed through gritted teeth. Cronus was doing this on purpose and—

He brought his hand to his mouth, unclenched his fist, and swallowed the devil whole.

Lili's cry made the whole mountain tremble, the force of her magic and grief ripping the ground apart.

I shook, reeling, unable to process the fact Lucifer was *dead*.

Wane. I needed to get my mate out of here, needed to—

A giant foot swung into my side, fracturing my ribs, and I screamed as Cronus kicked me out of the sky.

I flung my wings and arms out on instinct, and some higher power must have been rooting for me because one of my daggers embedded in Cronus's shin, stopping my fall. I shrieked so loudly I heard the sound even over the furious storm of power, dangling there for a precarious moment before my wings remembered how to work.

Panting, my head spinning, I ripped the blade out and drove both of them into an unblemished patch of skin on his back, venting my anger and terror on him until blood covered my hands and my blades glowed. Light blasted from both my curse marks, and I grunted as I stabbed him over and over, flying higher in a panicked zigzag so he couldn't grab me.

I was supposed to be able to kill him, but *how?* Why didn't this prophecy come with instructions, dammit? I jammed one blade into his throat, ripped it out, and sank the next into his cheek, ripping a gruesome hole.

That's what you get for eating people, I thought, and stabbed his eyes next.

Cronus let out a noise between a laugh and a snarl and knocked me back.

I dropped so fast my head spun, breath snatched from my

lungs, but I threw my arms out and caught myself with both blades buried in his stomach. Hanging like this was hell on my biceps, but my wings beat, taking some of the weight.

I couldn't get my dizzy head to form thoughts, but a tiny, vicious grin curled the edges of my mouth as I gutted Cronus from edge to edge. Blood poured down his stomach, inner light breaking through the slash in a myriad colours, but—he healed this wound too. Too fucking quickly.

Shit. Faster, Haley...

I drove the next blow into his hip, breathing rapidly, sweat dripping off my head and the world too cold around me. What happened to the spirits? Where was Poseidon? That fucker *owed* me; he needed to back me up so I could kill Cronus and—

I screamed when a giant hand snapped around me and ripped me away from his body.

So this is it. This is when he devours me.

I'll have this meal tenderised, he remarked in his cruel, pain-inducing voice.

Wait, what? I struggled in his massive hand, but my arms were locked at my sides, my daggers useless and—I screamed until my voice gave out when he threw me so hard and far that the world blurred.

Wind tore at my hair, clothes, and wings as I shot across the city. Light streaked from my daggers. I only had enough time to turn them away from me so I didn't impale myself before I slammed into the ground so hard my head rattled. Pain erupted through my knee, and the world turned black for a stretch of eternity.

Am I dead?

I groaned, testing my body. Death really ought to be more floaty and painless than this.

Ugh. Fuck. I was still alive.

Growls and voices clamoured around me, and I could have

sworn an enormous black wolf dog was hugging me, but I was too dizzy to turn my head and see if the dog was real.

The ground rumbled with an earthquake, but the dog pressed tighter to me, enclosing me in trembling warmth. My head swam and my whole body hurt, my knee especially brutal but—the scent registered.

I gritted my teeth, pulling myself back together, dragging a tiny scrap of strength from my bruised, broken body when I realised it was *Harvey* wrapped around me, not a wolf dog. Kai was here too, pressed close and livid with protectiveness.

My mates were here, and I might have been spiked with pain in every limb, but if they were here, everything was going to be okay.

I dropped into my bonds, desperate to feel Em and Wane and—

I was mad. Certifiable. I had to be.

My whole body started to shake, my chest cut through with so many emotions that I couldn't contain them. Denial was strong. Disbelief was stronger. But hope drowned them both out.

A sob crushed my throat and tore past my lips, and one gave way to ten, to twenty.

"What the fuck *is* that?" Kai hissed, his hand wrapping around my arm and pulling me to my feet.

I wavered, slumping into him as sobs broke apart my chest, but I forced myself steady through sheer will. We weren't safe yet. Far from it. And if Wane hadn't moved, he was too fucking close to Cronus.

I wasn't even thinking about the alternative. Not with the emotions howling through me and the way my soul buckled.

I shielded my eyes as I searched for my unconscious mate, moon-light white everywhere, washing out Olympus until I couldn't even see Cronus. Another sob smothered me.

"Touch her," a cold voice breathed, entirely lethal, "and you die."

I froze.

My breathing cut off.

Every atom in my body just ... stilled.

The words echoed around my head, louder and louder with every pass. They shattered me into broken pieces and forged each shard into something stronger, filling the cracks with gold.

I took a step without really meaning to. I couldn't feel my face, my knee was fucked, and my feet were numb but I took another step.

I was truly mad, wasn't I?

But that didn't stop me running towards that cold voice and the bright light as fast as my bruised, fractured body would allow. Kai swore and raced after me, Harvey growling as he did the same.

My skin prickled all over as sensation threatened to return, dragging pain back with it. I was wrong, I *had* to be wrong. But the viciously bright light cut out, allowing me to see more than two feet in front of myself and—

He was there, standing in the middle of the ruined road, dressed in pure black and wreathed in moonlight as he faced Cronus. Rage slammed his brows down over livid silver eyes, and his mouth was pressed thin, a thousand different threats carved into his harshly beautiful face.

Wynvail.

I ran faster, my heart beating erratically as I threw myself across the ruined road, Olympus blurring around me. I didn't care that my leg dragged behind me, or pain shot down my wings and my back where I landed when Cronus threw me.

He was here. Right here. Not unmade, not dead. Furious and blinding and *alive.*

Wynvail turned towards me, his nostrils flaring as he

marked the way I limped, maybe even feeling my pain if our bond was still intact. Gods, how was he here? He was unmade —I watched him die. He died *in my arms.* This had to be fake, there was no way it was real.

But I felt it then—the endless well of violence roiling through his chest as he stared at my face. I didn't want to know what state I was in, what made Wynvail's jaw clench and magic flash brighter.

I ran faster, so close now that I could see every detail of his face. My heart skipped, my bottom lip buckling when he opened his arms for me.

"Wyn," I choked out and slammed into him, throwing my arms around his waist as a sob ripped up my throat, followed by another and another until I couldn't breathe. He was warm, solid. I cried harder. "Are you—"

"Miraculously alive?" he replied softly, a tiny hint of amusement in his voice as he wrapped his arms around me and brushed a kiss to my forehead. "It appears so."

My lips quivered, hot tears burning my eyes.

"Ready to kill a titan, honey?"

A keening sound formed in my chest. I thought I'd never hear him say that name again, never thought I'd hear his voice again.

"You're dead," I rasped.

He kissed my temple again. "I'll explain later, but I need you to be strong for me now. Can you do that?"

I sniffled, swallowed the lump in my throat. "No."

"That's the spirit," he drawled, letting go of me and loosing a sudden beam of vicious light.

I pressed my face into his shoulder to shield my eyes, and dragged down breaths of his scent. It was him. He was really here.

"Where are your blades, honey?"

I blinked. They were in my hands when I fell and I—oh. I hugged him now with empty hands. Shit.

"Here, my rose," Kai said, making me jump as he appeared at my left, holding my blades out to me.

I sheathed one and accepted the other, but refused to let go of Wynvail.

"Don't you dare leave my side," I warned Wyn, my voice raspy and raw. I couldn't take my eyes off him, couldn't believe he was flesh and blood, not ashes stolen on a heartless wind.

I never knew what his reply would have been because Cronus came roaring at us—not just reaching out with giant hands but surrounded by a sheer, strange veil of sapphire magic.

It was only when I took a step forward and everyone else froze that I remembered Cronus's power.

He was the titan of time.

And he'd just frozen me here with no backup.

CHAPTER 33

I gritted my teeth and spun, searching Olympus for any signs of movement. My mates were immobile, and even Lili had frozen mid-rampage, her hand raised and light gleaming around her head. The only thing that moved was Cronus's enormous form as he took a step towards me, making the ground shake so hard that I stumbled back. I sucked in a sharp breath when pain shot up my knee. My back and wings throbbed in sympathy; I tried to breathe through it.

Wynvail was alive. My mates were frozen but *alive*. But how long would they stay that way if Cronus got his giant hands on them? I needed to fight—for them, for me, for everyone Cronus had ever hurt.

So even though my back blazed with pain and my right wing dragged along the ashen ground, I drew my other dagger and stared up at the titan bastard who had tortured my mates. Fury pounded through my blood, making my skin sear with heat at the thought of everything he'd done to them, and my magic surged in response.

"Do your worst," I spat, my breathing coming quick, hands trembling.

I wasn't strong enough to win, I knew that. But what was the alternative? Stand here until Cronus crushed me to death? Kai would resurrect me just to kill me if I gave up.

Darkness swirled off Cronus's mammoth body, but light flickered through the dark like tiny veins of lightning. I sucked in a breath, backing up and trying to come up with a plan. How did I fight a twenty-foot titan on my own, with no help?

He ate Lucifer, for fuck's sake! How long did I have before he ate me, too?

I twirled my blades in my hands, my heart hammering as I scrambled for a course of action. I'd already failed. Stabbing him in the eyeballs hadn't worked, slitting his throat and gutting him did nothing. He had no weakness I could see, and now magic shimmered around him, so powerful that I stumbled back a step when I should have been racing towards him.

Wynvail is alive, but not if this bastard gets his way. He's already killed him once; he'll do it again.

How did you do it, Halwen? Cronus demanded, that hideous voice slicing through the soft parts of my skull and ripping a sob up my swollen throat. *How did you remake Wynvail? I tore apart every speck of life in him, so how did you, tiny insignificant demon, undo his death?*

He thought I did it? I laughed, letting all my madness fill the sound, and spat blood on the ashen ground.

"You underestimated me, asshole," I taunted.

If he was giving me credit for Wynvail being alive, I wasn't about to correct him. I spun my long daggers again, stalling for time. I had no ideas. Nothing.

Kamikaze it is.

I pictured Wane curled up in the corner of his rank prison, and Wynvail collapsing to ashes in my arms, and Harvey and Kai trying to murder each other in the fighting pit, and Emlyn racing at me with zero recognition in his eyes, his whole life stolen from him. Rage and violence had always unlocked my curse's magic, and it was no different now. Crimson light erupted from both my marks, travelling up my blades until shards of it covered my knives.

I didn't wait for Cronus to laugh or drop another taunt; I launched at him, flapping my wings—and veering dangerously left when my wing buckled. Fuck!

Cronus laughed now, because of course he did. Pain thumped through my skull, but I clenched my jaw and breathed through it, letting rage wrangle my injured wing back under my control. It was agony, but agony was my longtime friend. You could even call us begrudging besties. So I screamed through gritted teeth and flew around the bastard's gigantic body, slashing my knives through his hamstrings.

I held my breath as I soared higher. *Please have an Achilles heal, please have an—*both healed after barely a second, and the titan didn't even grunt in pain.

Well, there went that. My tiny scrap of a plan. I was screwed.

I slashed at the closing wounds on his thighs, but the edge of my knife connected with the blue veil of power around him, and electricity charged up the metal, down the hilt, and burned the pink fabric Kai had lovingly wrapped around the hilts. I screamed as his magic lit up my body, charged through my bones, and fried every vein and synapse until all I knew was blinding pain and *power*. So much power.

It coursed through me, crashing into my blood magic until the only thing I could hear was the slow, endless drone of heartbeats. He'd really frozen everyone—not just the people I could see, but underneath the city there were *thousands* of people frozen in time, too. No, frozen was the wrong word. Their hearts still beat, but impossibly slowly. By the time any one of them took a single step, an hour would have passed here, and I'd be dead.

I pumped my wings, angling away from that sheen of magic on his skin, my heart pounding. My magic was more intense in Olympus *without* whatever just happened. My head spun, my breathing came faint and fast, and my magic felt like someone had doused it in petrol and thrown a match.

I retreated, gasping, shaking.

You respond to my power because you already possess a glimmer of it, Cronus said with an annoying amount of smugness.

"Fuck you," I gasped, burying my pain so he wouldn't see it when my wing almost collapsed as I flew higher, searching for a weakness to attack and knowing I'd find nothing.

Did you truly never wonder why your curse marks flare with magic? Or why being in Olympus unlocks a new level of your magic?

He *tsked,* sending a flare of pain through my skull and down my spine to the rest of my body, until no part of me was spared deep, slicing agony.

I choked on a cry, unable to silence it, and stabbed my blades into the meat of his upper thigh to stop myself falling. My wing was fucked. Lame, it refused to hold my weight. Cronus was twenty feet tall; if I couldn't fly, how was I supposed to fight him?

You're my kin, Halwen, Cronus continued his smug monologue, as I hadn't already worked that out. He was Rhea's abusive husband; I was her great-granddaughter. It didn't take a genius to put that together. *My power is your power. Your blades glow because of me.*

A scream ripped past my lips when one of my daggers tore from his skin, leaving me hanging by a single weak hand. My heart fluttered fast, making me lightheaded. I hung on by a single precarious blade, the cut making Cronus's thigh slippery and treacherous as blood coated my fingers. Wind thrashed faster, sharper around me like it was waiting for me to drop.

I hung so far above the ground that broken bones were guaranteed, and a broken neck was almost assured. It was a miracle Cronus throwing me across Olympus hadn't already snapped my neck. Some deity was definitely rooting for me.

"My blades," I panted, the muscles in my arms screaming as I held on by that single dagger, "glow because I'm *cursed*, you pompous twat."

Cronus just laughed, the sound filling my head until I couldn't bear it.

It's just like scaling a building, Haley, I coached myself, panting hard. *Just like scaling a building.*

With a stifled scream, I swung my other arm up, pulling my damaged wing to breaking point as I drove the knife back into Cronus's thigh. When I was stable, sweat rolling down my face, I did the same with the other knife, rising a few inches at a time.

And look at you, he taunted. *You turned out wonderfully even cursed. Almost like someone knew you would.*

Fuck that, and fuck him.

"Don't care," I panted, driving my daggers higher, climbing him like an ice climber on a giant, glacial cliff. I rose higher and higher, unsure how I'd kill him but determined to do the deed.

Electric blue magic fluttered like a shroud on his skin, grazing my daggers. *Fuck!* A scream of pain trapped behind my clenched teeth, desperate to break free. It was like touching the prison bars all over again, but I could have sworn this pain struck my *magic*, not my body.

Your curses made you who you are, Halwen. You should be grateful. You wouldn't have half your power or greatness without them.

He only let me have this *power and greatness* because he wanted it for himself.

I gritted my teeth, climbing higher, not daring to look

down. Heights usually didn't faze me because I could catch myself with my wings, but I knew today was very different. Cronus had assured that by throwing me halfway across the city. *I'll have this meal tenderised.* Asshole.

"There's nothing—great about—killing my mates," I panted, reaching his broad back and hauling myself up, driving my knives deep into his spinal cord. I hope it hurt like hell.

How can you know when you haven't done it? They can't kill you, Halwen. They never stood a chance. You're the daughter of titans and gods; an archdemon is nothing *compared to you.*

"Yippee—for me," I rasped, my arm muscles buckling as I dragged myself higher. If I could go back in time, I'd add a hundred pull ups to my workout routine everyday. Maybe my arms wouldn't be going numb, maybe I wouldn't be losing strength with every inch I climbed higher.

If you kill them—

I drove my dagger into his spine ruthlessly hard. "It'll break me."

You'll be reshaped into something invincible. No demon has killed their mate and survived, but a descendant of the king of Olympus?

I forced a snort even as tears gathered in my eyes. "Wow. *Zeus* is my ancestor?"

Cronus roared, my jibe hitting him in his weak ego like I knew it would. I didn't account for the pain that split my skull, tore through my body, and ripped my chest apart until I could only scream.

The sound tore from deep in my chest, bruising my vocal chords.

Cronus twisted, snatching me off his back in crushing hands, ripping my daggers out without even a hiss of pain. My fingers had locked around the hilts, pain freezing me like his cruel power had frozen my mates. The world twisted and blurred around me, pain carving itself so deep, so permanently into my blood and bones, that I barely even saw Cronus as he lifted me to his face. I was nothing compared to him. Powerless, small, breakable. I knew he wouldn't throw me across Olympus this time. This was it. I was going to be eaten by a megalomaniac titan.

"Not waiting—for me to kill—my mates anymore?" I rasped, my voice so fucking weak.

My hands started to shake around my blades as the numbness wore off. The pink fabric of the hilts had been burned off. My hands were raw, blood smearing my fingers—both his and mine.

Cronus's face was horrific up close, formed of night and shadows and evil, blue threading through his skin and magic like lightning. He had no features at all, just a flat plane that made my heart jolt.

Looking at him made my skin crawl, made a deep, buried instinct scream at me to flee. But he held me too tightly for me to escape. At least my arms were free this time; I took full advantage by driving my strong arm up and burying the blade in his throat for the second time tonight. This time I drove it all the way to the burned hilt, and blood sprayed, drenching my face until copper and power was all I could taste. I twisted the blade, but blueish magic thrashed from his skin and brushed my arm, that minor touch inflaming my magic so badly that I couldn't think.

My eyes rolled back. I screamed until my voice broke.

My curse marks flashed brighter, until all I could see was crimson light and my knife buried in Cronus's throat. It should have been enough.

God killers, Cronus mused, like he knew exactly what I thought. He probably did. *Not titan killers.*

Tears burned my eyes, slipping down my bloody cheek as I

twisted the blade again, desperate, shaking. I had nothing left, no last-minute tricks.

Nothing would kill him. He was truly, horrifically invincible.

I'd really believed my daggers would kill him when they absorbed the hippocampi's curses. From the second they lit up red, I thought they'd be his downfall. *God-killers, not titan-killers.* My heart crashed, tears flowing faster. I wanted to be strong and defiant until the end, but there was nothing to stop him devouring me, swallowing my power, and growing even more horrific.

He lifted me higher, his cruel mouth wide.

My heart stopped for a long beat.

The edges of his maw curled into a smirk and hate poured through my heart. All I'd ever wanted was to be happy with my mates, live a quiet life, maybe have a bar fight on the weekend, but no world-changing events, no life-or-death battles every other day. Why did Cronus get everything he wanted, but I didn't get to keep a single thing I'd dreamed of?

"Fuck you," I spat, staring into the pure void of his mouth.

I matched his smirk with the last bit of my strength and flipped my dagger until it pointed towards me. *You don't get to have this too, asshole.*

I didn't hesitate, driving the long dagger into my stomach so hard I screamed myself hoarse.

The pain was so much *bigger* than I expected, voracious as it spread to every part of me, agony howling through my middle.

Light filled my vision. I screwed my eyes shut to escape it. Screaming through gritted teeth, I threw my body onto the blade until I was fully impaled, until I was surely dead.

I get the final laugh. You can't devour my power if I don't have any.

The victory lasted about as long as Cronus's roar of fury.

He ripped me away from his unnatural face and stared at what I'd done. His face twisted, uglier than ever, the veil of blue magic billowing on his skin.

Yeah, asshole. I killed me. You're too fucking late. I win.

But the pain tore through my stomach, so bad that I couldn't think, couldn't do anything but cry. This wasn't bruises or broken bones; this was a slow, draining death. I should've aimed higher and hacked my head off. Not sure I had the nerve for that one, though.

Blood seeped out of me, hot and slick, and all my bravado and strength seemed to flee with it. Oh gods, I'd killed myself. I really stabbed myself in the stomach.

Weakness spread, leaching all sensation from me until the only thing I could feel was the hot throb in my stomach. My other knife slid from numb fingers, falling far below, and I went limp in Cronus's hand.

Spiteful little bitch, he snarled, making me cry harder as his voice tore apart anything left holding me together.

He pinched the dagger's hilt between his giant fingers and ripped it out, my answering scream so loud and violent that my voice gave out.

You think this will save them? I'll devour every one of your mates until there's no trace of you left behind.

My head spun, my body heavy and rife with pain. Cronus was angry—*furious.* It took me a moment for my sluggish brain to sort through his words and realise why my blades were glowing brighter than ever.

I'd stabbed myself right where my curse mark scrolled across my torso.

I broke the hippocampi's curse using these knives. Did I ... break the last curse, forcing me to murder my mates? Did I break theirs, too?

My thoughts grew sluggish. Pain and peace merged in my body. *I did it. I broke our curse.* And ... I was dying.

262

I didn't want to die.

I wouldn't get to spend the rest of my life with my mates, wouldn't get to rebuild our house near the Forest of Halwen.

But Cronus didn't get to steal my magic. He didn't get to take anything from me ever again.

The peace began to swallow the pain, until I couldn't feel the cruel fingers crushing me, or hear the horrible rattling sound in my throat, only a distant roar of agony and grief I could've sworn belonged to Emlyn.

Fine, Cronus seethed, *you win, Halwen Vakhara.*

I wanted to give him the middle finger and say *I told you so,* but darkness swallowed me before I could even twitch my fingertip.

It wasn't a cold, biting darkness like Cronus's. Wasn't cruel and bloodthirsty like Locke's. Wasn't even cool and velvety like Wane's. This was soft and careful. The darkness embraced me like a mother holding their newborn child, promising only comfort, only safety.

Only peace.

CHAPTER 34

EMLYN

*W*here the fuck was I supposed to leave Verena? There was nowhere safe on this mountain for a thirteen year old, and the responsibility of her safety weighed on my chest until my breaths thinned. My mate bond was going insane, panic and pain and endless fear coming from Haley. I needed to be with her right fucking *now*, but I couldn't leave Verena alone.

I certainly couldn't lead her back to Olympus, where Cronus would either trample her or devour her. But the only shelter on this side of the mountain was a forest, the trees thick and tall and endless. No structures, no buildings. I couldn't leave a child alone in the forest.

"I'll be fine," she bit out for the ninth time, her hands curled into fists at her sides and her face pink behind her freckles, her nostrils flared. "Just leave me here, I can find my own way."

"No," I argued, each of my replies growing sharper, deeper.

"I'm not leaving you alone when there are maniac gods and titans running around." When she opened her mouth again, arms crossed over her ashen band shirt, I snapped, "I said *no*, Verena. Stop asking me to leave you to your death. It's not happening."

She began to argue again, but I shot her a sharp look, my next step so forceful that I snapped a twig in half.

"I don't need your help," she muttered under her breath, aiming a sideways glare at me. "I'm fine on my own."

"Verena—" I began, but when she spun suddenly to her right, a gleam of light flickering at her fingertips, I cut off the lecture and immediately followed her. I didn't have a knife, but I sank deep inside myself to the place my shifting magic lived, one touch away from taking my bird form.

I nudged Verena behind me, scanning the dense tree trunks and the canopy high above. Whatever wildlife lived in this forest had been silent long before we entered, but it felt even more still now, like even the leaves on the trees had frozen.

There were no sounds to suggest something was out of place, but I opened up all my senses and—fuck, there were demons all around us. Alphas judging by the size and power of them. I straightened to my full height, my pulse thrumming fast and so forceful I felt it even in the tips of my fingers. I'd fought alphas for a hundred years, had killed many of them, but I'd almost been killed myself too many times. Did Wynvail make sure I survived? Were the fights ever really fair?

How long would I last against fifty alphas? Especially when I had a clear weakness to exploit—Verena. I needed to keep her safe. I'd promised my mate I would, and I didn't break promises.

"What is it?" she whispered behind me.

"Alphas," I replied quietly, scanning the trees for movement. "A lot of them."

"I can fight," she insisted, not for the first time. It pissed me off that she might *have* to fight. She was a kid; the only thing she should have been fighting was acne.

"How well? Where did you train?"

"Uh. In the yard of my second foster home?"

Shit. No training then.

"I don't have a knife for you," I murmured, keeping my eyes on the tree trunks, knowing we were surrounded. Cold trickled down my arms, warning death was near.

"I'll be fine," she bit out, but her breathing accelerated and she edged closer to me.

"I know you will," I agreed with full confidence, not letting her hear even a flicker of my panic. "Because I'll make sure of it."

Leaves rustled and I spun, a deep growl of warning vibrating my throat when my stare latched onto the massive, dark-haired man that stormed out of the trees. I didn't recognise him from the Alphaven fighting pit, but that didn't stop me charging forward with a roar, yanking hard on my shifting magic until feathers tore through my skin, my bones shifted, and my wings became blood red, tipped with black.

Now, I had talons and a deadly beak, and I dove right for the big alpha, ripping open a vicious wound on his chest. He came at me with a snarl, and relief crushed my chest.

Good, focus on me. Don't even look at the kid.

He was faster than I'd accounted for. Shit. My screech rent the air when claws raked across my underbelly, blood soaking through my wings until hot pain pulsed. But Haley's fear was still cutting off my air, and I needed to get Verena to safety and return to my mate.

I angled my wings to carry me back to the alpha, scanning the forest as more alphas poured out of the darkness of tree trunks.

Climb, I tried to yell at Verena, but all that emerged was a throaty screech.

Fuck. There were too many of them.

I swooped, talons outstretched. They sliced through the alpha's thick throat, blood spraying my feathers, before I swung around and shot at a woman who thought she could get past me.

"Stop!" a whip-sharp voice shouted, and the woman I was flying for sneered and stepped out of my path at the last minute.

I screeched in rage and defiance, turning to face this new threat and—I paused. I knew the grey-haired woman from somewhere, but I couldn't remember if she was a friend or an enemy. She hadn't been wearing thick armour or wielding a broadsword the last time I saw her—with *Haley.* Fuck, she was my mate's friend.

"Back the fuck up!" Verena yelled, fear obvious in her voice but not in her stance when she lifted her hands and curled them into fists. Golden sparks lit her fingertips, but compared to the magic I'd seen monsters wield lately it was nothing, compared to the violence of alphas, it was nothing.

I dove for the ground in front of Verena, my wings tucked tight to my body. Furious with protectiveness, I yanked hard on my shifting magic, magic rushing up and over me, bringing a threat of exhaustion with it. I landed hard on two legs, impact spiking up both legs and a rumble of warning in my throat.

But all the alphas had frozen at the woman's command; they didn't even twitch in our direction even if violence clearly shone in their eyes.

"You touch her," I warned them, looking directly in their commander's eyes, "and you die."

The commander tilted her head, her long grey braid falling over her shoulder. She was Renna's wife, I remembered, but I didn't know her name. "You're Halwen's man. The big, growly one. Where is she?"

"Fighting Cronus," I replied grimly, crunching grass and twigs as I positioned myself in front of the kid, every step venting my rage and panic. "Now get out of my way."

"Who's the girl?"

"She's ours," I growled. "She's family. I—"

I cut off, spreading my arms to shield Verena when an enormous three-headed hellhound tore through the forest, sharp teeth bared in each head and murder glowing in their eyes. The creature didn't glance our way, just sprinted through the trees and raced out of sight. My heartbeat quickened.

"Something's wrong," the commander said, alarm in her eyes. "I can feel—can't you feel that?"

I shook my head, but then a shift went through me, like an earthquake shuddered through every atom of my being.

"Lucifer," the commander breathed, her face pale. "That's —impossible."

"What?" I breathed, glancing back to make sure Verena was still behind me. She'd edged closer, her fists still raised but no longer flickering with golden magic. She didn't have nearly enough power to be fighting threats as deadly as these. I needed to get her out of here.

"He's—no longer our king." The commander shook her silver head and raised her voice, "Everyone to Olympus. *Full speed!*"

When I grabbed Verena's arm and twisted away from the city, the commander said, "You're not coming?"

"That's no place for a kid," I rumbled, picking up my pace, wanting Verena as far away from these alphas, the city, and the titan as possible. Even if it killed me to walk away from my family when they so clearly needed me.

What the fuck had happened to Lucifer?

"Wait," the commander yelled, stalking after us. "Take this."

I spun with a scowl, but Verena was already reaching out to snatch the shining metal thing from the woman's hand.

"This is a pen," she said flatly, her young face filled with an ire that better suited someone twice her age.

"It's an emergency portal," the commander corrected, her expression hard when she looked at me. "Get the girl to safety and come back. You're an archdemon, and you've survived death once. If Lucifer really is—we're going to need all the help we can get."

If Lucifer really is ... what? Dead? Shit, did Cronus kill *Lucifer*? The devil, the King of Hell?

My blood turned to ice.

"Go!" the commander barked at me, and I startled, instinctually jumping to obey a more powerful demon. She raced away from us and threw her hands out at her sides, an awful, chilling magic roiling through the forest.

"What the hell is she?" Verena breathed, staring at the pen in her hand.

I grabbed her wrist so she couldn't portal alone and murmured, "A demon, but no kind I've seen before. Let's go. The sooner I get you somewhere safe, the sooner I can go back for the rest of our family."

Verena narrowed her green eyes at me, but there was something fragile about her expression. "Our family? Don't you mean *your?*"

"Didn't we already claim you as one of us?" I chided, flinching when pain tore through my bond, slashing its claws so viciously through my soul that my knees buckled.

"Close your eyes," I said urgently, my heart skipping at the blind trust Verena placed in me by immediately obeying.

I wouldn't let her down.

I clicked the pen with my thumb and held my breath, my

eyes slamming shut when the world shifted and whirled around us. It worked. *Thank fuck.*

I flung my eyes open again when the sense of being pushed and pulled in every direction faded. I could barely breathe, but it was a small price to pay.

A quick glance told me we were in Lucifer's palace. What if he was really dead? What would we do? He was the only thing keeping peace in Hell. Without him...

"I'll be fine here," Verena said urgently, pulling her hand from mine and thrusting the pen at me. "Go. Save them."

It didn't sit right with me to leave her here, but another lash of pain cracked through my chest and I gasped, unable to hide my reaction.

"Go!" Verena snarled, shoving me back a step. She was tiny but vicious, brave. My chest tightened.

"Do *not* leave this palace," I ordered, my voice deeper than I meant it to be. "And if anything happens, hide. We'll find you. I promise."

Verena nodded, her face pale, freckles dark against her ashen skin.

"We're coming back for you. I promise."

She swallowed, then nodded. "Go!"

I sucked in as much air as my anxiety-crushed lungs would allow and clicked the pen, not sure how it functioned but praying it took me where I visualised: the ash-covered wreckage of Olympus where I'd left my mate.

The world pushed and pulled at me until I felt sick, but the sensation ripped away without warning. I threw my eyes open as I struggled to find my balance, catching myself on—on the dome where we'd split up. It worked.

I groaned in relief and pushed myself up, scanning the flattened city. Cronus was easy to spot, and so were my family. But they stood in place, like they were frozen by some cruel magic. No they *were* frozen. This was what he did, the titan of time.

A growl rumbled in my chest. But fear grew teeth and clamped around my chest. Why had he frozen them? What was he doing *to* them?

I ran closer to my family, the hairs on my arms standing in end. Something was very wrong here.

A crowd of people had been struck immobile in the act of racing down the street, some with hands raised, magic gathering in their palms, others with weapons. I wove around them as I ran, a shudder going down my spine. I didn't recognise any of them, but it wasn't hard to guess they were here to fight Cronus. And he'd frozen them.

When I got close enough to see Cronus, I slowed so I didn't draw attention, wanting to fly right to the bastard and peck his fucking eyes out. But the only person who could kill him was Haley. Where was she?

I vibrated with rage and panic as I searched the ashen ground for her, but when I didn't find her, I turned to the skies. Fuck, where *was* she? Where—

Oh gods. I found her, so small and fragile where that monster held her in his giant hand. My mate was so fucking vulnerable. What if he—

"No!" I cried, the guttural sound drawn straight from my soul.

Fuck being slow. I full-out sprinted down the street when he lifted my mate to his vile mouth, opening it to devour her. Something snapped inside me—my sanity or maybe my control.

I roared my rage and terror, shifting to my winged form between one step and the next, praying I reached her in time. My stomach revolted, but I couldn't take my eyes off his open jaw and the love of my life gripped in his hand, too small, too breakable. A strangled sound escaped my throat.

Please no.

I flew faster than I ever had before, my lungs fighting me, my wings screaming with exertion as I shot through the air, panic threatening to turn me feral.

Cronus opened his mouth wider, lifting my mate, poised to drop her. *No! Not her!*

I pushed myself to breaking point and still refused to give up. A shrill scream exploded from my beak when my wings gave out, dropping me two feet before I recovered in a panic. I felt tiredness circling like a hungry predator, but I kept my head lifted, my eyes fixed on my mate as—as light flared from her swords.

Yes, fight him! Don't you dare give up, Hales!

I soared higher, beating my wings as fast as I physically could, fighting the wind as it tried to keep me back. Or was it winning? Panic clawed my chest apart, and my heart skipped with a beat of hope when Haley lifted her glowing knife and— and stabbed *herself.*

No! I screamed, my shriek loud enough to split the skies. My hope died, decayed right in my chest. She hadn't fought him; she stabbed herself. *Why?* I screamed the word and didn't care that the word came out mangled and avian.

"Why?"

Pain ripped my chest apart and spread to every part of my body.

Please, no. Not again. I can't lose her again. I can't live without her. Please.

My wings were numb as I flew closer, too weak, too gutted to even yell when Cronus ripped the knife out of my mate's stomach and discarded her like an unwanted piece of rubbish.

I dropped through the air, following her body's path through the sky. Pain shredded my heart, crushing all the feeling out of my wings, numbing my soul. I barely even felt it when I arced under my mate's falling body and she crashed into my back.

It was too silent, too still. The whole world had frozen in grief.

But she was still alive, wasn't she? She had to be. It was only a stab wound; she'd survived so many of them that I'd lost count. She'd be fine. She'd be completely fine.

The ground raced up faster than I expected, my head a scrambled mess. I landed and shifted to my demon form in the same breath, twisting my body to catch Haley before a single strand of her hair could meet the dirty ground.

"Come on, Hales," I gasped, holding her to my chest, my arms numb but trembling, *all of me* trembling. Her stormy eyes were open, staring up at me. Empty. Oh gods, oh gods—

"Wake up," I choked out, staring into her slack face. "Don't leave me, Hales. Please."

Noise roared around me but I didn't even register it, and the movement that soared past me was meaningless. None of it mattered. Haley wasn't moving, wasn't breathing. Blood soaked her clothes, a ragged wound gaped in her stomach, and she wasn't *moving*.

"Emlyn?" a raw, broken voice demanded, shadows blotting out the world. I couldn't see anything but Haley. "We need to get her to a doctor. We need—"

"It's too late," I said, my tongue completely numb.

A cry rent the air, the whole mountain shaking under us. My dead heart skipped. Kai.

I stared at her empty eyes and couldn't look away even as voices reached my ears—Harvey, Kai, Wane, Wynvail. Wynvail was alive and my Hales was dead. Everything was wrong.

"Listen to me," the bastard hissed, his voice low. "We need to get out of here. I can't tell you why, but we need to leave *now*."

"No, *you* need to die," Kai snarled gutturally, movement in the edge of my vision suggesting they were fighting.

"Fuck," Wane sobbed, pressing closer to me, his side flush to mine. "What is the titan—what is *that*? In his hand?"

I lifted my dead eyes and stared, not seeing a single thing except—charred pink and volcanic metal. Her dagger.

I took a painful breath, clutching Haley closer to my chest. She wasn't dead. She'd wake up. Any minute now, her eyes would open and her chest would fill with air.

Any minute now.

But Cronus had shrunk to his former size and he held my mate's dagger. The other was sheathed at her hip, pressed to my stomach, but the sight of her dagger in *his* hand made the numbness shudder, rage buried underneath the emptiness. Waiting.

"You fucking *monster*," Kai screamed, his voice cracking as he threw himself down the street at the titan.

I stared emptily, knowing I should have stopped him but— I didn't have the strength. I didn't have *anything*.

A golden-haired young man intercepted Cronus before Kai could, power moving around him like a bright sunbeam, but it was clearly a weapon; it was aimed directly at the titan.

"Stop!" Harvey hissed, throwing himself after Kai, grabbing his shoulder and wrenching him back. I watched emotion- lessly as they tussled.

"Who is that?" Wane breathed.

"Hermes," Wynvail replied in a voice as empty as mine. He looked from the messenger god to Haley and then back.

Wynvail should have been dead. *She* should have been *alive*. If I killed him, would it restore balance?

"The gods are here," Wane breathed, trembling with fear. "They can fight him. We should run—"

Wane flinched, and a breath of surprise managed to leave

my chest when Cronus drove Haley's dagger forward, burying it in his stomach like—like she'd done to herself.

I stared down at her, my face crumpling. Why would she do that? *Why* would she take herself from me? Didn't she know how much I needed her? Didn't she know we couldn't function without her? Why would she leave us?

The golden-haired god staggered back from Cronus, clutching his stomach—and in my peripheral vision he dropped to his knees. *God-killers.* That's what they called her knives.

"We need to get her out of here," Wynvail hissed, his urgency abrasions to my ears, to my empty soul. "Come the fuck on. You two, over here. *Now!*"

Harvey wrestled Kai back towards us, and Wynvail held out his arms, a frozen expression on his face. I couldn't tell if he was furious or broken or both.

"Grab hold of me. I can't get us far; I'm still recovering my strength. But I'll get us as far as I can."

"Why the fuck should we trust you?" Kai snarled, his eyes glowing and the ground trembling around him. I knew I should reign him in but I didn't have the strength.

Wynvail's expression didn't flicker. "Cronus just killed our mate, and then slaughtered a god. Do you want to be next?"

Kai bared his teeth but he grabbed Wynvail's arm, hard enough to bruise.

"I'm not letting go of her," I rumbled in warning when Wynvail faced me, but I froze when he grabbed my shoulder. Wane and Harvey were already touching him.

Before I could say anything else, moon-white light tore us away. My stomach roiled. I clutched Haley tighter, her body too heavy, too limp, in my arms.

When the magic released us, even I knew it was far too soon. I stumbled, forcing bile down my throat and widened my stance so I didn't drop my mate. She'd wake up soon. Any minute now. She had to.

We were on a forested hill overlooking the shattered city of Olympus, far enough that I couldn't make out Cronus's features but close enough that I spotted him without effort. Too close.

"Shit," Harvey grunted, scrubbing his face with a shaky hand. "*Look* at the place."

There was nothing left of Olympus; it was only ashes. And people—gods? There were a hundred of them, and even more streaming from the mountains behind the once-city. Alphas and their commander, led by Cerberus, the three-headed dog. My heart festered with poison. If they'd been faster, would my mate still be breathing?

"Let me look at her," Wynvail said in his horrifically flat voice.

I bared my teeth, clutching her closer to my chest. I'd rip his throat out if he tried to take her from me.

"What is—what's happening?" Wane whispered, utterly still as he stared at Olympus, the city flattened and—

Dark, glassy structures rose from the ground, growing at an alarming rate. I blinked, and there was a city full of black, mirrored glass where it had been ruins moments before.

I took a step back, the sheer scale of power it took to make something like that happen quickening my breaths, freezing my blood in my veins.

Another second, and there were skyscrapers towering over the city, reflecting the dark trees and stormy skies around Mount Olympus. Power thumped from the dark, shining stone like a heartbeat, hideous and fell. My stomach roiled with each thump of magic.

"He remade it," Wane whispered, spiralling. "He remade Olympus."

"And if he can do that, what else can he do?" Harvey asked bleakly.

"Anything," Wynvail replied, staring—at Haley, not the city. "He just killed a god, and probably absorbed all his power. There's no hope of saving them when they're killed by that knife He's—" Wynvail's throat bobbed, lifting his hand to reach for my mate. I snarled, clutching her closer. "He's the true king of Olympus now. The king of all gods."

Even from here, I could see Cronus return to his heinous giant form, towering over the dark, dreadful city with Hermes clutched in his hand. I couldn't watch as he lifted his arm, his intention obvious. My gaze fixed instead on my mate.

Come on, Hales, wake up. Wake up.

I snapped my hand up when a bronze hand neared her face, but I swallowed my growl when I found *Wane,* not Wynvail. He brushed pink hair out of her face, pure devastation written in his eyes.

"She's not coming back, is she?" he choked out.

"Shut the fuck up!" Kai snarled, twisting to us with a dangerous wildness that made my instincts pulse with a warning I was too numb to heed. "You shut the fuck up *right now!*"

"They're bowing," Harvey said, backing up from the edge of the hill, brushing his wing against mine. "Why the fuck are they bowing?"

But the answer came a moment later when power swelled from Olympus and charged through the forest we stood on the edge of. It slammed into my body and my knees buckled, dropping me to the ground with a thump.

My head was forced low, cruel power pressing on the back of my neck, but I growled and held Haley tighter, refusing to give her up.

Wake up, Haley. Come on, you have to wake up.

"He'll find us," Wane breathed. "He'll kill us, too."

"Good," Kai bit out, fighting like a rabid dog against the power pressing us into the ground. "I'm not staying anywhere my mate isn't. But I'm taking the bastard with me. He's fucking *dead.*"

"Wake up," I breathed, kissing my mate's cheek. My stomach twisted when cold skin met my lips.

"We have to get back to the safe house," Wynvail urged, trying to cast off the dark power pinning us with a flicker of light. "We're running out of fucking time."

"Who cares?" I replied, my voice hollow as I stared at Haley, cold and still and unmoving. Wane was right. She wasn't coming back. She was dead—really, truly dead. "Haley's gone. Kai's right. Let him kill us, too."

THANK YOU SO MUCH FOR CONTINUING HALEY'S SERIES, you're amazing! Shadow Fall: Part 1 will release in January, swiftly followed by the final book!

While you wait for Shadow Fall, you can read the Fae of the Saintlands series - it's enemies to lovers fantasy romance, with fated mates, steam, fae rebels, adoring men, a dangerous heroine, and four books out in KU!

Thanks again for continuing this series with me. If you need to talk about the series or share your theories, come join me in my reader group. (Just mark any spoilers, so we don't ruin any twists for other readers.)

Leigh x

FREE VAMPIRE ROMANCE STORY!

Hybrid's Curse is a stand-alone paranormal romance.

As a vampire-witch hybrid who can never be killed, Emilio is used to pain and suffering. But when Aislin, an innocent faerie healer, is kidnapped because of him, Emilio will do anything to stop her suffering too. Especially because she's been dreaming of him for seven years, and claims to be his mate.

If you love romantic stories with a healthy dose of suspense, and pairings of dark, gloomy men and sunny, optimistic women, you'll enjoy this happily-ever-after story.

JOIN MY MAILING LIST FOR YOUR FREE STORY

THANK YOU FOR READING!

Need the next book ASAP? Let me know – the more demand for a series, the more likely I am to bump the next book to the top of my list! To stay updated with what I'm working on next, come join me in my Paranormal Den on Facebook, or sign up to my fortnightly newsletter! (Links on the next pages, so keep reading, loves.)

Reviews make the world go 'round - or at least they do in my world. If you loved this book and you can spare a minute, please leave a review on Amazon or wherever else you like to review. Even the smallest, one-line review has an impact, and helps me reach new readers like you awesome people.

Thank you to everyone who's already reviewed. Your words mean I can keep writing the books you love!

LEIGH KELSEY

WHERE THE MEN ARE *PSYCHO* BUT THE WOMEN ARE *WICKED*

INSANELY PRETTY SPECIAL EDITION HARDBACK!

If you're like me and LOVE a stunning collector's edition, check out this GORGEOUS Fae of the Saintlands hardcover, with brand new covers, colour illustrations, and the chance to unlock foil and SPRAYED EDGES!!

Find the hardcover exclusively on Kickstarter!

COMPLETE TWISTED PARANORMAL RH SERIES

Here's a tip: don't mess with the demon girl who kills people for a living.

The four self-proclaimed kings of Orchid Vale apparently never got that memo, and now my self care retreat is about to become a bloodbath.

READ FREE IN KINDLE UNLIMITED

JOIN MY READER GROUP!

To get news about upcoming releases before anywhere else, and early access to my books, come join my Leigh Kelsey's Paranormal Den group over on Facebook!

ABOUT LEIGH KELSEY

Leigh Kelsey writes about psychos with questionable morals and addictions to shiny, stabby objects, but she's perfectly harmless, she swears. She can be found in Yorkshire, England listening to K-Pop, watching serial killer documentaries, and writing as much spicy paranormal romance as she possibly can in a day. (Where's that Time Turner when we need it…?)

LEIGH KELSEY

WHERE THE MEN ARE *PSYCHO* BUT THE WOMEN ARE *WICKED*

f

FIND THESE OTHER PSYCHOS BY LEIGH KELSEY!

Feared by Monsters: A stand-alone twisted paranormal romance

Killers and Kings series
(Complete Twisted Paranormal Demon RH)

Crazed Candy

Sweet Violence

Sugar Rush

Kissed By Brimstone series
(Twisted Paranormal Demon RH)

Hellborn Angel

Midnight Descent

Eternal Night

Cursed Dawn

Shadow Fall: Part One

Shadow Fall: Part Two

Rebels and Psychos Duet
(Complete Twisted Paranormal RH)

Complete Series Box Set

Killer Crescent

Blood Wolf

Lawless Angels series
(Dark Biker Apocalyptic RH)

Vicious Legion

Sick and Twisted series
(Twisted Death Gods RH)
All Hallows Night

Broken Alphas series
(Complete Rejected Mates Dark Paranormal RH)
The Omega's Wolves
The Omega's Mates

NOTES

CHAPTER 2

1. Not through it. Smart man—my hair was one solid matt of muck, grime, sweat, and blood.
2. I knew for a fact Wane or Harvey had made it, because it wasn't cut into perfect triangles by Em or hacked in half by Kai.
3. Did whales even eat sharks? Ugh, why was I thinking about sea creatures when my legs were wrapped around Wane?

CHAPTER 3

1. And I could clean her after.

CHAPTER 5

1. Speaking of, what the fuck happened to Bevan? Was he still locked up in Lucifer's dungeon being *mined for information?*

CHAPTER 6

1. Was she keeping snacks in her bra?

CHAPTER 8

1. Yeah, I might have *accidentally* stroked a sensitive spot...
2. Hopefully literally.
3. Because *holy shit,* there was a second tongue licking me.
4. It didn't when I was so sensitive. It really didn't.

CHAPTER 9

1. Sweated like I'd just run a marathon too.
2. That was a *prop* grenade, right...? No way was that real...

3. *Woman up*, I snapped back at them. *If I want more cocks, make it work.*
4. Fuck he was right, did I really not get enough cock last night? I know I had a hundred years to make up for, but being this horny was insane.

CHAPTER 10

1. And yes, I *was* still annoyed about that.
2. I'd learned that phrase from Tali. Love language. She'd learned it from Renna of all people. That woman was a scary mystery.
3. I wanted him inside me right the hell now, his heavy body pressing me into the sofa cushions, his cock filling me and—goddamn, had I taken a horny drug? Actually, I wouldn't put it past Kai to dose me with something so I was constantly needy...
4. I was ninety percent sure he'd been using some of the fancy-as-fuck lotions and potions Wyn stocked the bathrooms with.
5. Was I in heat? Demons could go into estrus but my species never had. This was insane, though. I was like a horny cow just waiting for a bull to come and fertilise—ugh, cutting that thought off before I had a spontaneous orgasm.
6. Not friends anyway.

CHAPTER 11

1. It was weird right? It wasn't just me? We had a monster in our house, and he was ... normal. *Shy.*
2. What kind of monster said 'I've put my foot in it?'

CHAPTER 13

1. I didn't know what to think about my twin's best friend being a guy with dragons for arms, who could melt into a puddle of black fluid. But Wane had always had a weakness for picking up strays. This was no different than the broken-winged bird he brought home and nursed back to health.

CHAPTER 17

1. Dramatic much? Besides, I'd already died, and there was nothing abyssal about it. There was *nothing* about it; it was emptiness, absence.

CHAPTER 20

1. True fucking love right there.

CHAPTER 21

1. Okay, so it wasn't permanent, but it damn well *felt* it.

CHAPTER 22

1. My eyes were drawn to it again, snagging on the peacock feathers and cows. *Cows.*

CHAPTER 25

1. Fuck was Mount Olympus even a city? Calling it a *mount* was fucking weird. City would have to do.
2. See that just didn't flow right, it sounded weird. I'm going back to city.

CHAPTER 26

1. I swear, if Haley started hovering without flapping her wings, I was calling a damn exorcist. And coming from a demon, that was bad, bad news. That shit was *creepy.*
2. Hera couldn't have flown us to the doorstep? Really?

CHAPTER 30

1. Okay on second thoughts, let's never land again. The air was the place to be. No terrifying waves of shadows and silver up here. Just a twenty-foot-tall titan
2. I was trying really fucking hard to be okay. Was it obvious?
3. Literally hungry.

CHAPTER 31

1. My body was turning against me, and I was not a fucking fan of it. Zero out of ten. Miserable experience.